"Where did you learn to kiss?"

"I...well..."

"It occurs to me that somehow, in between your French lessons, you neglected kissing entirely," he said. "It would be cruel of me to let you go without a lesson." He began walking toward her. She should have run, but instead she raised her chin, too proud to let him intimidate her.

"Thank you, but I do not need a lesson, Mr. Bentley."

"Oh, but I think you do."

He'd reached for her at this point, but still she held her ground. His dark gaze roamed boldly over her face.

"First, we'll have to take that ridiculous thing off your head." She stayed very still as he gently lifted the wig, desperately trying to tamp down the feelings churning inside her.

"Now, that's much better. Do you know how long I've wanted to kiss you?"

* * *

The Wayward Debutante
Harlequin® Historical #884—February 2008

The Wayward Debutante

SARAH ELLIOTT

HARLEQUIN®

TORONTO • NEW YORK • LONDON
AMSTERDAM • PARIS • SYDNEY • HAMBURG
STOCKHOLM • ATHENS • TOKYO • MILAN • MADRID
PRAGUE • WARSAW • BUDAPEST • AUCKLAND

ISBN-13: 978-0-373-29484-8
ISBN-10:   0-373-29484-0

THE WAYWARD DEBUTANTE

To Meg and Stan: congratulations!

Chapter One

1 July, 1818

"**Y**ou've always been so good, Eleanor," Beatrice Summerson said appreciatively as her eighteen-year-old sister entered the sunny drawing room bearing a silver tea tray. "Between Ben and Helen and me it's a mystery how you ended up so well behaved. Father thinks of you as an absolute miracle."

"Oh, I don't know…I'm not *so* good," Eleanor replied as she laid the tray on a side table. She began organizing its contents without looking at her sister.

Beatrice cocked her head, her eyes slightly worried. "Now, now, you mustn't protest. You're perfect, and you couldn't be a more agreeable guest. Charles and I are grateful to have you."

"I hope so," Eleanor said uncertainly. "Would you like a slice of cake, Beazie?"

Beatrice smiled, her concerns momentarily allayed by the prospect. "Well…I *am* eating for two at the moment."

Eleanor cut a very large slice, and brought it to her sister, who patted the spot next to her on the yellow damask sofa. "Do have a seat, Eleanor. I've been wanting to talk to you."

Slowly, Eleanor sat. "Oh?"

"Well…I've been feeling rather guilty. I know it might seem that Charles and I are terribly busy and distracted with Mark, and with the new baby on the way, but I hope you don't feel too neglected."

Eleanor looked down at her lap. "I can entertain myself all right." There was, she hoped, a melancholic note to her voice.

"*And* our household must feel very chaotic to you at the moment," Beatrice continued apologetically: "It's such a shame that our butler, Cummings, absconded with our downstairs maid. We're completely disorganized as a result, and I've no time to hire new staff. I'm afraid it's become a bit of a burden to you. You shouldn't have to help out as much as you do, especially during your first season."

Eleanor shrugged. "You'll get a new maid soon enough. Besides, Cummings was kind enough to recommend his father."

"Yes," Beatrice sighed, "but while Mr. Cummings Senior is very polite and correct in his manner he's also completely deaf."

Eleanor frowned. "You mustn't let him go. I'm very fond of him." Realizing her response seemed disproportionately heated, she added, "He's kind to me."

Beatrice narrowed her eyes. "Eleanor? Is something matter? You're behaving rather strange."

It was Eleanor's turn to sigh. "No, no, Beazie. Everything's fine. I've just been thinking about the ball this evening."

"You're looking forward to it, I hope."

"I'm afraid I am not."

Beatrice sank back in the sofa. "Nor am I. But we must do what we must do."

"Would you like more tea?" Eleanor asked, rising.

Beatrice nodded contentedly. "You're in an obliging mood this morning. Just a drop of milk, please."

Eleanor poured the tea in silence, then asked hesitantly, "Would you think it the *worst* thing if I didn't go tonight?"

"You're feeling well, aren't you?"

"Oh, yes. It's not that. It's just, you see, a friend of mine asked me to come for a visit, and I already told her I would—"

"A visit on the night of the Montagu-Dawsons' ball?"

"Miss Pilkington won't be going to the ball. She took ill yesterday."

Beatrice cocked her head slightly. "Pilkington? Have you mentioned her before?"

Eleanor smiled patiently. "Yes. Jane Pilkington. I introduced you to her at the Nortons' party two weeks ago. Surely you remember."

Beatrice obviously remembered nothing of the sort, but she agreed nonetheless. "Oh, yes. Of course. You know how scatterbrained I can be."

Eleanor nodded sympathetically. "I met her at the beginning of the season. She's come all the way from Yorkshire and doesn't think her family can afford to send her so far from home next season if she doesn't meet her match this time. So this ball actually meant a lot to her and she's devastated she'll have to miss it. She needs cheering up."

Beatrice frowned. "I understand your sentiments, but I hope her illness isn't contagious."

"Oh, no. It's just a mild cold, and you know what my constitution is like. It's her spirits, really, that suffer most. I know I *should* go to the ball, but I'm sure I won't be missed in that crush."

Beatrice shrugged. "I suppose I don't mind if it's just this once."

"Must I go?" her husband, Charles Summerson, asked hopefully from the doorway.

She turned around, making a face. "Absolutely. Lady Montagu-Dawson would never forgive us if we all deserted."

He groaned and sank down into a chair. "Doesn't seem a bit fair. Eleanor's the only reason we're going in the first place."

Eleanor sniffed resentfully. "You've no idea how fair—produce a sick friend yourself and then you may complain. Besides, I'm the one who's been to some affair nearly every day for the past two months, aren't I?"

"She's right, Charles." Beatrice stepped in to defend her. "Eleanor is willing to go, but she's sacrificing her time to help her friend. You, on the other hand, haven't an unselfish bone in your body."

Charles regarded Eleanor with mild skepticism but didn't comment. Beatrice turned her attention back to her sister, concern again on her face. "Are you not enjoying yourself anymore? I'm sorry, but I haven't even asked you until today…it's just that you always seemed so eager to have your first season and I only assumed…"

Eleanor hadn't been enjoying her season for some time now, but she wasn't going to admit it. "Of course I'm having a good time, a splendid time. Really. I only said that because I've been overcommitting myself recently."

"You're lucky you're staying with Charles and me rather than with Aunt Louisa—she'd have you go tonight even if *you* were the sick one."

Eleanor knew that was true and said a silent prayer of thanks that she'd avoided lodging with her domineering great-aunt. "As it is Aunt Louisa hardly leaves me alone. Every time I see her she asks me why I'm not engaged yet, knowing, of course, that no one's asked me. She called me a disappointment the last time I saw her."

"She didn't!" Beatrice gasped in outrage.

"She did, too—said everyone expected better things of me. I'm *trying,* Beatrice, really—" She broke off, allowing her lip to tremble convincingly. "I'm not like you, Bea…six proposals in your first season alone…"

Beatrice blushed. "Oh, come, now. We all know you're trying. You deserve a night off, and it sounds as if Miss…oh…"

"Pilkington."

"Yes. Miss Pilkington could use your company. Go right ahead."

Eleanor suppressed the urge to crow with joy. Instead, she folded her hands demurely. "You are the best sister in the world. Jane's sending her carriage round later and I'll also be driven home, so you've nothing to worry about."

"I never worry about you, Eleanor. If you were our dear sister Helen, on the other hand, I'd be worried indeed. But not you."

"Really?" Eleanor should have been pleased her sister thought so highly of her, but instead she was rather disappointed. Being sensible and dependable was all very well, but…

For a moment they sat without speaking, the only sound provided by Beatrice finishing off her cake. Eleanor began to drum her fingers on her lap. Catching herself, she said, "Oh, my."

"Yes?" Beatrice asked, her fork poised midair.

"The time, Bea. You're going to be late."

"Oh, dear. You're right. When will I learn?" She deposited her plate on a small satinwood table and Charles helped her rise. As they walked to the door, Beatrice turned around to remark, "By the by, those items arrived from Father's house early this afternoon. Meg brought them to your room. What on earth do you intend to do with all those clothes? They're not suitable to wear."

"Probably planning to rope us into more of her drawing room theatricals," Charles suggested. "Don't think for one moment that you'll get me into that blond wig, Eleanor."

She grinned, imagining her tall, handsome brother-in-law in the straw-colored woman's wig that was a staple of her costume collection.

Beatrice just rolled her eyes. "*Do* try to enjoy yourself with Miss. Pilkington tonight, darling."

"I will," Eleanor said, following them out of the

room. Indeed, she had a most marvelous evening planned—even if she couldn't help feeling nervous.

Of course, there wasn't any Jane Pilkington.

Eleanor started changing her clothes the moment she heard the front door close behind Beatrice and Charles. She didn't ring for a maid to help. Her wardrobe for the evening was designed to be put on without assistance. A serviceable gray cotton dress with a simple linen collar. Sturdy black boots. The outfit had belonged to a past governess and had been moldering in her father's attic until she'd rescued it for her costume chest last year. She'd known it would come in useful.

She examined her reflection in the mirror. She looked…passable. She pulled on the blond wig and grimaced. Each of her three siblings was blond. Tall, blond and stunning. Eleanor was quite pretty, she supposed, at least when she wasn't standing next to one of them. Her hair was brown; she was of medium height; her eyes, at least, were a striking blue. For the time being, however, her less impressive looks were a godsend. She must not be recognized.

She removed the wig and looked away from the mirror with a sigh. I really *am* a disappointment, she thought as guilt settled over her. As Beatrice had said, she'd always been the good child in the Sinclair family. Ben had been a terrible rake before he'd married, while Beatrice found wedded bliss only after being thoroughly compromised first. Helen promised to be the worst of them and she was only fifteen.

But her family had always assumed that Eleanor

would do her duty and wed with relative ease. If only they knew that she didn't give a fig about getting married, not that anyone seemed interested in proposing to her, anyway. She was far too much the bluestocking, and although men seemed to enjoy her conversation, few glowed with pride to be seen in her presence.

No, the reason she'd longed for a London season was precisely what she was preparing to do tonight. She was going to the theater. It was her favorite thing in the world and had been ever since she'd seen her first play with her family in Bath at the age of nine. She'd have liked nothing more than to be a playwright herself, although that would probably never happen. She'd even like to be an actress, and that would *definitely* never happen…even though tonight's performance proved she was perfectly capable.

The closest she'd ever get to these aspirations was sitting in the audience, and since she'd turned sixteen, every trip to London had included as many plays as she'd wanted, provided she could convince a family member to act as chaperone. She'd always imagined her coming-out would basically resemble these earlier trips, but now she was here and Beatrice and Charles were too busy to escort her. A London season, she was dismayed to learn, was serious business. Her life was carefully regimented, and she had little time to attend plays, not unless there was a very good reason to go. The only acceptable reason for her to go anywhere these days was that hordes of eligible men would be there. Getting married took priority.

And she was bored.

So she'd invented Jane. At first, it'd seemed a simple idea: tell Beatrice that she was visiting her dear sick friend but go to see a play instead. She'd disguise herself, and she'd probably only do it once, so what could possibly go wrong? Only now that she'd lied to her sister and dressed up in someone else's clothes, she knew that everything could go wrong, and probably would. But she was already committed and she was excited, too. She *had* been well behaved her entire life, and it was about time she experienced a bit of rebellion.

She pulled her cloak around her shoulders, stuffed the wig up one of its voluminous sleeves and headed downstairs. At the bottom of the main staircase the ancient Mr. Cummings dozed fitfully. He jerked awake as she passed him.

"Good evening, Cummings."

"Good evening, Miss Sinclair," he responded in his reedy voice. Reluctantly, he began to rise.

"Please, don't get up," she chided. "I saw the Pilkingtons' carriage approaching from my window and am perfectly capable of opening and closing the front door myself."

"But, miss…" Despite his protests, he had already resumed his seat and showed no sign of rising again.

Eleanor was hard-pressed not to smile. "I insist, Cummings."

"Very well, miss," he said, nodding with gratitude, his eyelids already beginning to droop.

Eleanor walked briskly to the door before he could change his mind. Her plan would never have worked if not for Cummings. A younger butler would have insisted on accompanying her to the carriage.

And in this case, there was no carriage. This part of the plan worried her most. She would have to hire a hack. The very idea was scandalous, and she wasn't even sure how one went about it. She glanced up and down the empty street to see if anyone was watching, pulled her hood over her head and descended the short flight of steps. She hoped she didn't look too odd. A cloak was one thing, even a lightweight one like hers, but a hood was something else entirely. It was summer, after all.

She tried to look confident as she began to walk, hoping she wouldn't have to go far. Luckily, the well-lined pockets of the average Belgravia resident meant that hacks wandered down even the less-traveled streets fairly frequently.

That was what she was counting on, anyway, and after a few minutes she spotted one slowly approaching, its driver scanning the street for customers. Holding her breath, she raised her arm and prayed he would stop. Miraculously, he did, and with only a slight tremor in her voice she told him her destination. He didn't bat an eye.

He didn't help her into the coach, either. That was a first, but she supposed she'd better get used to it. No proper young lady would dream of riding alone in a hired hack, and the fact that she'd requested one of London's playhouses as her destination…as far as he was concerned, she wasn't proper at all.

The hack jerked into motion and Eleanor eased back into the leather seat, feeling more relaxed. She'd just sailed over the first—and biggest—hurdle, and the rest of the evening should be trouble-free. In fact, she couldn't remember ever feeling as independent as she did at that moment, watching the stately homes of Belgravia gradually give way to the bustle of central London.

She took the wig from her sleeve and pulled it onto her head, carefully tucking away her chestnut hair. Then she removed a small hand mirror from her reticule and examined her reflection. The face that looked back wasn't any more interesting than it had been before, but she couldn't help smiling. It was rather nice being a little bit bad…at least as long as luck was running in her favor.

Chapter Two

The play was supposed to begin at seven, and when the curtains hadn't parted by half past Eleanor started to get very nervous. Lady Montagu-Dawson's ball would last until the early hours of the morning, but Beatrice and Charles wouldn't stay beyond midnight and might leave much earlier. If they returned home before she did…oh, it didn't bear thinking. She couldn't let that happen and, much as she'd dislike it, she'd have to leave the theater prematurely if the play didn't start soon.

It didn't help her nerves one bit that the surly driver was supposed to be waiting for her; although she'd paid him extra to do so, she didn't have much faith in his patience or his honor. If he didn't keep his word, she'd have to go through the ordeal of finding a hack once more.

To keep her mind occupied, she let her gaze wander over the audience around her—as best she could, anyway, without turning her head too much and attracting unwanted attention. She was aware that a few inquisitive looks had already been aimed in her direction, since even if she were a member of the lower classes, it still wouldn't be proper for her to be there alone. She sank down in her seat, hoping to make herself less noticeable. She'd deliberately seated herself on the extreme right side of the theater where the crowd was sparse. Her view was impaired, but in the interest of avoiding eye contact and conversation it was worth it.

Theatergoing was primarily a social experience, and most people there were too involved in their own conversations to worry about her. She was becoming worried, however, about a rowdy group of young men seated in the center of the audience. Their cultured accents betrayed them as society gentlemen, and she paled at the possibility that one or two might recognize her. They were obviously drunk, and certainly beyond caring whether they made a spectacle of themselves or anyone else. A pretty orange seller made the mistake of getting too close and was pulled onto one man's lap. She laughed good-naturedly, but Eleanor could see that she was scared and only playing along.

Lucky for the girl, the curtains parted at that moment and she was able to escape. A hush spread over the audience as the first actor walked onto the stage. The quiet didn't last very long, but Eleanor was able to block out everything but the play. For the first time in months she was doing exactly as she pleased, and she felt gloriously liberated.

This lasted almost an hour.

At first the woman's laughter, coming from just a few rows behind her, was like the buzz of a fly: annoying, but perfectly ignorable. But then she kept giggling, as if she had little more than a dried pea rattling around in her head. It wasn't even a proper laugh. It was a simpering, grating titter.

Eleanor gritted her teeth. She couldn't turn around and tell her to be quiet. Chances were the woman would respond with a few rotten cabbages that she'd brought along just in case.

A sharp squeal burst from the woman, followed by another round of giggles.

This was more than Eleanor could bear. Pulling herself up straight, she turned around with as much hauteur as she could muster. She wasn't going to say anything, but she would make her displeasure known with a pointed, dignified look. Then she would turn back around and enjoy the rest of the play in peace.

Only it didn't work that way. She forgot about the pointed look completely, and she even forgot to turn back around. She forgot the reason she'd turned around in the first place.

The irritating woman was there, and her gaudy dress, cut low to reveal her generous attributes, was to be expected. But beyond that Eleanor noticed nothing about her. She noticed instead the man seated next to her, and she continued to notice him even as it slowly dawned on her that she was staring. He was the most beautiful man she'd ever seen and she simply couldn't help herself.

His head was bent to whisper something in the woman's ear—she might have responded with another giggle but Eleanor was temporarily rendered deaf. His brown hair, so dark it was almost black, was fashionably cut but just a bit too long. Long enough to brush against his temples and make Eleanor's fingers itch to do the same. Nearly everything about his features proclaimed a high birth—his faultless nose and high, chiseled cheekbones, his straight, dark brows—but his full mouth intimated nothing but sensuality. And the way his perfectly tailored blue jacket caressed his broad shoulders…

Caressed? Eleanor cringed at the choice of word, but good heavens, it was true. Something about him made her think in terms of…well, *touching*. How very odd. Something about him made her rather flushed, as well. She wondered if he'd be hot to the touch, if his skin would feel soft, or his hands, perhaps, lightly callused. He was again whispering something into the woman's ear, and his lips were so close that they must have brushed against her skin. What did that feel like? She watched, enthralled, as his head dipped slightly and his lips trailed down the woman's neck, stopping at her shoulder.

And then he turned his gaze in her direction.

Oh, dear.

She knew she should have looked away the very second their eyes collided, so why was she still staring, only now with her mouth ajar like a simpleton? Her mind told her what to do, only her body was slow to respond. It didn't help that he was staring right back at her, looking every bit as surprised as she felt. And why shouldn't he be? She'd been ogling him. His gaze traveled over her face as if remembering every detail, and she blushed deeply as his bemused expression gradually gave way to something far more sensuous. She couldn't tell what color his eyes were from such a distance, but she could easily discern that they were dark and sinful. His lips curved appreciatively.

Her jaw snapped shut and she turned around so quickly that her head hurt. *Dear God. What had she told herself? Do* not *look at anyone, particularly not men who look like that. Particularly not handsome rakes who seduce women in public places.*

She wrinkled her nose at that last thought. Was that really what he was doing? Seducing that woman? What she would have given to be able to turn around to double-check. She'd certainly never seen such a thing before, and here was her chance to find out the precise mechanics. But she clearly couldn't do that, no matter how curious she was. Especially since she sensed that he was still watching her. No, she couldn't turn around. Not again, and she shouldn't even be thinking such unchaste thoughts. What would her family think? She was Eleanor, the good, studious child, and although she'd strayed that evening she'd since learned her lesson.

All she could do was wait for the intermission. It seemed like an eternity, and she was too flustered to pay attention to the action onstage. She just counted the minutes and endeavored not to think about the wicked man behind her.

As the curtains began to close at the end of the first act, Eleanor quickly rose from her seat. She tried not to look too agitated as she walked down the aisle, her eyes trained on the floor and her heart pounding in her chest. He was still watching her. She could feel his gaze on the side of her face.

She was the first person out the theater doors, and

once into the foyer she began to run. The street outside was still busy but she had no trouble picking out her driver. In her current state he shone like a beacon.

Thank heavens she'd be home soon.

James Bentley's office was situated on the south side of his large home. Its floor-length windows filled the room with bright sunlight, light that was gradually bleaching his mahogany furniture of its original dark sheen and endowing it with the warm and weary look of age. Shades of brown and green dominated the office, but were tempered—if one wishes to be strictly honest—by dust. The sunshine brought the dust to prominence, although this fact often went unnoticed by the occupant's selectively unobservant male gaze. His maid, a girl of about twenty, was too scared of him to enter most days, although he couldn't fathom why. So the dust quietly collected on the skirting boards; on the chairs and desk; and on the randomly placed piles of books, stacked three, four or five high. It was a cluttered room, but it was an intelligent clutter, a masculine clutter. It was exactly as a productive office should look.

That's what James told himself as he regarded the room from his desk, even though his day thus far had been marked by inactivity and distraction. He'd accomplished little more than a good lunch at his club.

He rose from his seat and crossed the room to look out the window, onto the well-appointed houses that faced him from across the street. He'd been living at this address for just over a year. Just a year since he'd returned to London after twelve years away. It had been a busy time: furnishing a new home, rekindling old friendships, helping finance a friend's business and sorting out his own neglected finances. But now the novelty and challenge of these endeavors had begun to fade. He feared he was getting bored.

That thought worried him—he'd been having it too often, and he couldn't put his finger on the source of his discontent. He supposed taking advantage of the season's entertainments might help. Despite his lengthy absence, he still received piles of invitations every week—to dinners and balls and every other type of social torture imaginable. And, if he ever decided that standing around in a hot room with a gaggle of silly girls whispering about him behind their hands was a pleasant way to spend an evening, then someday he just might accept one of these invitations.

He ran a hand through his dark hair and glanced at the papers scattered across his desk. He still had work to do, but it could wait until tomorrow. A brisk walk would clear his head, and besides, he was supposed to have dinner with his older brother, Will, in a few hours. William Henry Edward Stanton, now the seventh Earl of Lennox, to be exact.

James grabbed his jacket in preparation to leave, but just as he started walking to the library door it opened. His butler, Perkins, announced, "Mr. Kinsale to see you, my lord."

Jonathon Kinsale, his best friend and now a business partner, too, was right behind him, not waiting for permission to enter. "You're not leaving?" he asked in his mild Irish brogue.

James resignedly draped his jacket onto the back of an armchair. He wasn't in the mood for company, but Jonathon was already helping himself to a glass of brandy. "I'm dining with my brother tonight. Thought I'd take a constitutional first."

"Oh? And how's Will?"

"Just returned from six months in the country. Haven't seen him yet. Why don't you come along? You'd be doing me a tremendous favor."

Jonathon made himself comfortable on the worn sofa. "Why, so I can play buffer between you? No thanks. You can handle him perfectly well on your own."

"He's bloody persistent, though. Every time I see him, he brings up things I don't want to talk about."

"Like Richard."

James shrugged. Even in the privacy of his home, with his best friend, he still didn't want to talk about his eldest brother. "Richard is dead. He doesn't concern me anymore."

"Of course," Jonathon said, obviously unconvinced.

James sat back down, wishing Jonathon wasn't so bloody astute. But the truth was, he didn't think Richard would ever cease to concern him.

Both Richard and William shared the same mother, but she'd died giving birth to Will. Their father, the fifth Earl of Lennox, had remarried one year later, this time to Diana Bentley, a renowned Irish beauty and his lifelong love. Unfortunately, she'd also been an actress.

James was born a year later and Will, only two at the time, had adored his little brother instantly. But Richard was another matter. He'd been eight when his father remarried, old enough to be aware of the traces of infamy that clouded James's mother's past. He'd despised her, and he'd hated James, too. To his sneering and slightly mad eyes, she was a lowborn whore, and her son carried her tainted blood. He'd told James this every chance he'd got. Although James hated Richard right back, these words dominated his childhood. He'd always been afraid that despite a polite facade, the rest of society felt much the same way.

Unfortunately, Richard concealed this side of his personality well, and when both parents died in a fire, no one questioned his ability to be guardian to James and Will, who were only nine and eleven. As the eldest son, Richard would control their education and incomes. He also inherited the title and the bulk of family estates until they came of age.

Will hadn't fared too badly, but for James, the years that followed were marked by unhappiness and abuse. Will did what he could to protect his younger brother against Richard, but he, too, was just a child. James bore his brother's cruelty as long as he could, and if only he could have borne it for a few more years he would have come into his inheritance—not a great fortune, but enough to pay his commission and become an officer in His Majesty's service, like every other third or fourth son. Instead, he'd run away at sixteen, with only the money in his pocket. He'd slept on the side of the road for two days, but then came across a recruiting party at a public house. A red-coated captain had urged all able-bodied men present to protect their fair island from the French scourge, but what sounded most attractive to James—

who'd had one pint of ale too many for his youthful head—was the promise of a clean uniform and a hot meal. At least he wouldn't starve, and although he was presently unable to buy his commission, perhaps he could earn his place as an officer through honest hard work.

"Will just refuses to accept that I've created a life for myself separate from everything he values," James said finally. "I've no love for titles and inherited privilege."

"He just wants to correct past wrongs. Feels guilty because you had to struggle for so many years while his life was easy. Richard was mad."

"Mad, yes, and not too fond of me, either. I know all this, so let's drop the subject."

When he'd left home, he'd thought nothing could be worse than life with Richard, but two years in the army had proved him wrong. The life of a professional soldier was a far cry from the more comfortable existence of an officer. Jonathon had been in his regiment, and they'd become friends whilst sitting in a muddy ditch trying not to be killed. It turned out that Jonathon knew several members of his mother's family. James's grandfather owned a Dublin theater, and Jonathon had worked there as an actor and playwright. They'd spent hours plotting ways to escape the service, but these plans became irrelevant when a Frenchman fired a bullet straight at James's heart; Jonathon shoved him out of the way, taking the bullet himself. James would be forever grateful for this act, although by the end of the day he, too, was struck down. Wounded but alive, both were released from further duty. They'd traveled to Ireland, where Jonathon promised to introduce him to the family he'd never met.

And they'd embraced him. He'd felt for the first time in many years that he had a family. He'd even adopted his mother's maiden name, a change that Will took issue with; his name would certainly be a topic of conversation at dinner that night. He'd stayed there for almost a decade, until news of Richard's death arrived.

When he'd returned, Jonathon had come with him, hoping to pursue his dream of owning a London theater. He'd saved a bit of money, and James had helped him with the rest.

"You *are* being rather stubborn, James, I must say," said Jonathon, unwilling to let the subject drop that easily. "Will has a point. Richard's gone. You've moved back to London, you've claimed your inheritance. So start using your real name, too, and pretend to be respectable."

James rose, picked up his jacket once more and headed for the library door without responding to that suggestion. "Sure you won't come tonight?"

Jonathon reluctantly rose from his comfortable position and followed him out of the room and across the marble hall. "Theater won't run itself. By the by, did you enjoy yourself last night?"

James's head experienced a tiny pulse of pain at the memory. He knew exactly what Jonathon was referring to. He opened the front door with a quiet groan and stepped outside. "You witnessed my shame?"

"Kitty Budgen is rather conspicuous, I'm afraid. Laughs like a jackal."

"A real friend would have stopped me."

"It was too amusing to stop."

James hadn't intended on spending his evening with

Kitty Budgen, sometime actress and notorious flirt. He'd gone to the theater merely to sign some papers and had been about to leave when he'd spotted a lone woman seated in the audience. Unaccompanied women were invariably prostitutes and not good for business, so he was going to ask her to leave. He'd been waiting for the right moment, but the longer he watched her the less convinced he became. He couldn't see her face, but her tight, priggish hair and drab clothes didn't correspond to a prostitute's colorful appearance. Furthermore, she definitely wasn't trying to solicit anyone's attention. He'd started to lose interest, and then Kitty had come along and he'd forgotten about her altogether…

How surprised he'd been when he finally surfaced from Kitty's charms to see the woman now turned around in her seat, staring at him with a mixture of shock and opprobrium. Any doubts he'd had about her status vanished—he didn't think he'd ever seen such a sincere display of maidenly outrage. He couldn't blame her, either, all things considered.

And he'd been damned shocked himself. She was remarkably pretty, a fact he would never have guessed from the back of her head. She was beautiful in a way that Kitty, with her garish clothes and painted face, could never be. He rather regretted the fact that he'd held back from approaching her. He had an idea she'd have been a far more interesting companion.

"James?"

He looked up, realizing he'd become lost in his thoughts once more.

Jonathon sighed. "I said that if I were in your

position, I certainly wouldn't be wasting my time with the likes of Miss Budgen. I'd be dancing with a different heiress every night and fathering weak-chinned, aristocratic brats. What about marriage?"

James frowned. "You're as bad as Will. I'm not sure that any self-respecting heiress would waste her time with me, nor am I interested in the least. Now—" he paused, looking north, in the direction of Hyde Park "—I'm walking this way."

Jonathon took the hint, but he couldn't help calling out over his shoulder as he headed in the opposite direction, "Perhaps you should try to be interested. It might cheer you up."

Chapter Three

Eleanor didn't exactly know what she was doing there, seated once more in the shadowy outer edges of the theater, just two weeks after her first ordeal there. She'd anticipated spending a quiet evening at home with Beatrice and Charles as no social events had been organized. Only that had changed late in the afternoon when Charles's mother, Lady Emma Summerson, invited them all to dinner.

"You'll come, of course, won't you, Eleanor?" Beatrice had asked. "The invitation is rather tardy, I know, but that's because something novel has come up. Mrs. Parker-Branch visited Emma late this afternoon with her latest protégé in tow—she fancies herself a great patron, as you know. He's a Florentine tenor and has agreed to sing for Emma tonight."

Normally Eleanor would have agreed immediately, but something—she wasn't sure what—had made her hold back. "It sounds like a late evening."

"I suppose, but you've done nothing all day. It won't be anything too formal, I promise. Say you'll come."

Indeed, Eleanor had *meant* to say just that. But when she'd opened her mouth something else came out entirely.

"Perhaps I'll give Miss Pilkington a visit."

A braying voice coming from the center of the audience bought her attention back to the present with a snap. Her first instinct was to turn to see what was happening, but she caught herself in time. She'd been coaching herself all night to practice restraint, only it wasn't as easy as it sounded. She'd been raised to speak her mind, not to lower her eyes demurely.

The curtains parted, and she took a deep breath, trying to relax.

Only she couldn't, nor could she concentrate. She glanced over her shoulder to look at the rows of seats behind her, but they were still empty.

Don't be silly, Eleanor, she chided herself as she turned her head back around. *He will not be here this time. That would be too great a coincidence.*

The evening's play was *As You Like It,* again. She'd returned for a second viewing—not that she'd been able to see it properly the first time—and the chance that he'd also be there a second time was too slim to worry about. It was highly unlikely that she'd see him again in any context. His physical appearance might have suggested he was a gentleman, but his behavior certainly did not. She'd never seen him at any *ton* events before, and she would have remembered.

So why couldn't she stop thinking about him? He was no longer a threat; he was nothing more than a spine-tingling—make that *very* spine-tingling—memory. She wasn't unused to attractive men, either. Her brother, Ben, was terribly good-looking and Charles, until two weeks ago, anyway, was the handsomest man she'd ever seen. But, well, that was *Charles,* for goodness sake. It wasn't the same.

Eleanor closed her eyes and tried to remember the stranger's face. Since she'd dreamed about him just the other night it wasn't that difficult. She sank back into her seat and looked up at the plasterwork ceiling. She couldn't help grinning. *Dear God, why have you made me so depraved?* His boldness had shocked and thrilled her, and all he'd done was smile at her with a little more masculine approval than she was used to. Few men had ever flirted with her; she wasn't used to that sort of attention.

The sound of a large form easing into the seat in front of her drew her attention back to earth. That form was a very tall and spherical man.

Oh...!

She frowned at his broad back and leaned her body to one side and then to the other, trying to see around him. How dare he not only come in late but obscure her view, as well? She stared at the back of his bald head, willing him to change his seat. *She* certainly wasn't going to move. In the first place—just as a matter of principle—she'd sat down before him. In the second place, however, looking for another seat would require standing up, searching about and drawing attention to herself in the process. Just when she'd been avoiding notice so well.

With an annoyed sigh, Eleanor realized she had no choice but to crane her neck.

* * *

From the comfort of his private box, James looked out over the audience. He wasn't really paying attention since he'd already seen the play, and had actually only come along because Jonathon had invited him for a closing night drink. With each successful play, he came closer to repaying the loan, and he liked to celebrate.

His gaze faltered as it drifted across a blond head. A woman, seated on the right side of the theater. Unlike most of the audience, her face was turned toward the stage, and she appeared to be following the play with interest. She was also completely alone. He narrowed his eyes, instantly certain he'd seen her somewhere before, although he couldn't remember where. Other than the fact that she was alone there wasn't anything remarkable about her. Her body, what he could see of it, anyway, was slim and covered in a dreary, gray dress. Her hair was pulled into a severe knot.

He watched with amusement as she shifted her weight, apparently trying to see around the large man seated directly in front of her. If he'd been any closer, he was certain that he would have heard her huff in annoyance.

Where had he seen her before?

With a frown, he reached for Jonathon's opera glasses. As he watched, she leaned forward once again, trying to crane her head around the impenetrable form blocking her view. He chuckled as she sat heavily back into her seat in frustration.

As if she heard him, an impossibility from that distance, she turned her head to the side quickly, almost suspiciously. He stopped laughing, his eyes on the face that was now presented to him in profile. Suddenly, he remembered.

"See anything unusual through those?" Jonathon asked, regarding him with mild interest.

"Perhaps."

Jonathon glanced down at the audience toward the nondescript blond woman. She still fidgeted miserably. "Really?" he asked dubiously.

"Have you seen that woman before?"

Jonathon frowned. "Don't think so…honestly can't remember. Have you?"

He shrugged. "When I was here last…about two weeks ago. She was unaccompanied then, too."

Jonathon sighed. "What a nuisance. Do you want to remove her, or shall I?"

James didn't respond. He wasn't going to throw her out, not until he'd satisfied his curiosity, anyway. He didn't know why she so intrigued him, but he'd thought about her several times since he'd first seen her. She was quite pretty, but she definitely didn't seem out of the ordinary. Yet he remembered a slightly different picture from before: bottomless azure eyes; flushed cheeks; full, parted lips…he hadn't expected to see her again, and he wasn't going to let her run away so soon this time.

With a departing nod to the still-doubtful Jonathon, he left the box, heading down the dimly lit flight of stairs to the seats below. It took only a moment to locate her, and he had to hold back another grin as he walked slowly down the aisle. If she'd been paying attention before, that was no longer the case. Her attention now seemed to be entirely focused on boring holes with her eyes into the man's thick neck. She was so absorbed that she didn't even notice as he took a seat directly behind her. She just exhaled loudly in frustration and craned her head once more.

James watched her for several minutes, enjoying her irritation. The act soon ended, and the man rose and walked off, presumably to stretch his legs before the second half of the play began. With a relieved sigh, she leaned back into her seat.

And he leaned forward, his lips only inches from the back of her head. In a whisper, he asked, "Why don't you change your seat if you can't see?"

She didn't turn around. He wasn't sure if he'd expected her to. For an instant she looked as though she was about to jump out of her seat, but then she merely stiffened her shoulders. She was pretending not to have heard him.

He narrowed his eyes. The volume in the theater had increased as the scenery was changed, but it wasn't that loud. She'd heard him, and it wasn't as if she had anyone else to speak to, either. She was just sitting there, intentionally ignoring him. James wasn't used to that sort of treatment. He slid from his seat, stepped over the row of seats in front of him, and sat down right next to her.

Eleanor kept her neck as rigid as a flagpole. She'd no idea who this beastly man was, and she certainly wouldn't dignify his presence by looking at him. Making eye contact would only invite further liberties; better just to ignore him and hope that he'd go away. She'd rehearsed this tactic many times in her head just in case such a scenario should pass.

"Are you enjoying the play?"

She made no answer and still didn't turn her head. Instead, she imagined what he'd look like. Pudgy. Ugly. His nose would be bulbous and lined with red veins from too much drink.

He sighed elaborately next to her, leaned back in his seat and stretched out his legs. In turn, she edged sideways in her own seat and tried to make herself as small as possible so she wouldn't accidentally touch any part of him. Odious man.

"Well, you must like it, as I've seen you here before," he said. His voice was deep and rich and didn't fit the unattractive physique her mind had conjured up. "Unless, of course, you just make a habit of wandering around the less savory parts of London by yourself at night."

She hoped he didn't notice her eyes grow slightly wider as the meaning of his words sank in. Had he really seen her there before? Her muteness was positively killing her, but she refused to speak, hoping that if she ignored him long enough he'd get bored and leave.

But he didn't get bored. He got impatient, and he reached out and grabbed her hand, tugging gently.

She gasped and pulled it away with a jerk. She was so outraged that she completely forgot about ignoring him and turned her entire body around to rebuke him. But the nasty words that were ready at her lips died before they were ever formed.

Oh, no.

"Hello again," he said, his voice laced with humor. She didn't reply. She was still too stunned. He wasn't supposed to be there, but there he was. Right next to her, regarding her with curiosity and waiting for her to say something. And she could think of nothing to say. Her head felt as if it had been emptied of all intelligent content and all she could do, again, was stare. She'd thought he was handsome the first time she'd seen him, but now, up close…she really *shouldn't* be looking at his lips. She lifted her gaze from his mouth but instead became trapped in his eyes. Mesmerizing eyes, not dark at all as she'd previously thought, but leafy green with veins of gold and brown.

"What's your name?" he asked, his voice growing softer.

She didn't know how or when it had happened, but he'd reclaimed her hand; with his thumb, he lightly stroked her palm. If not for that fact, she surely wouldn't have answered him. But with his hand covering hers she couldn't think too clearly. Her voice didn't sound quite like her own. "Eleanor."

He cocked his head, waiting for more. His fingers drifted up her arm, across her shoulder, to trace a gentle line along her jaw.

"Surely you have more of a name than that?"

Did she? What was her name? "Um…Smith."

"Are you newly married, Eleanor…um, Smith?"

"Why do you ask such a question, sir?" Her sense was finally returning, and she pulled her head away from his wandering hand.

He smiled, his eyes darkening wickedly. "You stumbled a bit over your name, Eleanor Smith," he explained. "I thought perhaps it might be…new to you."

She blushed deeply, but her voice was sharp. "I stumbled because I am unused to such rudeness."

"I see. Are you married at all, then?"

She just glared at him before turning her head away to face the stage. She would not answer him this time. Doing so had obviously only encouraged further impertinent questions.

"I don't believe you *are* married."

She could hear the laughter in his voice and cursed him silently. She picked up the thin program she'd been given upon entry and began reading it for a second time.

"If you're not married—and you're not—then you must be employed."

Still without looking at him, she gritted out, "I never said I wasn't married."

He chuckled. "But you're not, of course. You're lucky you aren't, too…if you were, your husband would be obliged to give you a thorough spanking for coming here alone. It's not at all proper, you know."

Eleanor didn't turn her head for a moment. She was too shocked, not believing he'd really said what she thought he'd just said. Spanking?

Spanking?

With the word raging in her mind, she turned on him, eyes flashing, forgetting for the moment the dangerous effect he had on her. "You, *sir,* are not at all proper!"

He was unfazed by her indignation. "How are you employed, did you say?"

"I did not."

"I see. Then shall I guess?"

"I am a governess," she answered shortly, hoping

that austere and respectable occupation would change the direction of his lecherous thoughts. Scathingly, she added, "And you are...what, a professional libertine?"

She'd meant to insult him, but her remark seemed only to amuse him further. "No...I rather wish, but..." He paused, perhaps realizing he'd baited her too much. "Don't think I've introduced myself yet—perhaps I should start over. I'm James Bentley."

"Do you intend to sit here all night, Mr. Bentley?"

"Just until I figure something out," he said thoughtfully, his gaze roaming over her face. "You see, it's a rather odd thing that a governess should be here alone. I mean, you ought to have an untarnished reputation, oughtn't you? You *ought* to be at least as proper as the brats you look after."

Eleanor swallowed hard, wishing she hadn't come up with that particular profession. He was right. No governess would traipse off to the theater alone—not if she expected to keep her position, anyway. "It is not a crime to enjoy the theater. And I'm not employed. Currently, that is," she blurted out. "I am looking for work."

James leaned forward. "I can help you with that," he said, his voice low and slightly thick.

"You can?" With his face so close to hers, she felt her train of thought begin to slip carelessly away. Her eyes wandered to his mouth. She was watching him speak, but not really attending to what he said.

"You've overlooked one crucial point, Miss Smith. You're far too pretty to be a governess. No one will ever hire you."

"No?" Her voice sounded small and faint.

He shook his head. "Afraid not. But I'd be happy to employ you."

She blinked, not understanding at first what he meant. But when the meaning of his words slowly became clear, all the anger and embarrassment she'd felt that evening came back to her in one large dose. She opened her mouth to retort, but she had no insult to equal the one he'd just dealt her. So instead she said nothing and rose. He didn't try to stop her as she pushed past him. What a fool she'd been. She knew he was watching her, but she didn't care. All she cared about was leaving the building, finding her hack, and getting home as soon as possible. With her head down, she picked up her pace.

And then the next thing she knew she'd crashed into a large, solid object. It was the man who'd been sitting in front of her, the one who'd started her disastrous night off on such a sour note. She glared up at him. He was coming back to his seat for the second act, but unfortunately, he seemed to have had several pints of ale in the interim. He wasted no time latching his fat hands on to her shoulders.

"Well, 'ullo. What's the 'urry, luv?" he slurred. She backed away from him quickly, but she tripped on the hem of her dress as she did so. With a startled cry, she fell backward.

She should have hit the floor, and she braced her body for the inevitable pain, but it didn't come. She found herself instead being held by a pair of strong arms. She didn't have to look behind her to know to whom they belonged. She went rigid, trying to ignore the unfamiliar sensation that washed over her, a feeling of both helplessness and safety, of anger and, most frightening of all, of thrilling pleasure. She took a deep, steadying breath and regarded the large man in front of her. Although she couldn't see it from her position, something in Mr. Bentley's expression—that handsome face that had been laughing and mocking her until just a moment ago—must have told him to retreat. Any menace the man had possessed was now replaced by an almost comic apprehension, and he nodded apologetically as he backed away. She shivered, wondering if Mr. Bentley really could be dangerous if provoked.

He turned her around in his arms and looked down at her face with concern. "Are you all right?"

She nodded shakily and tried to straighten. He was too close, and she had to crane her neck to look at him. Heavens, he was tall. She hadn't noticed when he'd been sitting.

He brushed a finger across her cheek, and she realized he was wiping away a tear. She hadn't been aware that she'd been crying. There was something…almost tender in his expression, something truly apologetic for having upset her. It only lasted a second— perhaps she'd even imagined it—but it sent a shock of uncertainty through her body. Was he to be her friend or her foe? At that moment it wasn't clear which. One minute he was arrogant and insulting, and the next he was protecting her from harm. A tiny inexplicable part of her wanted to bury her head in his arms, even though prudence told her to kick him in the shins and run.

He was still holding her, still looking down at her

face. She couldn't look away. His head dipped and she was certain he was going to kiss her; it felt inevitable, like a force she was powerless to stop and didn't want to stop, anyway. She'd never been kissed before and she didn't know what to do. She closed her eyes and waited.

Nothing happened.

"Miss Smith?"

She opened her eyes. He was looking at her questioningly and holding up a long, chestnut-colored curl. With a startled intake of breath, she reached her hand up to feel her wig. It had slipped to the side just slightly, probably when she'd run into that man. He reached out his hand, too, and she stepped away quickly, concerned that he was going to pull it off.

They faced each other. She didn't know what he was thinking, but she knew how she felt: nervous. There was no telling how he would react to this discovery. He might be angry, or feel deceived. He'd obviously be suspicious. But instead all that emerged from his guarded expression was…the same look of intense curiosity that she'd seen on his face several times that evening.

"You're a bit of a puzzle, aren't you, Smith?" he said, taking a step forward and stopping when only a few inches separated them. "But I'm afraid I'd rather like to figure you out." His head dipped slightly again, only this time to whisper, "I was going to kiss you a moment ago. Unless you want that to happen you'd better run."

She still wasn't at all clearheaded, but for the first time that night she had no trouble making a decision and acting upon it. She took him at his word and turned and fled. She didn't look back.

And James didn't follow. He would have liked to, but he could tell from her expression that he'd frightened her. He just watched her dash up the aisle, long enough for her to disappear through the doors. Then he sat down on the closest seat, not yet ready to return to his box. Jonathon had doubtless observed the whole encounter and would be waiting to rib him. Normally James would have no problem handling his jokes, but for some reason this situation was different. He felt…disappointment at her leaving, and regret that he was the one responsible for her departure. It was an odd sensation since he didn't even know her. She remained a mystery, and he'd stupidly frightened her off for good. He believed that she was exactly what she claimed to be: a governess who, for whatever reason, simply liked a bit of Shakespeare. Nothing wrong with that. It was actually rather endearing. Like a lot of governesses, she probably had no family and therefore no chaperone. So why, having determined that she was *not* a doxy trolling the theater, had he treated her like one?

The answer was pretty obvious. Because, in the short time he'd spent with her, she'd intrigued him more than any woman he could remember. Because she had the most remarkable eyes, and a face that was both sensual and intelligent, a rare combination. Because he *did* want to kiss her. Because he knew, whether she knew it or not, that she'd wanted him to kiss her, too.

The curtains parted for the next act and he sighed. He didn't really want to sit through the play once more. He rose, but as he stepped into the aisle something caught his attention: a reticule, abandoned on the floor. She must have dropped it. He bent over to pick it up, noting that it was made of cream silk and embroidered with birds and flowers. It was obviously expensive. Perhaps it wasn't hers after all….

He didn't mean to snoop, but there was only one way to find out. He opened it, looking for some clue. It contained a long piece of frayed blue ribbon, a small leather-bound volume of the plays of William Wycherley, a mirror and several coins.

It also contained an invitation: to The Right Honorable Marchioness of Pelham, 5 Belgrave Square.

Now who was that?

Chapter Four

It was a perfect morning for a walk in the park. The sun shone softly through the trees, dappling the path with light, and a mild breeze gently teased Eleanor's hair, loosening it from the knot at her nape. She carried her scratchy straw hat in her hand, at least for the time being. Eventually, Louisa would notice and insist she put it on once more.

Right now, though, Louisa was about ten paces ahead of her and gaining distance with every step. Beatrice walked stiffly by her side. They'd been arguing until just a few minutes ago, although Eleanor had been unable to hear what about. It hardly mattered, since Louisa picked fights just for fun. Beatrice had made a few murmurs of appeasement but now, knowing her efforts were pointless, had given up in favor of stony silence. Eleanor was thankful that her sister had come along, although she would have preferred to be alone with her. They hadn't had a meaningful conversation in ages, and could hardly do so with Louisa listening in. Beatrice tended to understand her better than anyone else, and not that long ago, she'd also been a reluctant debutante. She'd have some words of encouragement or advice. And good heavens, did Eleanor need it, at least if she was going to survive the rest of the season. Of course, she couldn't confess everything that was on her mind: James Bentley, no matter the impression he'd left on her, was simply out of the question.

For the moment, though, their conversation would have to wait. She hummed quietly, letting herself be lulled into daydreams by the satisfying crunch of her kidskin boots hitting the gravel path. She allowed herself to lag even farther behind and began to imagine herself away from Hyde Park, away from the stifling governance of spinster aunts, uncomfortable hats and tight stays. There was so much more to life than her petty existence. She had a mind of her own; she had interests that had nothing to do with finding a suitable husband and producing suitable children. What was all the fuss about getting married, anyway?

And why did the only man to excite her have to be distinctly *un*suitable? What on earth did that say about her taste? Granted, he was handsome. Granted, he had wanted to kiss her, and that was certainly a novel experience. No one else had wanted to kiss her before; all the young men she'd met so far only wanted to kiss Lady Arabella Stuart or Lucinda Cator, the season's two Most Desirables.

"Eleanor!"

She looked up with a small jerk, anticipating the reprimand that Louisa's sharp tone promised. Louisa and Beatrice had halted several paces ahead, but were now standing, waiting for her to catch up. Both women looked annoyed.

"How many times must I say your name? And where is your hat?" Louisa demanded. She squinted directly into the sun, which made her look even crosser than normal.

Eleanor immediately began to rearrange her hat and walked briskly to reach them. "I'm sorry, Auntie. I wasn't attending. Is something the matter?"

"I asked, Eleanor, why your sister denies having received an invitation to my dinner next week."

Eleanor thought carefully before answering, not having the faintest idea how this question pertained to her. Both Louisa and Beatrice were staring at her impatiently. Hoping for a clue, she said slowly, "I didn't know you were holding a dinner, Auntie. I'm afraid I haven't put it in my diary."

"You're not invited. It's for married ladies only. What have you done with the invitation?"

Eleanor wasn't prepared for this interrogation, not right now, not when her mind had so recently been indulging in far more pleasurable thoughts. What did they want from her? "But I thought I wasn't invited. Why would I have the invitation?"

Beatrice sighed at her continued confusion. "You aren't invited, Eleanor. Louisa insists she gave you the invitation to pass on to me several days ago, but I never received it. Did you forget?"

"I knew I should have entrusted it to my footman," Louisa added resentfully before Eleanor could reply. "But your sister was at my house for a visit, anyway,

Beatrice, so I gave it to her instead. Useless girl. I repeat, Eleanor, where is the invitation now?"

Eleanor had gone pale as the memory came back. She knew where the invitation was, or at least where it had been when she'd parted ways with it. It had been in her reticule, along with other useful things like money to pay her driver. Luckily, she knew where Beatrice's housekeeper kept a small supply of funds for day-to-day sundries, so she'd been able to pay him on arrival. But given the events of that evening, the invitation had been insignificant enough to slip from her mind entirely.

Louisa was still looking at her, waiting for an answer that she didn't actually have. She certainly couldn't admit that she'd left the invitation at the theater when she shouldn't have been there in the first place. All she could do was be vague, but that would only send her aunt into a greater rage.

"It is possible I lost it, Auntie."

"It is possible? Did you or did you not?" Her nostrils flared slightly.

Vagueness wasn't working, so she tried bluntness instead. "Well, I don't know where it is now. So I suppose that means I did lose it. Yes."

Beatrice sighed deeply. "It no longer matters, Aunt Louisa. I never received it, and I've made other plans. Just this morning I told Lucy that I'd spend the day with her."

Louisa shook her head. "You will have to change your plans. Your sister-in-law will understand."

"I can't just change my plans. I made a promise."

"I'm so sorry," Eleanor said, quietly but sincerely,

hoping that her apology would placate her aunt enough so that they could change the subject.

"Your apology is noted, Eleanor, but not particularly helpful at this stage. I *must* have even numbers. Who ever heard of seating thirteen around the dinner table?"

"Well, I *am* sorry, Auntie."

"*Thirteen!* It's preposterous."

Eleanor bit her lip, not wanting to retort. But she hadn't slept well the night before and didn't have her usual patience for her aunt's histrionics. "Don't you think 'preposterous' might be a bit strong?"

"What?" Louisa spluttered.

"It is hardly a crisis. No one will even notice."

Louisa's mouth opened and closed a few times, fishlike, before she could speak. "I…I am not accustomed to this impudence from you, Eleanor. Where does this boldness come from?"

Eleanor refused to answer her. She was sick of being treated like a child. She crossed her arms and stared back stubbornly.

Louisa's gray eyes narrowed. Still looking at Eleanor, she said, "Beatrice, I am going home. We will finish our discussion there. I do not approve of flippant girls."

And with a curt nod, she turned and marched off.

Beatrice shook her head as she watched her walk away. "Why did you provoke her, Eleanor? She's going to be in one of her sulks for the rest of the day, and I'm the one who'll have to talk her out of it."

"It's not as if I meant to lose your invitation. I hate the way she talks to me, and I can't let her do it forever."

"You won't think that when she decides you're

becoming undisciplined and need to stay with her instead of Charles and me. I know it was an accident, Eleanor, but you've been terribly absentminded. Louisa has apparently been planning this dinner for many weeks. You weren't very sympathetic."

Eleanor wished she could explain why she'd responded as she had, but she couldn't tell Beatrice how she'd really lost the invitation. Hopefully, she said, "You'd rather spend the day with Lucy, anyway. Perhaps I did you a favor."

"That is *not* for your carelessness to decide."

She flinched. Beatrice had never spoken to her so sharply before.

"I am sorry," she said quietly.

Beatrice flushed with guilty embarrassment. "You needn't apologize. I shouldn't have spoken like that. Forgive me."

"If you forgive me. I *haven't* been myself…I don't know what's wrong with me."

"Yes, well, one's first season will have that effect." Beatrice looked up the path, where Louisa's rigid figure was gradually growing smaller. "I have to go now if I'm to catch up. Don't worry about Aunt Louisa. I'll calm her down. Come home soon."

Eleanor watched her sister move hurriedly off. She walked over to the nearest bench and sat down, feeling wretched. She'd never stood up to Louisa before, and she'd hardly ever fought with Beatrice. What did it take to please everyone? Perfect obedience? Perhaps her taste of independence *had* made her bold. At any rate, her reinforced backbone didn't seem to be going over at all well.

* * *

Who was she?

James was growing more confused by the minute, and to make matters worse he was beginning to feel rather absurd, as well. He'd been following her, after all, for half an hour now. He'd first seen her when she'd emerged from the stuccoed portico of number five Belgrave Square, preceded by the two stately creatures who'd just left her stranded. Finally alone, she was sitting forlornly on a bench. And he was standing behind a tree, looking, no doubt, like a complete fool. He'd ducked behind the tree when her companions had turned around to remonstrate with her. Now that they'd both left he supposed he could emerge, only he still didn't know what to say to her.

His intention had been merely to return her reticule, and it was a matter of pure coincidence that he'd arrived at the house just as she was on her way out. He hadn't even been certain that it *did* belong to her, as he could come up with no explanation for why she'd be carrying around someone else's invitation, or for why a governess would own such an expensive item. As he'd mulled the possibilities over in his head it had even occurred to him, albeit briefly, that she might actually be the Right Honorable lady herself. She certainly talked like a marchioness. But he quickly discounted that thought: she was too obviously innocent to be married. Some rudimentary detective work, carried out the day before—well, he'd just asked William—had revealed that the Marchioness of Pelham was tall, blond and visibly pregnant. She could only be the woman he'd just seen Eleanor talking to.

If she was an Eleanor at all. Perhaps she was a Jane, or a Maria. He still didn't know why she'd be carrying the marchioness's invitation, nor could he explain why she looked so different today. It wasn't just that the horrible blond wig had been replaced by her own rather nice, sleek brown hair. She wasn't dressed as she had been before, either. She didn't look like a governess.

But the way those women had been bossing her about, not to mention the way she'd been walking ten paces behind them, suggested they didn't regard her as an equal. He hadn't heard most of their words, but it was obvious they were taking her to task for something. Words like *impudence, carelessness* and *useless* had a way of carrying.

So, again, who was she?

He began walking in her direction, his hands in his pockets. He hoped he looked nonchalant, but he didn't feel that way at all. Although he kept telling himself that he had the upper hand, with both age and experience on his side, it didn't change the fact that he was starting to feel like an untried schoolboy. He didn't exactly have a plan, and there was a very real risk that she'd bolt the moment she saw him.

Luckily, that didn't happen. She noticed him just before he reached her, but although her eyes registered surprise she didn't so much as start. Perhaps her mind was too busy with other matters for her to react quickly; he thought he detected a fleeting trace of sadness in her expression, although it vanished before he could be sure. As he halted in front of her, her expression became masked. She straightened warily in her seat, as if preparing herself to spring at the slightest sign of impropriety.

James hadn't assumed she'd make things easy, and clearly she wasn't going to dash his expectations. He suppressed a sigh of frustration. "Miss Smith. What a pleasant surprise."

She didn't respond right away. Just continued to stare levelly back at him, allowing no indication of her feelings to enter her face. But inwardly, she was reeling. How was this possible? Was she dreaming him up...every detail down to his disheveled hair and gold watch chain? Was he as much a figment as Jane Pilkington?

No, no. Be reasonable, Eleanor. He is real, and he is dangerous. Find a way to leave, and do it quickly.

Only instead of following her mind's advice by nodding a curt goodbye and departing immediately, she responded with a question of her own. She was too bewildered to do otherwise. "What are you doing here?"

James raised an eyebrow at the accusation in her tone, but her suspicion was perfectly justified. He probably *should* answer her question honestly and immediately by removing her belongings from his jacket's inner pocket, but he thought it would be unwise to reveal his hand so soon. Better to pretend he was equally surprised by this meeting.

"I always walk in the park at this time of day...live quite close by, in fact. And you, Miss Smith? I don't recall seeing you here before."

"I rarely walk in the park," she lied. She often walked in the park, but would now obviously have to change that habit. Blast him. Furtively, she glanced up and down the path. An elderly couple, some distance off, was strolling in their direction. They were hardly a threat, but what if someone she knew came along? What if she should be seen talking to him? She had to leave, and if he tried to stop her she'd…

Probably expire on the spot, but she'd worry about that later.

She rose. "Do enjoy the sunshine, Mr. Bentley. I wish you a good day." But as she took her first step, he moved to the side to block her.

"Not so fast, Smith. I'm starting to think you're following me. You'll have to explain yourself first."

Eleanor glared at that absurd suggestion. Speaking quietly through clenched teeth, she ordered, "Move out of my way, Mr. Bentley, or I will scream."

He arched an amused eyebrow, almost daring her to make good on her offer. After a few seconds he asked, "Well? I'm waiting."

She opened her mouth slightly, but not a scream, or even a peep came out. Her cheeks suffused with color. Of course she wouldn't do it; she had no desire for public humiliation. The horrible man had called her bluff.

And he knew it, too. He looked altogether too smug.

"You grow tedious, Mr. Bentley," she said finally. "Have you no one else to bother?"

"Not when you've so unexpectedly improved my morning. Who were those women?"

Surprised by the sudden change of topic, she blinked in confusion. "Which women?"

"The ones speaking to you. The stern gray one and the blond one who stayed behind with you for a minute. Do you work for the younger one?"

A sudden wave of dizziness forced her back down on

the bench. This was very bad news indeed. He'd seen her family, and finding out her identity and theirs was just a short step away. Work for Beatrice? What exactly *had* she told him? Oh, yes. Eleanor Smith: governess.

"I look after her two-year-old son." She didn't feel at all confident as she told this falsehood, but hoped he would believe it since she resembled neither her sister nor her aunt.

He let his eyes wander down her body and then back up. "Dresses you rather well, doesn't she?"

She stiffened under his disconcerting gaze. "I simply benefit from her castoffs. She is very generous. I…I just have her clothes altered to fit me. This dress is two seasons old."

He nodded slowly. "And as she appears to be enceinte, presumably in a few months you will have another charge."

"Yes. I can hardly wait."

"And how long have you worked for her?"

She felt as if she was being quizzed under oath, only she didn't have any answers to give since every word she uttered was spur-of-the-moment perjury. "Not very long."

"Two days ago you said you were looking for work."

"Yes, well, I lied." She had no trouble coming up with that answer—it was the first bit of truth she'd spoken since they began this ludicrous conversation, and the words came out easily. But, oh God, now she'd have to explain why she'd lied….

He sat down on the other side of the bench. He was looking at her skeptically. "It's not nice to tell falsehoods, Miss Smith."

"I don't care," she said defiantly. "Why should I have told you the truth?" She didn't exactly know how she'd explain herself out of this mess, but desperation helped the words to flow, as did the fact that he was too close to her and she *really needed to leave*. "I believe it was you, sir, who pointed out how improper it was for a governess to be at the theater alone. I simply didn't want you to know who my employer was, so I told you I had none. But now you've found me out. You may tell her if you like." She sincerely hoped he wouldn't take her up on this challenge, and she was relieved by his answer. He even looked a tiny bit contrite.

"I have no desire for you to lose your position."

She rose again, this time determined to leave. "Now, you will forgive me, but I really must go. She will wonder what has kept me."

He rose, too. "I'll walk with you."

His words caused a swirl of unfamiliar sensation deep down in her stomach, but she tried to ignore it. "That won't be necessary." She started walking briskly, but he paid no heed to her refusal and began walking with her.

She stopped and turned on him. "What do you want, sir?"

It was a reasonable question, and he wasn't even sure of the answer himself. He could hardly confess that he wanted to kiss her, that he wanted to take her home with him and keep her there until he grew bored. She was completely adorable, especially when her cheeks filled with color and she looked as though she was ready to stomp her foot in irritation. He certainly wasn't ready to see the last of her.

"I have a confession to make, Miss Smith. Thought you'd want to hear it before you left."

She was extremely curious to hear it, but it didn't matter. As much as he infuriated her, his was the most thrilling company she'd ever experienced and her self-possession was vanishing fast. "I don't care."

But before she could turn away, he reached into his pocket and removed her reticule. He held it out to her. "My confession is that I didn't just stumble upon you. I found this after you left the theater…there was an invitation inside, addressed to your mistress. I was on my way to return it, but you were leaving the house just as I arrived."

She took the reticule from his hand, but just looked at it dumbly. Slowly, she started walking again, trying to digest this new set of facts. He knew where she lived. How disastrous. What if he should seek her out there? Or change his mind and decide to tell Beatrice after all?

She looked at him from the corner of her eye. She didn't actually think he'd do either. In the first place, he had no reason to go to the trouble of seeking her out, not when he was handsome enough to have his pick of beautiful women. And second, she didn't really think he'd tell Beatrice. Doing so would be deliberately cruel. But then again, he'd already proved he was capable of a certain amount of underhandedness in order to get what he wanted.

She needed a strategy, and provoking him further would obviously get her nowhere.

She stopped walking and turned to face him. He stopped, too, and waited.

She swallowed nervously, and then spoke. "I'm sorry if I've been rude to you this morning. I mean, you deserve it, but nevertheless it is remiss of me not to thank you. For rescuing me from that horrid man the other night. And for returning this. The invitation inside is very important."

James smiled, and her heart fluttered. "Don't thank me too soon."

She furrowed her brow. "What do you mean, 'too soon'?"

He began to walk forward again and, unaware of what she was doing, she followed his cue and began walking with him. "Well," he said slowly, "I have another proposition to make."

"What kind of proposition?" Eleanor asked. She quickly amended her words, however, realizing that she probably didn't want to know the answer. "Actually, you don't need to tell me."

"I assure you it's nothing sinister, Miss Smith. Do you always think such base thoughts?"

"Base thoughts!"

He stopped once more, leaning this time against a tall oak tree. "Yes. It's a perfectly innocent proposition and you won't even let me begin. It's precisely what happened when I tried to make the same proposition at the theater—you misunderstood me badly, you know, and maligned my character in the process. Instead of waiting to hear what I had to offer, you dashed off like a scared deer."

She bristled at the comparison. "Do you refer to your gallant offer of employment? As you now know, I've no need of work."

"Shall I tell you what my offer was? Or would you prefer to go on thinking the worst of me?"

She glanced over her shoulder suspiciously. They'd entered one of the more secluded parts of the park, and she hadn't realized it until then. "I'm not remotely interested," she said, but she made no move to leave. She leaned in slightly.

James smiled. "Yes, I can see you're not at all interested. You enjoy the theater very much, don't you?"

"What has that to do with anything?"

"It's obvious you'll go to great lengths to attend."

"That's not true," she lied stubbornly. "I like it no more than most."

He sighed. "Then explain your ridiculous disguise and your multiple deceptions. You know you'd lose your situation if your employer ever learned of your outings, but you're willing to take the risk anyway."

"Yes, well, I have decided I won't be doing so any longer. Too risky, as you've just pointed out."

He moved a step closer. "You could go, if you wanted to. You could go if you were with me."

She countered by taking a step back, unable to think clearly when he stood so close. "I don't think that's possible."

"But it is. I hold a very large share of that theater, you see. I'm one of its owners, and if you were with me I could provide you with better protection than you have now, sitting alone in the audience. As your last experience showed, you need protection."

Eleanor just stared at him for a good five seconds as she attempted to make sense of his words. She felt rather sick. How could this be possible? She'd wondered how she'd been unlucky enough to encounter him there twice, and he owned the theater. She was a fool.

"I don't think that would be wise," she said, her voice weak.

"Look, Miss Smith, you needn't act so maidenly about this. It's a simple business proposition. We both have something to gain."

"I fail to see what either of us would gain."

"We both require the other's company."

"I do *not* require your company, sir, and you can go alone."

"Of course I can go alone. I don't have to go at all—I helped finance the theater, but I have little to do with its day-to-day running. But I've been thinking of late that I ought to take a more active role, and I would do so more readily if I had someone pleasant to sit next to on a regular basis. Make it feel less like work, don't you think?"

It was outrageous. Jeopardize her reputation so he wouldn't be bored? "Get someone else to sit next to you—you didn't seem to have any difficulty finding companionship before."

He smiled. "Perhaps. But it *is* a problem finding someone intelligent enough… I must admit to being a bit of a philistine, Miss Smith, and I need someone to help me understand the plays properly. Someone who'll have something improving to say at the end. Someone like a…governess."

Her heart was pounding so loudly that he must have heard it, but somehow she managed to sound calm.

"You're a bit old for a governess, sir, but I wish you luck in your search. I must go."

She turned away, but he caught her hand. He was beginning to look impatient. "What I'm really trying to do is help you. Will you accept my help?"

"How on earth would this help me? Please don't tell me you're concerned about my welfare."

"Well, I am. You need a chaperone."

"And you think you're qualified?"

He frowned at her sarcastic tone. He was making everything up as he went along, but it all sounded like good sense to his ears. He'd almost convinced *himself* that his motives were benign, so why wouldn't she believe him? "Maybe not in the conventional sense, but it's not safe for you to go alone. People make certain assumptions about women who do such things. You are aware of that, aren't you? If you step foot in a theater alone, everyone there will assume you are a woman of easy virtue."

She turned pink. She'd known respectable women never attended the theater alone, but she hadn't actually taken the time to consider why that was so. She'd thought it was just another of society's conventions.

"I already told you, I won't be going again."

"But you'll want to." He still held her hand, and the light, warm pressure was beginning to make her feel dizzy. He stepped closer again, and his voice dropped an octave. "Give me an answer, Eleanor. I know I haven't behaved like a perfect gentleman to you, and this is my only way of making up for it. Let me help you. A new play starts next week. Come with me. I promise you'll enjoy it. I even promise I'll behave. You'll be perfectly safe."

She knew she should refuse; that was the only sane thing to do. But his voice was gentle and cajoling, and his leafy eyes had grown dark. She wanted nothing more than to acquiesce. She was thinking about kissing again, thinking about how close his face was to hers. He was right: she would want to go again, and he was offering her the chance.

She knew she should refuse. That's what any sensible, gently raised young lady would do. But the tedium of being a sensible young lady had been doing her in for many weeks now. There really was much more to life.

"I can't come. It's too difficult to get out of the house without being detected."

He sensed her resolve was fading. "You must have a night off."

She shook her head.

He rolled his eyes. "This habit you have of lying… *everyone* has a night off. Tell me when yours is."

This couldn't be happening to her. He was asking her to sneak away and meet him secretly. She wasn't supposed to do that sort of thing, but here she was, actually contemplating it. She knew she shouldn't…but why shouldn't she? There were so many rules she had to follow, and she hadn't invented a single one herself. Besides, what if he should reveal her secret? Thanks to that invitation, he knew where she lived and he knew who her relatives were. Her voice was small and uncertain. "Wednesday?"

He seemed surprised that she'd actually provided him with an answer. "Wednesday? Shall we meet then, next week?"

She was already shaking her head vigorously, wanting to take everything back. She hadn't agreed to anything. "I...I don't know my answer yet. I will think about it, but I can't make any promises."

"I'll send my carriage. There will be no risk at all."

"I will not be alone in a carriage with you!"

"Oh, for... I won't be in it. I'll meet you at the theater, so you'll be perfectly alone. I'm just trying to be helpful."

"It will never work. You cannot send your carriage to my house. I could never explain such a thing to my mistress."

He frowned. Of course his carriage couldn't simply arrive at the doorstep to whisk the governess away for an evening of dubious entertainments. But he also knew that if he left transportation up to her she'd never come. "I don't think you'll have to explain yourself, but if anyone asks, say you're visiting an elderly relative. My maid goes somewhere every Tuesday night and I haven't the faintest idea where, nor do I care. She can do what she likes during her own time. No one will miss you."

Except she wasn't a servant, and she would be missed. "I don't know...."

"Six o'clock," he said, his voice quiet and brooking no argument. Eleanor looked into his eyes and knew he'd won. How had it happened? Everything had moved too quickly, and she just couldn't keep up. And now he was standing so close to her, his head bent toward hers and his changeable eyes meeting her gaze. He still held her hand, and the gentle, almost imperceptible caress of his thumb made her shiver.

He really was going to kiss her this time; she was sure of it. But he didn't, not on the lips or cheek, anyway. He lifted her hand to his mouth and kissed the back of it softly, never taking his gaze from hers.

"I believe you have somewhere to go, Miss Smith, so I will bid you good day. Don't make my driver wait, or he'll come find you."

As he walked away, she took a deep breath, trying to calm her racing heart. What had she allowed herself to be talked into?

Chapter Five

Six o'clock had come and gone, and Eleanor still wasn't ready. She couldn't find her gloves, and in light of James Bentley's disturbing habit of grabbing her hand at unexpected moments, they would be an indispensable part of her armor. She'd practically turned her bedroom inside out looking for them. Where were they? And where, for that matter, was he? *If* he was coming, he was late.

She walked over to her window and looked out onto the square; it was the sixth time she'd done so in as many minutes. Perhaps he might not come at all. That was a reassuring possibility. His promise may have been nothing more than an empty threat meant to scare her. Perhaps he'd met some other hapless girl in the week since she'd seen him and had forgotten all about her.

But just in case he hadn't...*where* were her gloves? She was ready in every other way: gray dress, blond wig concealed in the folds of her cloak. The carriage might arrive at any second, and it wouldn't do at all for her to keep it waiting. What if James's driver really did come to the door looking for her? She didn't particularly care to put that threat to the test, even if Beatrice and Charles had already gone out for the evening and wouldn't be there to witness anything. In fact, she was supposed to be with them, and at that moment she desperately wished she'd never requested permission to visit Miss Pilkington instead.

She moved away from the window and sat on her bed, furrowing her brow as she tried to remember everything she'd done that day and hoping for some clue as to her gloves' whereabouts: ate breakfast, wrote to her father, bought a new hat, returned home and read a book in the sitting room…

Right. Sitting room. She'd look there.

She dashed out her bedroom door and down the front staircase. She slowed as she reached the bottom, giving the hall a cursory glance. Cummings, not surprisingly, seemed to have gone on an extended break once Beatrice and Charles had left and was not to be seen. She exhaled slowly with relief as yet another obstacle disappeared and threw open the sitting room door. She immediately spotted her gloves, in a crumpled heap on a Pembroke table on the other side of the room.

But she took only one step into the room before stumbling to a halt. It was already occupied. Charles was leaning back comfortably on the sofa, a rumpled newspaper spread out in his lap.

She backed up immediately, so that only her head and shoulders poked around the door. He'd be sure to wonder why she was wearing her cloak.

As it was, he was already looking at her curiously. "Eleanor? Is something wrong?"

She didn't answer right away. Why was he still there? She'd said goodbye to them over an hour ago, but now Charles was back, looking as though he had no immediate plans to go anywhere. Although he was still in evening dress, he'd loosened his cravat and removed his shoes.

Trying not to sound anxious, she said, "I'm fine. Why are you not at the Dalrymples' ball?"

He smiled rather smugly. "I've been granted a reprieve. Your sister felt unwell, and we returned home before we'd even got out of the carriage. She's resting upstairs. You might bring her some tea since we're short staffed. Do it m'self, but she blames me for her queasiness."

"I'm afraid I have to leave."

He frowned. "Why are you hovering in the doorway?"

"I...I'm visiting Miss Pilkington tonight, remember? Her carriage has just arrived and I don't have time to talk." Eleanor hardly looked at him as she answered. Her eye was drawn to the large south window, the one that faced the street. It was true: a carriage *had* just pulled up in front of the house, only it didn't belong to Jane. It was quite a grand one—although not ostentatious—and it definitely wasn't the sort of carriage a humble governess would take to meet her relatives. James seemed not to have worried about such details.

However, from Charles's perspective it seemed perfectly natural that one of Eleanor's friends should own such a smart contraption. "Oh, yes. Has she improved?"

"She's convalescing slowly."

"Don't know how you manage to avoid your social duties, Eleanor. Thought Louisa would've forced you to go tonight."

She shrugged noncommittally, hoping to mask her annoyance. *What* a time for him to start feeling expansive. "Bea's very sympathetic. She knows what it's like to be in my position, and she never told Louisa that I wouldn't be going. But, Charles, I really must leave. I don't want to keep her driver waiting."

"I'll walk you to the carriage," he offered. "Cummings seems to have vanished into the ether again."

Her eyes widened in alarm. "What ridiculous ceremony! There's absolutely no need for you or for Cummings. The carriage is right outside and I can walk to it perfectly well on my own. Besides, you haven't any shoes."

He looked down at his feet, realizing she was right. But when he looked back up at her, Eleanor was afraid she saw a tiny hint of suspicion in his eyes. Was it her imagination or had they narrowed just a tiny bit?

Luckily, though, she was saved by Beatrice's lady's maid, Meg, who walked briskly passed her into the room. Like all good lady's maids, she was a snob, but she gave Eleanor's unseasonable outfit nothing more than an unconscious look of disapproval before going straight to Charles. She appeared anxious, but Eleanor was unable to hear her whispered words. Beatrice obviously needed something, and for a blessed moment, Eleanor no longer mattered.

"Charles, I'm sorry, but I really must go. Give Bea my love."

He nodded distractedly and waved her away, his concern now entirely focused on his wife's condition. Eleanor crept out the door.

Eleanor's deep blush began the moment James's driver greeted her politely and helped her into the carriage, and lasted the whole way to the theater. Now, sitting in the parked carriage and waiting for the driver to open her door, she began to feel ill. And where was James? A large crowd had formed in front of the theater, and for all his promises of chaperonage, he was nowhere in sight.

She closed her eyes and slid back into her seat, allowing her head to fall back despondently. The whole situation still didn't seem real to her; perhaps she'd wake up in bed any minute now, having dreamed the whole thing. It wasn't *her* fault that she was there, considering he'd pretty much blackmailed her. If she hadn't complied with him, he might have told Beatrice, and that would have meant that she'd be shipped back to her father's house in disgrace or, even worse, that she'd be forced to spend the rest of the season with Louisa. She'd had no choice but to do as he told her.

She opened her eyes and sighed, knowing perfectly well that she was making excuses. She *could* have refused, if she'd really wanted to. It was just that a tiny bit of her wanted to be there, despite her nervousness. She wasn't afraid of James, strictly speaking, even if she was afraid of the way he made her feel. But she could control her feelings for one night, right? What could he do to her in a crowded theater, anyway? She should be perfectly safe, as long as no one recognized her, *and* as long as she didn't do anything stupid like talking to him or looking at him unless absolutely necessary.

And if he tried to kiss her again, well…it wouldn't kill her, would it?

She closed her eyes miserably. She could not succumb to such reasoning or she'd really be doomed.

When she opened her eyes, the door was ajar and James was looking in. In the dim light he seemed positively sinful. His white cravat made him appear even darker, and the wind had tousled his hair. She wondered dumbly if he'd walked there. And she was staring. Again.

Why, oh why…

"Is everything all right, Miss Smith?"

She realized with a renewed blush that she was practically reclining in her seat, and she pulled herself up quickly to restore her composure.

"I…I was just getting bored of waiting. You're late, Mr. Bentley." She didn't mean to scold, but she was so embarrassed she couldn't seem to help it.

He smiled rather ruefully, and her heartbeat quickened. "Have you been longing for my company?"

"Like I've been longing for measles."

"I do apologize. Shall we go inside?" He held out his arm to help her from the carriage.

Her mind was now clear enough for her to be wary of his chivalry. "I can alight unassisted, thank you."

He shrugged. "If it pleases you."

It was actually a rather difficult feat to climb from a carriage in long skirts without help, or to do so gracefully, anyway. By the time Eleanor had reached the pavement, she could plainly see that he was biting back laughter.

"Do I amuse you, Mr. Bentley?"

"Not at all. Will you be warm enough?" He waited for her answer, but her stubborn eyes told him it wouldn't be forthcoming. He gave up. "Right, take my arm." It was an order.

She looked at his arm, and then she looked at the large, jostling crowd gathered by the theater's doors. She swallowed, gingerly placed her hand on his sleeve and pretended that doing so made her feel nothing. And they started to walk, left, right, left, right. She concentrated on her feet so as not to think about his arm. They'd nearly reached the entrance.

If only she'd been concentrating on what was happening around her, rather than keeping her gaze fixed on the ground, then she would have seen the scuffle that began between two men, just behind her right shoulder. She would have stepped out of the way before they crashed into her.

But she didn't notice them soon enough, and the impact spun her around and sent her flying, right into James's chest. She grabbed on to his shoulders to stop herself from falling, and she stayed there for several long seconds, steadying herself but also becoming all too aware that the front of her body was pressed rather snugly to his.

And then he groaned. Not very loudly, but she heard him.

She quickly realized the reason why and stepped away, embarrassed. "I'm so sorry. Your foot."

"My foot?" His voice sounded a bit hoarse.

"I stepped on it, didn't I?"

He shook his head slightly, as if only just understanding what she was referring to. "You weigh nothing. Are you all right?"

"I'm fine. I've wrinkled your jacket, though—"

"Where are they?"

"They? Those men?" she asked in alarm. She didn't know what he proposed to do to them, but he was starting to look quite angry. "Oh, please forget about this incident. It was just an accident." She took his hand instinctively, wanting to lead him inside, away from any altercation, but she immediately blushed once she'd realized what she'd done. She tried to pull her hand away, but he stopped her by squeezing it tight.

"I think you'd better hold on for now. Come with me."

He led her through the theater doors, straight through the foyer, and up a small flight of stairs. She could barely take in her surroundings—a burgundy carpet, cream painted walls with gilt highlights—as she struggled to keep up. He was so tall that he seemed to take one step for every two of hers.

"Where are we going?"

"It'll be safer for you up here."

"Up where?"

But the answer became self-evident even as she asked the question. They'd arrived at a closed, red velvet curtain. It was a private box. She stopped. "Oh. Oh, no."

"What?"

"I think we will have a better view down below."

"I can assure you we will not," he said, irritation entering his voice. "Furthermore, your identity will be completely protected if no one can see you, and you'll be out of public view sitting here, at least if you keep your chair back enough. It's the only sensible thing to do."

She had to admit that he had a point. At least in a private box she'd have only him to worry about. But he was her biggest concern....

He *had* promised to behave, but Eleanor didn't rate that promise too highly. To him, she was just a governess, a powerless female. She'd heard many stories about the way men treated women of that ilk. He would have no compunction about trying to…to make love to her, if he wanted to. She didn't actually know if "make love" was the right term, nor did she think he could possibly have any real interest in her, but still…

He leaned in closer, as if reading her thoughts, and his eyes took on a challenging gleam. "Don't you want to be alone with me?"

She said nothing.

He sighed in a bored manner. "I assure you, Smith, you've nothing to worry about."

She raised her chin. "If you should act in any way improperly I…I will scream. I really will this time. Loudly." And she meant it.

Unfortunately, he just looked as if he wanted to laugh again. "I believe you. Now are we finally ready to sit?" He parted the curtains and ushered her inside. "Any other demands?"

"Not presently," she said, her tone probably a trifle too imperious to belong to a governess. She perused the small room and was relieved to note that the seats were spaced generously apart. She sat, and the box settled into stubborn silence. Neither she nor he would be the first to speak.

She glanced at him covertly. His profile alone was enough to make her feel flustered. He, however, seemed completely uninterested in her presence. She should be thankful.

The play began after just a few minutes, and she exhaled slowly; she hadn't even been aware that she'd been holding her breath. She couldn't help smiling with anticipation as the first actor walked onto the stage, and after a few more minutes, she quite nearly forgot who she was sitting next to. She leaned forward to concentrate on every word and action. It was a comedy, and even though her personal situation wasn't particularly comical at the moment, she managed to giggle the whole way through the play nonetheless.

It could have lasted much longer and she'd have remained amused, but the play was just two hours long, and therefore without intermission. As the curtains closed James turned to her. "Well, Miss Smith? Satisfactory?"

"Extremely satisfactory," she said, eyes shining with pleasure, before she remembered where she was and with whom. Masking her expression, she asked politely, "Did you enjoy it?"

"I did."

She nodded, feeling shy once again. She didn't know what to say, and she actually rather suspected he hadn't been paying attention to the play at all. She shifted uncomfortably in her seat, feeling suddenly aware of the smallness of the room. Of the size of him and of every inch that separated them. Of the muted candlelight that shone from the sconces, making him look even more handsome. The silence that ensued felt tangible and heavy. The only noise was the background murmur of people rising and preparing to leave.

"I should go," she said, awkwardly breaking the silence. "I mustn't be late."

"Just sit for a spell," James suggested, leaning back nonchalantly in his seat. "There will be a crush to leave."

She took a steadying breath. Continuing to be alone with him was a frightening prospect. "Well…*just* a few minutes, maybe."

And then they settled once more into an uncomfortable silent void.

At a young age Eleanor had learned never to let a conversation die. *Never stop talking to your neighbor,* her father had instructed her at the first dinner party she'd been allowed to attend, *even if you have nothing to say.* That advice had never seemed more suitable than now. She'd just pretend this was a formal dinner party and she'd be all right.

"Um, how did you come to own this theater?" she ventured politely, looking at him only obliquely.

He paused for a long while before answering, as if choosing his words carefully. "It's a rather complicated story…my mother was an actress."

"Really? An actress?"

He raised an eyebrow at her surprised tone. "Don't look so scandalized, Miss Smith. What was your mother? A duchess?"

"No, of course not," Eleanor replied quickly, blushing. "I meant no offense. It… I think it sounds exciting."

"The rest of her family were also on the stage, and I went to live with them in Dublin when I was eighteen.

I actually tried acting once myself, but I forgot all my lines and was roundly jeered off the stage."

"Why would you try to act? I thought you said you didn't care for plays."

"Ah, but I was trying to persuade a pretty girl to join me tonight."

"Mr. Bentley—"

He sighed. "Yes, I know, I said I'd behave. Anyway, my best friend in Ireland was an actor, and when I returned to London last year, he came along. I helped him finance this theater, although he's gradually buying my share. Within a few years he'll be the sole owner."

"And what will you do then?"

"Try something else, I suppose."

"Oh." She wanted desperately to hear more, but she sensed he'd revealed as much as he was willing to for the evening. How curious it was. The background he described didn't sound like one of great privilege, but he looked and spoke like a gentleman. Money seemed not to be a problem, but where did it come from? Was he a criminal? She'd heard tales of dashing highwaymen, of gamblers, of people who could appear to belong to polite society, but who all the while inhabited its murky fringes. She glanced at him warily. It wouldn't surprise her.

"And how did you become a governess?" he asked, turning the tables on her.

She'd prepared for this question, and responded easily. "My father was a tutor. He taught me French and Latin, and I managed to pick up a smattering of needle-work and music and other useful arts on my own. I suppose the idea came naturally to me."

"You might have found a husband instead."

She blushed. There was something uncomfortably pointed in his tone, something altogether too interested in her answer. "I'm afraid it is not that easy."

He just nodded slowly, his gaze never leaving her face. She wished she knew what he was thinking, but she was grateful that he took pity on her and let the subject rest. "Are you in town for the season with your mistress?"

She nodded. Actually, she'd be leaving London in August, well before the season officially ended. Beatrice and Charles would be traveling to their country house in Kent for her confinement, and she planned to go with them, to be with her sister when the baby was born.

"So tell me something else about yourself, Miss Smith. I don't really know that much about you, except your fondness for wigs and sneaking out to the theater."

"I have brown hair."

James sighed. "I'd noticed. Do your brothers and sisters have brown hair?"

"I haven't told you if I have brothers and sisters."

"Yes, I know. I'm asking you to do that now."

She wanted to smile at his obvious frustration. "Ben is the oldest. Then comes Beatrice, myself, and finally Helen. They're all blond."

"Ah. So if Ben and Beatrice are older, and Helen is younger, then that would make you…?"

"Are you asking, in your circuitous way, my age?"

He smiled. "I am."

"You're not supposed to ask that sort of question, you know."

"Don't be so pedantic. Pretend, for the moment, that you're not a governess."

"I'm twenty, with a birthday in November." She'd seen no reason to lie about her siblings, but she couldn't reveal her real age. In fact, she'd be nine and ten in November. But if she'd already been working as a governess, even for a short while, she'd have to be a bit older.

"And you, Mr. Bentley?"

"Nearly thirty. Practically ancient."

She blushed again. "I meant do you have any siblings."

"I have two half brothers, or had, anyway. Richard, the eldest, died last year."

"I'm sorry." She meant it, too. She adored her family, and she couldn't imagine losing any one of them.

James just shrugged. "I don't miss him. We weren't close."

Eleanor couldn't understand his unemotional response. "Do you share the same…?"

"Father. My mother was his second wife."

"But what about your other brother?"

"William. We get on very well."

"I'm pleased."

He looked at her sharply. "Why do you care?"

"I…I don't." She stumbled under his scrutiny. "I mean, it's just that I'm very close to my siblings, and it would be a pity if anyone did not have that sort of relationship."

"Even me?"

She swallowed hard. "Even you."

"Must you always wear that awful wig?"

She blinked at that sudden change of subject. "Blond hair is very fashionable."

"I prefer you without it," he said, his gaze roaming slowly over her face. "You're rather beautiful without it."

A wave of heat rushed through her body at that compliment, even though she was sure he didn't really mean it. "Well, I have no one to impress. And, as you know, I mustn't be recognized."

"Fair enough," he said, "but what I've been wondering is who would recognize you, anyway? You're not exactly socially prominent."

Again, Eleanor drew upon rehearsed answers. "Just in case. I have met several of the marchioness's friends in the course of my employment, and one of them might recognize me."

"Would they?" He didn't seem convinced.

"With brown hair, yes, they might. And I can't even wear many of my everyday clothes because, as you know, some are her castoffs, and so someone might identify me with her even if I wasn't myself recognizable." Even to her own ears this sounded far-fetched.

"You could plunder the wardrobe room backstage for another disguise. It must contain something more attractive. You could do it tonight if you like."

Eleanor cocked her head to the side. "Really?" She would have loved to go backstage—ever since she was a little girl she'd wondered what it would be like. Her imagination conjured up a colorful vision of bosomy actresses unabashedly changing their costumes and practicing their scales. It would certainly be like nothing she'd seen before.

Of course, she couldn't go backstage.

"I'm afraid I'd better stay on this side of the curtain."

"No doubt you're right." He paused thoughtfully. "It

occurs to me, actually, that you might be trying to make yourself less appealing for my benefit."

She grinned cheekily. "An added bonus."

"Oh, really?" With one swift movement, he'd pulled the wig from her head.

She glared at him. "Why did you do that?"

He looked entirely satisfied. "I told you I prefer you without it."

"What if someone sees me?"

"If you haven't noticed, we're the last people here."

She rose to look down into the empty seats below. He was right. She'd actually been having the best time she'd had in months and had completely lost track of the hour. "I must go. Oh, dear. Is it late?"

He looked at his watch. "Midnight is three hours off, so you needn't fear my carriage will turn into a pumpkin."

She held out her hand. "My wig, sir. You promised you'd behave."

He sighed and rose. "I suppose I did."

He handed over the wig, and she pulled it onto her head. He frowned. "It's…uh…it's rather crooked. Here."

Before she could stop him he'd reached out to fix it. He tucked away a stray brown curl, and his fingers lingered by her temple. She wanted to close her eyes, but her gaze was tangled up in his and she couldn't look away.

"I enjoyed myself, Eleanor." His voice was soft.

She liked the way her name sounded on his lips. She should insist that he address her properly as Miss Smith, but since that name wasn't even her own, in a way it seemed even less appropriate. "I enjoyed myself, too," she responded, feeling suddenly shy.

"Shall we do this again?" His hand had left her forehead and was now on the small of her back, leading her out of the box and down the stairs.

Should they? No was the obvious answer, but she couldn't bring herself to say it. She wanted to come again. He'd behaved himself—not perfectly, but she didn't think he'd be capable of any better. All they'd done was talk. He'd been infuriating, but it was…nice. She hadn't had an enjoyable conversation with anyone recently, not even Beatrice.

So why not? How splendid it was to do something without her aunt or sister in tow. How much she enjoyed being the one to decide what she did, and where and how. At least he paid attention to her, which was more than could be said about the countless gentlemen she'd met so far. And since she was only in London for another month…how much trouble could she possibly get into? Coming one more time wouldn't hurt her.

They were crossing the empty foyer. She nodded uncertainly.

"Another play will begin next week. Would next Wednesday suit you?"

Wednesday…Wednesday…did she have anything to do? Just a luncheon in the afternoon…she could get away later…it had been so easy tonight…

She nodded again as they stepped out into the cool summer night. She couldn't actually manage the words.

"Six o'clock then? Wednesday next week?"

"Yes."

"I'll send my driver again. Good night."

He helped her into the carriage and closed the door. With a rap on the window, the carriage jolted into motion.

She closed her eyes and sank down as far as possible into her seat. She didn't know what she was getting herself into, but she was too far along to stop now. She hoped she could trust him. He hadn't even tried to kiss her this time, and she should be relieved. So why did she feel so disappointed?

Chapter Six

"James?"

James looked up at his brother. William had obviously asked him a question and was waiting for an answer. "Sorry. I wasn't paying attention."

Will sighed. They were sitting in his library, digesting their supper over brandy. The conversation had been remarkably one-sided all evening. "I said that if I'd known you'd be staring off into middle distance all night I'd never have invited you. What's wrong? Not in love, are you?" He grinned at this suggestion.

James just frowned. "Don't be an ass."

"But you are looking rather lovesick and distracted like—who was it? Some rot about his wrinkled doublet and foul stockings...you must know the one. Hamlet, I think."

"Do be quiet, Will," James said irritably. He had been inattentive, but he didn't care to discuss the reason why. He knew it had nothing to do with love. It was lust, plain and simple. He hadn't been with a woman in weeks and, frankly, he needed one. That was the only explanation for why, at odd moments throughout every day, his mind wandered off into inappropriate daydreams involving Miss Smith, the primmest, bluestockingest governess in London.

He'd attended the theater with her twice, every Wednesday for the past two weeks, the second time just last night. Each time he'd exhibited, with great effort, the most unimpeachable behavior—or, if not exactly unimpeachable, then at least pretty good by his standards. As he'd hoped, she was slowly lowering her guard. She was even beginning to smile at him regularly: sweetly, innocently, trustingly. And each time he'd wanted, in the most primitive way, to carry her off to some dark corner and ravish her. Not being able to do so was driving him distracted.

But in spite of these urges, her smiles also made him feel something else. Pleased that he'd been witty enough to amuse her, and proud that he was sitting next to such a lovely girl. He felt generally…well, pretty damned lucky, and he often found himself watching her from the corner of his eye, feeling a strange tug of pleasure at seeing her happy. He hardly paid attention to the plays himself, even though he wasn't the philistine he'd claimed to be. He simply enjoyed sitting next to her too much to pay attention.

So maybe it wasn't *simple* lust. It was lust and… affection, perhaps? He liked her, but love? He was still confident that once he bedded her—and he would, if he were patient—then these conflicting feelings would disappear. Problem was he was beginning to feel like a monster for even entertaining such thoughts. Most women he knew were older and experienced, and he'd wager a hefty sum that Eleanor was completely innocent.

Hoping to direct the conversation away from himself, he remarked, "Haven't seen you in many weeks. Been busy?"

"Yes, I have been, actually," Will said, a touch of defensiveness entering his voice. "Busier, I'm sure, than you." He rose to refill his glass.

James raised an eyebrow. "You're normally one of the least busy people I know."

Will mumbled something without turning around, and James asked him to repeat it.

"It *is* the high season, if I must point that out, James," he replied testily as he returned to his chair. "One has certain obligations."

"What kind of obligations?" James asked warily.

"If you must know, I've been to Almack's twice since I saw you last, as well as to a variety of other dull entertainments. Going to some other blasted ball tonight. Laugh if you want. I don't care."

James didn't laugh. He was too nonplussed. "I don't understand. *Why* are you doing this?"

William was beginning to look truly distressed. "Why? Because I just can't bear the pressure anymore."

"Is there pressure?"

"Not for you, maybe, but you don't have our irritating cousins, Venetia and Henrietta, coming round to your house three times a week to remind you that duty has called and you've failed miserably."

"Just ignore them," James said, mentally cringing at the thought.

"I can't. They make me feel guilty, and Venetia is threatening to blackmail me."

"I see." James rose to fill his own glass, wondering vaguely what she was blackmailing him about. It could be anything, given his brother's reputation. He didn't ask, though, since Will was looking too distraught. "Well, then keep going to Almack's, though frankly I'm surprised you're even allowed in. It won't kill you, and it'll placate them enough to leave you alone. The season won't last forever, and then you can go about your business."

He appeared to think that over. "I suppose…but then, I also wonder…"

A long pause.

"Yes?"

"I wonder…what would you say if I told you that I was seriously considering going through with it this season?"

"Going through with what?"

"Getting married."

James returned to his seat. "I'd say I didn't believe you."

Will swirled his drink thoughtfully. "I don't *want* to get married, now that I think about it. It's inevitable, though—I have to produce an heir sometime, and I *am* one and thirty. Maybe it's better just to get it over with, like most unpleasant things. Why are you smiling?"

"Because I have never heard such utter rubbish in my entire life. *You* are not getting married."

"No, not yet. Can't say I've met anyone even remotely suitable. Don't know anyone who's looking, do you?"

"Me? I'm afraid I don't even know the type."

"No, don't suppose you would."

They were silent for a moment while James realized that his brother was, at least on this occasion, completely in earnest. He shouldn't be so surprised. Although Will rarely took anything seriously, he made an exception for his family, particularly since he'd inherited his title. Carrying on their name was his burden.

How odd it would be, though. Since his adolescence women had been succumbing to William's roguish, sandy-haired charm, and although he might be willing to marry, James didn't think for a minute that he was ready to settle down. He was already beginning to pity the bride, whoever she might be.

"I don't envy you, Will," he said finally. "It's times like this that I most appreciate being an unimportant third son."

"Yes, well, I hate to remind you, but you're *not* unimportant. If I should fall off a cliff tomorrow, you'll be the next earl—God save us all. That's another thing Venetia and Henrietta keep nagging me about because clearly you'd be utterly useless in that respect. What do you think about that?"

"I think the chance of you falling off a cliff is too remote for me to bother thinking about it."

Will snorted. "Yes, well, you can see why I feel so compelled to start producing. If I don't we're bloody well done for, and you'll be directly to blame."

"You'll make a rotten father."

Will sighed. "I'm inclined to agree. Look; why don't you come along with me tonight?"

"Where, exactly?"

"The Countess of Thrushton's."

"That woman? You must be joking."

"It won't be that bad."

"It will."

"All right, all right, it's true. But if you would conform *just* a tiny bit then our cousins might leave me alone. I mean, if they could be convinced that you weren't a total reprobate, and that you, too, were thinking of marriage and children—"

James cut him off before he could say any more. "Absolutely not."

"You merely have to pretend, James. And, perfectly seriously, there are several very pretty girls out this season. It's not such a hardship."

"I'm not interested in empty-headed little girls."

"Of course. You save all your energy for jades."

James tightened his grip on his glass but didn't otherwise respond.

"Are you involved with anyone at the moment?" William asked. "Anyone giving you an excuse *not* to come with me tonight?"

Only Eleanor, James answered silently, *and our involvement consists of nothing more than sitting next to each other and talking.* Strangely enough, talking to her was pretty satisfying in itself. She was perceptive and intelligent, and he'd found himself telling her things that he reserved for his best friends. About his parents dying when he was young, about joining the army when he was sixteen and deep in his cups. That tidbit had scandalized her to her toes, and he was quickly realizing that scandalizing her was a hugely amusing endeavor.

He hadn't told her too much, of course. Certain things would always remain off-limits. He'd mentioned Richard, but he'd never reveal the true, abusive nature of their relationship. And he didn't want her to know about William, the earl, or about his own large house. Those things were only a tiny aspect of his life, and he didn't want her to perceive him differently because of them.

Oh, damn. He was thinking about her again....

"No. Not involved. Look, maybe I will come along tonight."

"Really?"

James shrugged. He didn't want to go, but wallowing in thoughts of Eleanor wasn't exactly productive. "Why not."

Lady Thrushton's was just a short carriage ride away. Most balls held during the high season were a thin excuse to exhibit silly young women to wealthy potential mates, and as James stepped inside the hot ballroom everything he'd believed was confirmed. There were more women present than men, although he quickly realized that their number was inflated significantly by anxious mamas. Anxious mamas who turned to stare at him and Will as they entered, sizing them up as potential sons-in-law and making silent calculations about their finances, their connections and their pedigrees.

"Oh, God," William muttered. "I *do* hate these things—sorry to drag you along but I couldn't bear to go through with another one alone. Look, I'll go get us a drink. I suspect Lady Thrushton allows gentlemen champagne by the thimbleful." He walked purposefully off, leaving James alone.

The stares didn't bother him. Most of these women wouldn't know who he was, since even before he'd run away he hadn't spent much time in London. He leaned nonchalantly against the wall, allowing his own gaze to roam over the gathered guests. As James had promised, there were several very attractive young ladies, but he couldn't manage to feel even the slightest bit of interest.

But then he caught the eye of someone faintly familiar. She was tall and thin, with her gray hair pulled severely back, and she was looking directly at him. He didn't know at first where he'd seen her before, but then he remembered. It had been in the park, about two weeks ago. She'd been barking at Eleanor while he was hiding behind a tree.

He looked away, suppressing a groan. He was certain she hadn't seen him at the time, so why was she staring? Perhaps it was possible she wasn't even the same person and that he was imagining the whole thing—he'd hardly had a good glimpse of her before. It seemed that just about anything made him think of Eleanor these days.

He tried to locate his brother through the crowd. He was at the refreshment table, at the end of a very long queue of suspicious-looking matrons. He must have sensed James's gaze, because at that moment he looked back beckoningly.

James refused to be drawn; this had been Will's idea, and if he wanted to stay, he could bloody well stay by himself. James needed a drink, and he'd sooner get one at his club. It gave him perverse pleasure to know that his brother was staring daggers into his back as he walked out the door.

Eleanor wasn't having much fun. She'd been at Lady Thrushton's for nearly three hours, melting in the late-July heat, and to make matters worse Louisa was her chaperone for the evening. That would be the case for the rest of the season, since Beatrice now considered herself too large and unseemly for public display. She'd stayed home with Charles, and Eleanor would have given just about anything to join them. But Louisa would never have allowed that, and besides…she was supposed to meet James at the theater next week and she needed to save up her excuses.

When would she be able to leave?

She'd only danced once that night, but that wasn't the cause of her restlessness. She didn't care about dancing, not with anyone there, anyway. All she wanted to do was go home and lie in bed, stare at the ceiling and dream up romantic thoughts. She'd spent most of her free time thus incapacitated since meeting James. It was really rather pathetic since he wasn't exactly Prince Charming.

She hoped it was just a passing infatuation, but she wasn't so sure. The problem was, she thought she might actually like him. She'd joined him at the theater twice now, and each time had returned home transported by clouds. He *was* insufferably arrogant, but he was also intelligent, witty and oh-so-handsome. In fact, he was the most interesting thing that had ever happened to her, and for whatever reason he seemed to be interested in her, too. He asked her opinion, and he listened to what she said—lies, from start to finish, but he listened nonetheless.

She sighed unhappily. The longer she told her lie, and the more elaborate the story became, the more tangled up in it she seemed to become. At first, she'd lied simply to protect herself, but now she longed to admit the truth. She had to do it quickly, too, since Beatrice and Charles would be returning to the country soon, and she'd be going with them. She'd remain in London for less than a fortnight, and she was afraid their next meeting, planned to happen in nine days' time, would also certainly be their last. She'd meet with him sooner if she could, but Beatrice and Louisa had crammed her final week with engagements and that was the only time she could get away. She'd just told him something had come up and her night off had been changed.

She'd have to tell him the truth then, but revealing who she really was would alter the whole nature of their relationship. She rather liked being Eleanor Smith. That identity certainly had advantages over her real one, particularly at this very moment. Right now, she was standing on the outskirts of the ballroom with her aunt Louisa and her equally fearsome friend, Lady Barbara Markham, although they'd long since forgotten about her presence.

"Haven't seen that one in many years," Lady Markham was saying, her voice lowered. "By the door, Louisa— the tall one with the dark hair. Do you remember him?"

Louisa frowned, annoyed that she didn't immediately recognize the man in question. "Haven't seen him in my life. Who is he?"

"Youngest son of the old Earl of Lennox, if I recall correctly. Was friends with my grandson, Philip, when they were very young. Always thought he was the hand-somest of the boy's contemporaries."

"Seems to be getting his share of attention right now, too," Louisa said wryly. "Look—Susannah Lidgate is positively gawping. Her mother must do something about that habit. So why have I not seen him before?"

"Well, he simply disappeared about ten years ago! Ran away, apparently. There were rumors…some said that he'd gotten some poor girl in trouble, or that he'd been disowned—even that he'd stolen his own departed grandmother's jewels to fund some depraved habit. Don't know the truth myself. I'm surprised you don't remember this."

"I must have been in the country at the time," Louisa said, defensive in the face of her friend's smugness. "He sounds like a rake, anyway. And from the look of him I'd imagine he's inconvenienced more than one girl."

Eleanor was too curious to keep quiet any longer. She tried to find the object of their conversation in the thick crowd, but could see very little. "Who are you talking about, Auntie?"

Louisa regarded her as if she were something to be scraped from the bottom of a boot. "You're still here?"

She smiled impudently. "I thought I'd take a respite from the throngs of gentlemen pestering me to dance with them. Although perhaps I should make an exception for this one. He sounds entirely suitable. What do you think?"

"I think he'd eat you alive, chit. Doesn't matter, though, since he just saw me looking at him and went straight out the door." Louisa sighed. "I'm afraid, Eleanor, that's something we have in common."

"I don't know what you mean by that," Eleanor said rather coldly.

Louisa smiled. "All you or I need to do is look at a man to make him retreat in the opposite direction. Lady Markham and I were discussing this earlier."

Eleanor blushed furiously, wishing Louisa would keep her voice down. "That isn't true, Auntie," she whispered back. "I'm perfectly nice to everyone. And it's none of your business, anyway."

Louisa tutted. "'Tis true. I've been watching you. You do not know how to flirt."

"You intimidate men," Lady Markham chipped in. "You betray your superior intellect and that makes them most uncomfortable."

Eleanor thought of James. She intimidated him about as much as a mouse did a cat. "I don't know what you're basing this accusation on."

"Observation," Louisa said. "We saw you dancing with Oliver Murray—he practically ran away from you once the music ended. Men like girls who smile and agree with them. They like to feel cleverer than their dancing partners, and you don't let that happen. Your father should never have allowed you to acquire this useless education. Smile and agree, Eleanor. That's all you have to do. Good heavens, now you're positively glowering."

"I'm sorry, Auntie, but on this issue I must question your expertise."

Lady Markham gave a bark of appreciative laughter, but Louisa didn't look at all amused. "I'm afraid that I see a good deal of myself in you, Eleanor. And, you will witness, I am a sharp-tongued spinster with no children of her own, just a collection of ungrateful nieces and nephews, of whom you're the worst. I don't know why I'm the only one to be subjected to your impertinence. In front of Lady Markham, no less."

Eleanor stubbornly refused to apologize.

Louisa was not yet ready to let the subject rest, but her expression softened ever so slightly. "Your sister tells me you think the reason you haven't found a gentleman yet is because you're not pretty enough, but I will tell you that is total rot. You're as pretty as any girl in this room, and if only you believed it so would everyone else—and by everyone I mean *men*. The first rule of flirting is confidence."

"I'm going to get a glass of lemonade, Auntie," Eleanor replied, an obviously forced smile on her face. "Good evening, Lady Markham."

Louisa just sniffed. "I am watching you, Eleanor."

Eleanor stalked off, trying to keep a pleasant look on her face but not doing a very good job. She nodded reluctantly to several friends as she crossed the floor.

She took her glass of lemonade and turned around to face the sea of dancing couples, feeling even lower. Was she really turning into Louisa? Good heavens, what an appalling prospect.

"Have we met?"

She turned her head and was surprised to see a very tall and exceptionally handsome blond-haired man smiling at her, waiting for her response. He held two glasses of champagne.

She was immediately suspicious. Handsome men never approached her at these events, and it was considered exceedingly forward for a gentleman to introduce himself. He could only want something from her. She was probably blocking his view of some more attractive girl and he wanted her to move.

Still, she followed Louisa's advice and forced a smile. No reason to be rude. "I do not believe so, sir."

He frowned slightly. "Are you drinking lemonade? Oh, *do* have champagne instead." Without waiting for her to concede, he took her glass from her hand, deposited it on a table, and then handed her one of his glasses. "There. That glass was for my brother, but he seems to have deserted me. Drink it quickly, and you'll feel much better."

She was so taken aback by his bizarre informality that she sipped it as requested. She'd had champagne only a few times and it made her nose wrinkle. But immediately she *did* feel better.

"Look, I know I oughtn't come right up and introduce myself, but I'm rather bored and you seem to be without a partner. No gentleman would ever leave a lady in such a position."

She might have thought him a gentleman when he

first approached her, but she'd already abandoned that thought. Cheekily, she pretended to look around the room. "Oh? Have you seen any of this rare breed?"

"Touché, my dear. Now, would you care to dance?"

"With whom?"

"With me, you silly fool."

"I don't mean to split hairs, sir, but you haven't introduced yourself. *Who* are you?" Was *this* flirting? Eleanor wasn't sure, but she was enjoying herself.

He frowned at her rather sternly, but she wasn't at all intimidated. "I am William Stanton, Lord Lennox, here to rescue you from the disrepute of being partnerless. And you would be…?"

"Eleanor Sinclair," she replied with a curtsy. Lord Lennox was very affable—if pompous—and as long as she was being accused of not knowing how to flirt, she might as well practice her technique on him. She was always too scared to attempt flirtation of any sort with James, although she'd come close a few times. Practice would help.

"So, Miss Sinclair, will we dance? You realize, of course, that the only charitable answer is yes. My heart hangs in the balance."

Eleanor scoffed. "Your heart won't be affected in the least. But I'll dance with you anyway, even if you are a liar."

She went to take a final sip of her champagne, but realized it was gone. Before she had a chance to worry about how quickly she'd imbibed it, he'd whisked her off onto the dance floor.

"Is this your first season, Miss Sinclair? I don't think

I've seen you before, not that I come to this sort of thing very often if I can help it."

"Why? Do you not like dancing, my lord?"

"I don't like mothers." He stopped dancing altogether for a moment. "Pray, tell me, is your mother here?"

"I'm afraid my mother died many years ago."

He looked appalled at his blunder. "I'm so sorry."

"You needn't worry. I was very young when it happened. I'm staying in London with my sister and brother-in-law, Lord and Lady Pelham. They are my usual chaperones."

He nodded approvingly, although Eleanor didn't know if it was her lack of a mother or her lofty connections that pleased him most. "Right, but you still haven't answered my first question. Why have I never seen you before?"

Eleanor shrugged. "Yes, this is my first season, and I, too, avoid this sort of thing whenever possible. Now, is *your* mother lurking somewhere?"

"Just my brother, although as I said earlier he seems to have left after barely setting foot in the place. Can't get him to do anything he's supposed to."

"Oh?" She instantly remembered Lady Markham's words about the dark-haired Lennox brother. "I think I've been hearing about him."

"I'm afraid it's all true. A total black sheep." He smiled as he said this, indicating that he didn't entirely mean it, or at least that he forgave his brother's misdemeanors.

She smiled back, thinking of her own roguish brother, Ben. "Brothers can be a bother, I know, although I think yours has got the right of it in this case. I'd leave if I'd the option."

"Is that why you were looking so disagreeable when I approached you?"

She blushed. "Was I? I'm sorry."

"I didn't take it personally."

"I wasn't *trying* to look disagreeable. It's just that I was having a rather difficult conversation with my great-aunt."

"You didn't mention an aunt. Is she still here?"

"Sadly, she is. Watching my every move so she can criticize me later."

Lord Lennox, who had perhaps been dancing a fraction of an inch closer than was considered proper, moved away slightly. "Aunts are worse than mothers."

"Mine is worse than dragons," she whispered.

"Then I'd better start behaving myself," he whispered back.

Eleanor giggled. "Why don't we talk about the weather?"

"The weather is a fascinating topic, Miss Sinclair. Did you notice it didn't rain today?"

She gasped in pretend shock. "Astounding. Tell me more."

In the end—surprising after such an inauspicious start—Eleanor enjoyed her evening tremendously. William Stanton had kept her laughing through two dances, and he'd definitely flirted with her, albeit in an entirely unromantic way. It was merely friendly banter, but that would be enough to soothe Louisa for the time being. She wasn't attracted to him, nor, she was confident, was he to her, but he had promised to dance with her again at Lady Lauderdale's ball the following week. For once she wouldn't have to worry about being without a partner.

And, thankfully, for the time that those two dances had lasted, she'd almost been able to put James from her mind. But in the dark carriage at the end of the night, with Louisa snoring at her side, her mind traveled to forbidden territory and lingered there, over memories of soft black hair, of a warm hand gently clasping hers and of twinkling green eyes that promised her things she couldn't even begin to imagine.

Chapter Seven

Eleanor looked at her reflection in the mirror. The dress was made from plum-colored cotton, a color that suited her well enough. It was high-waisted, and its long, full sleeves were its only mildly extravagant feature. On the whole, it was fairly functional and not at all the sort of dress she'd normally consider buying.

Betty, Beatrice's new downstairs maid, certainly seemed to think it an odd choice. Upon Beatrice's insistence, she'd accompanied Eleanor to the dressmaker's, and now she was frowning at the dress in the mirror, wondering why Eleanor would even contemplate it when she had so many prettier gowns.

She was also wondering, no doubt, why they'd come to this particular shop. It was a large establishment and stocked a broad range of moderately priced items—dress and upholstery fabrics, buttons and trimming. Eleanor had been there once before with Beatrice, when she'd been setting up her London household. She'd bought crimson velvet for her dining room curtains and blue wool for the servants' livery. But it was not the sort of place where most fashionable women would normally buy their own gowns.

Of course, she wasn't shopping for herself today. She was shopping for Miss Smith, who possessed, to date, just a single dress. Miss Smith also had a limited budget, and she had to wear modest clothes befitting her status. She needed something nice, but not *too* nice.

Eleanor didn't really want to examine why she'd decided to expand Miss Smith's wardrobe. She kept telling herself that the decision was purely practical; James might grow suspicious after seeing her again and again in the same dress, no matter what sorry excuses she came up with. But mostly she knew that she wanted to look attractive for him, just once. Especially since she'd see him tomorrow night, and it would very probably be the last time. Unless, of course, she returned to London immediately after Beatrice's baby was born. She could do that—in fact, she didn't *have* to leave London at all. It wasn't as if this was Beatrice's *first* child....

"It's very nice, miss. Um, where exactly would you wear something like that?"

Eleanor ignored Betty's question, astute though it may have been. "Thank you, Betty. Did Beatrice have any errands she wanted you to run while we're out?"

"To Mr. Larrimor's shop, to collect some books."

Eleanor nodded slowly. "I plan to try a few more things here before I leave, so perhaps you should run along and collect those books now. You can meet me here when you've finished. That will be a more efficient use of your time, don't you think?"

Betty didn't look terribly enthusiastic, but she nodded. "Yes, Miss Sinclair."

Eleanor softened, worried she'd sounded too imperious. "Come with me. I'll point you in the right direction." She led her to the door and stepped outside into daylight. "If you go to the end and turn right…it's about a quarter of a mile down Maddox Street."

She still felt guilty as she watched her walk off. She prided herself on treating servants with consideration, and since they'd pass Larrimor's on the way home anyway, she was sending poor Betty unnecessarily out of her way. But for the moment it couldn't be helped, not if Betty was going to start asking questions.

She reentered the shop.

"Can I assist you with anything else, miss?" the plump shopkeeper asked helpfully. "There are a few more ready-made items in the back, if that's what you're looking for. Are you sure that's really what you want? We could make something up by the end of the week if you're in a hurry."

Eleanor nodded. Since she'd been to the shop only once before, the woman did not recognize her, and she was obviously trying to understand why Eleanor had arrived in an expensive morning dress only to ask to try on such an ordinary garment. "No, ready-made is precisely what I require. I…I'll just keep looking."

The shopkeeper looked truly puzzled, but obligingly retreated behind her desk.

Eleanor sighed. Telling lies, or at least avoiding the truth, was becoming a habit, and she was beginning to worry about her soul.

The shop consisted of two large rooms. She casually wandered toward the back room, letting her hand trail across several bolts of printed cotton as she passed. Huge rolls of fabric lined the walls, and baskets full of colorful braid and spools of ribbon were artfully arranged in groups on the floor. She didn't have the faintest idea where to begin, never having bought a ready-made gown before. She paused in front of another mirror and sighed at her reflection. The plum-colored dress that looked back at her wasn't perfect, but she supposed it was time to give up her search. In fact, she didn't really *need* a new dress at all. She turned her attention instead to a pair of dove-gray gloves on a shelf beside the mirror. She pulled one on and admired her hand. Then she picked up a rather pretty straw bonnet from its stand and placed it on her head. She looked in the mirror once more, this time in order to tie the ribbon under her chin.

"That's very becoming," a male voice said from behind her. "I much prefer it to your wig."

Her fingers stopped moving and the ribbon trailed down uselessly. She dropped the other glove. She stood very still and didn't bother stooping to pick it up. She needed to calm her beating heart first.

When she finally turned around, James had already retrieved the glove for her. He held it in his hands, but he didn't give it to her right away.

She narrowed her eyes. It was one thing to see him at the theater, but she didn't appreciate it at all when he unexpectedly appeared in her life. "What are you doing here?"

He ignored her question, and instead just looked her over slowly, thoroughly. His mouth curved with appreciation.

"You look charming. Is that a new dress?"

She blushed, not at all sure how to respond to his compliment. Instead of thanking him, she just mumbled, "It's awful."

He cocked his head slightly to the side and regarded her thoughtfully. "Maybe it's not the most beautiful garment I've ever seen, but it's certainly an improvement. Are you going to buy it?"

"Um, no," she said, removing the hat and replacing it on its stand. "Just imagining what it would be like if I could. It's silly."

He was quiet for a moment, understanding on his face, and perhaps a bit of tenderness, too. She looked away, feeling awful for deceiving him.

"I don't think it's silly at all. Of course you would want pretty things. Or, prett*ier*, I should say, since we agree this dress leaves something to be desired. Shall I help—"

She would not let him offer to pay for it. "What are you doing here?"

"I was on my way to my club when I saw you step out the door of this shop. Wasn't even sure it was you, but naturally I came in to investigate. I must say I'm surprised to see you here. Who was that girl you were talking to?"

"Betty. A maid. I work with her."

"But you don't seem to be working now."

"I was lucky enough to get the afternoon free." *How many lies did that make? Two hundred and forty-six?*

"I probably shouldn't even be here. I'd have to save my wages for months to afford anything."

"I see." He seemed to be mulling over this bit of information, and she fidgeted nervously. "Then you can have lunch with me."

Her stomach did a little flip. "Lunch is not part of our arrangement."

He took a step closer. "It could be."

"I don't think so." *Flip, flip, flip...* "Betty will return soon."

He sighed with regret. "More's the pity."

She felt as if she was turning into liquid under his gaze. She began pulling the glove from her hand, desperate to provide herself with any occupation that didn't involve looking at him. But from the moment she'd seen him her palms had begun to sweat, and the glove refused to come off easily. Without asking for permission he took her hand to help. She was so startled she didn't even think to protest, and she simply allowed him to tug gently on her fingertips

Slowly, it came, and her hand lay bare in his. He'd removed his own gloves for the task, and she was completely mesmerized by the contrast of her smooth skin against his large palm. Her mind went numb and tiny waves of pleasure washed over her body. She still couldn't meet his gaze, but she knew he was looking down at her, that his eyes had grown dark. She should say something, do something, but she felt paralyzed. Even the noise of the door opening and of the shopkeeper offering warm greetings didn't immediately break her trance.

But then...oh, God...reason slowly forced its way

into her brain, and Eleanor turned her head as it dawned on her that Betty had returned, at the worst possible moment. Mr. Larrimor's shop wasn't that far, and her business there would be brief.

But it wasn't Betty. It was Lydia Lethrop and her mother, far worse. Lydia was eighteen, like Eleanor, and she was pretty and vicious. If she saw her in this compromising position….

Eleanor certainly wouldn't wait to find out. Not bothering to explain, she yanked her hand away and started walking. Without thinking she ducked behind the velvet curtains of the commodious dressing room at the very back of the shop.

And then James stepped in after her. "What's gotten into you?"

"Get out!" she whispered furiously.

He looked around the dressing room as if only just realizing that he'd encroached on a purely female—and definitely private—domain. Botanical prints decorated the papered walls, and a suite of mahogany chairs and a matching chaise longue, each upholstered in pink-striped silk, lined the periphery.

By the time his gaze returned to her, he was grinning wickedly.

"Whatever for, Miss Smith?"

She just glared at him before walking back to the curtains. She parted them slightly, just enough for her to peer out, but not enough for anyone to see in. Lydia and her mother were conferring leisurely over several samples of upholstery fabric in the front room. "Oh, dear God," she moaned.

"What is wrong with you?"

"*Me?* What is wrong with *you?* Why did you follow me here?"

"To be perfectly honest, I had no idea where you were taking me. I simply followed you because you suddenly dashed off as if you'd seen a ghost. *What* is wrong?"

Eleanor started pacing. This was her chance to be honest. "Nothing. I just…" *She just what?*

He crossed his arms on his chest and waited.

She began again, accepting that the truth would have to wait. "You see, my mistress knows the women who just entered the shop, and word would have gotten back to her if they'd seen me talking to you. Oh, but now you're in a dressing room with me and it's much, much worse… Will I fit out that window?"

"Maybe just, although I daren't imagine what the passersby will think when they see you exit the building that way," he said drily.

"What if she needs to come back here to look at more samples?" She was really panicking now, her eyes big with worry.

"Hmm…that's an interesting prospect. We might have to hide in this dressing room forever." He leaned in close as he made this remark, obviously enjoying her distress.

She frowned, not appreciating his sense of humor. "Be serious. This is your fault, you…you…"

"Cad?"

"Exactly."

"Look, Smith, I think you're overreacting. So what if they know your mistress? They're still unlikely to recognize you. I suggest we simply leave—me first, and then you follow when you're ready."

She didn't like that idea one bit, but didn't see an alternative. At any rate, they had to do something quickly, before Lydia started working her way to the back of the shop.

"All right…but just not yet. I…I'll just have a look first to see what they're doing." She parted the curtains once more. He stood next to her.

"You can't go now. They're facing this way and they'll see you," she whispered, trying not to think about how close he was.

He nodded, and leaned forward to look through the curtains, as well. But her face, just a few inches from his, caught his attention instead. Her skin looked smooth and soft and creamy, except along the gentle rise of her high cheekbones, where it was flushed pink. Her hair was pulled back neatly and demurely, and she smelled of soap, which unfortunately called up an image of her, unclothed and damp with steam, in a slipper-shaped bath.

God, it was painful.

"They're talking to the shopkeeper. Get ready."

"I'm ready." He was ready to turn her around and kiss her senseless. To lay her down on the chaise longue—

"All right…wait…wait… Their backs are to us and they're standing by the front door. You can go now. Quickly."

"Hmm?"

She turned to rebuke him for not paying attention, but her words never came out. He was close, so close that her breast brushed against his arm as she straightened, so close that she had to crane her neck to see his face. His proximity made her aware of how large he was, how broad his chest.

"James? Will you go?" Her voice was small and uncertain. She'd never used his Christian name before, and she didn't know why she did so now. It sounded too intimate, but why did that matter, since she couldn't even drag her gaze away from his?

And his eyes…they'd smoldered to darkest emerald green, making his thoughts and emotions indecipherable to her. She thought she saw indecision, as if he wanted to say or do something, but was unsure. She felt light-headed, and she thought he might kiss her. She hoped he would. She wanted to cling to his chest and absorb his heat. She thought she'd explode if he didn't wrap her in his arms.

His hands, warm and strong, were on her shoulders—she didn't know how they got there—and she held her breath, waiting for him to draw her near. But he didn't. He just squeezed her lightly, his gaze never straying from hers.

"Tomorrow night, then, Eleanor?"

And then he was gone. Trembling, she watched him leave through the curtains. Lydia looked up at him as he walked out the front door, as did the shopkeeper—he would never be inconspicuous—but as far as Eleanor could tell no comment was made. Betty reentered the shop just a few seconds later. And then, after another minute, the Lethrops left. Luck was finally going Eleanor's way.

"Miss? Do you need some assistance?" It was the shopkeeper. Her tone sounded slightly less friendly this time.

"If you could undo the back of this gown, please," Eleanor said weakly. "I don't think I'll take it after all."

The shopkeeper entered, her face flushed with embarrassed hostility.

"I am pleased," she said, her voice clipped as she started working efficiently on Eleanor's buttons. "It does not suit someone of your…ilk."

Eleanor didn't miss the implied insult. The woman had guessed that they were back there together and thought she was a…

Oh, my.

The shopkeeper finished her job quickly and left the dressing room. Eleanor knew she wouldn't be welcome there again. She wasn't particularly worried, since the woman didn't know who she was and therefore wouldn't be able to spread any rumors. But, oh, she did feel ashamed. Not just for what the shopkeeper had seen or assumed, but for what she'd felt. She might be a total innocent who'd never even kissed a man, but she wasn't so stupid that she didn't recognize the feelings inside her. He could have made love to her in the dressing room and she'd hardly have protested.

And he must be aware of it, too. How humiliating. How would she survive their meeting tomorrow? It was too late now to call it off—he'd send his driver to collect her and if she wasn't at the door…

His original threat rang again in her ears: *don't make my driver wait, or he'll come find you.*

Chapter Eight

James had been in a foul mood since he'd left Eleanor in the shop, the day before, and his mood had worsened since she'd stepped out of his carriage that night, looking so pretty that he'd had to hold his breath. The wig didn't matter, since he knew what she looked like without it. Nor the awful dress, which he could imagine away altogether. He still thought she was the loveliest, sweetest girl he'd ever seen.

The persistent stirring down below wasn't helping his humor, either. He'd been painfully aroused when he'd left her in the dressing room yesterday, and so he was again, doing nothing more than sitting next to her in his private box and looking at her profile whenever he could be certain that she wouldn't notice.

Will was right. He was acting like some lovesick fool. It was a disconcerting state to be in, and he didn't like it one bit. It was just that she was so unlike the other women he'd known—jades, Will called them, without Eleanor's intelligence or grace. She had all the charm and poise of the well-bred young ladies he'd spent years avoiding, only she wasn't a young lady at all. That meant she was accessible, but also…well, damn it, definitely *not* accessible at the same time. It was enough to drive a saint mad, and he wasn't saintly by a long distance.

He hadn't kept his mood to himself, either. He'd gone out of his way to be gruff and unpleasant—anything to keep her from extending any gestures of friendliness in his direction. It was a matter of self-preservation, since her sweet smiles and shy blushes made him feel as if a knife were being twisted in his gut each time. If she were any other girl, he'd simply bed her and get on with his life, but that just wasn't an option. Not yet.

So far his plan had worked. He'd been taciturn all evening and now, as the play's final act drew to an end, she sat stiffly in her seat, obviously annoyed. She was probably counting the minutes until she could go home. After their charged encounter yesterday, he'd half expected her not to come at all, and he almost wished that had been the case. Seeing her, and not being able to touch her, was torture. He wanted to punish her for making him feel this way.

And yet, he couldn't bear the thought of her leaving him at the end of the night.

The curtains closed, and she turned to him. "Well, thank you, Mr. Bentley. I think I will go now."

"Wait until the crowds clear."

She sighed loudly, letting him know what she thought about his company. For several minutes they sat in electric silence, all too aware that they were completely alone.

When she finally spoke, she sounded hurt and angry.

"I am sorry if I have offended you in some way, but you needn't be so unkind."

"Of course you haven't offended me." He, too, sounded irritated.

She just shrugged, and he wondered what she was thinking. Why would she believe she'd offended him? What an idiotic idea. He stole another glance at her face, but it revealed nothing. It occurred to him that she might be embarrassed. He knew he hadn't been the only one to feel something yesterday, and knowing that she'd also been aroused had added to his torment a great deal. Perhaps she felt ashamed by her response. She was innocent, after all, and such feelings might be new to her.

He hated making her unhappy, even if that had originally been his intention.

"I'm sorry, Eleanor. I'm just in a foul mood, but you've done nothing wrong. How can I make it up to you?"

"I think I should just go home." She sounded sad and resigned. "But I—"

"What?"

"There is something I must tell you first."

He didn't want to hear it. Not if it had anything to do with going home. Or with never coming again, which he half suspected it would. So he just ignored her words. "No, no, I must make it up to you. Did you enjoy the play?"

"Despite myself."

"Would you like to meet the actors?"

She blushed, but he could see that she was starting to thaw. "That wouldn't be remotely proper."

"Now since when has that stopped you?"

"I'm sorry?"

She looked wounded again, and he knew he was making a mess of this. "I don't mean to insult you…all I meant was that you're not the sort of person to worry about propriety for propriety's sake alone. Would you agree with that?"

She waited several long moments, but then she nodded reluctantly.

"So come backstage with me, Eleanor," James said, his voice quiet and coaxing. "Don't go home yet."

Her reply didn't really matter, since there was no way in hell he was letting her go so easily, but luckily he didn't have to resort to tossing her over his shoulder.

She nodded again. "Very well."

Eleanor should never have agreed to James's outrageous suggestion, and she wouldn't have, either, except she really didn't want to go home. Beatrice had been in bed when she'd left, and Charles was at his club with friends. No one would miss her, provided she didn't stay out too late. But she could certainly stay until eleven without causing anyone to start to wonder. She wanted to be there—she'd be leaving London the day after tomorrow and she didn't think she'd be able to see James again before that time. And before she left the theater that night she had to tell him that she was leaving, and who she really was. She'd been trying to do so all evening, but she hadn't found the right moment, not when he'd spent most of the time glowering at her.

Thus there she was, walking down a dim, narrow corridor, her hand in the crook of his arm. He was providing her with a running commentary, but she'd been too nervous to mind his words.

"I'll introduce you to my friend, Jonathon. He's Irish…I think I told you about him—I helped him buy this theater."

She nodded, remembering. And she remembered again the mystery of James's funds: his mother the actress, and his stint as a soldier…although army officers often came from genteel backgrounds, the lower ranks of the military were usually made up of desperate young men. But he dressed and talked and spent money like a gentleman—how was it possible? *Was* he a criminal? And what sort of people would she be meeting backstage?

"Do you gamble?" she asked.

"What?" The look on his face told her just how odd and abrupt her question was.

"I…I just wondered—"

"Are you inviting me to a game of whist? I'd probably win, you know."

"No, Mr. Bentley. I just…" But she couldn't think of a way to ask him if he'd won all his money at cards without running the risk of insulting him. "I only play piquet."

"Then piquet it will be. I should remind you that you called me James yesterday."

She blushed. "James."

"That's better. You've no reason to look so nervous, Eleanor. With Jonathon there, it'll be like you have two chaperones."

She raised a skeptical brow. "Is he as qualified as you?"

They'd reached a gray-painted door. "I'd say he's

only adequate, but I will remind him that your virtue is entirely in our hands."

Eleanor blushed at his words, but before she had a chance to chide him he'd opened the door. And then…well, it was as if a whole new world had appeared before her, a place completely unlike the protected milieu she usually occupied. The room was large, high-ceilinged and slightly smoky, and she immediately realized that she'd never been so out of place. The room buzzed with voices, but no one was paying her much attention, anyway. That much wasn't so unusual—it was rather like being at a large ton party, only here the guests were definitely *not* of the ton, and some weren't even fully clothed. All the women present appeared to be actresses, as she would have expected, but there were men, too. Some were actors, but there were also a few well-dressed but rather louche-looking gentlemen who'd come, no doubt, to meet their mistresses or to make new conquests. She hadn't expected to see anyone from her social background at all, and she quickly averted her eyes. Although it was highly unlikely that she'd be recognized, she didn't want to take any chances.

James felt her hesitate and squeezed her hand as he guided her through the crowd. "You don't need to worry about anything, Eleanor. I'll be by your side the whole time."

They were approaching an auburn-haired man who appeared to be about thirty years old. He was in the midst of a lively conversation and was really quite handsome, she thought, although not as handsome as James. When he noticed them coming his way he excused himself from his companions, and his animated expression changed to one of wry humor.

Eleanor tugged on James's hand, begging him not to introduce her, but it was too late.

"James," the man said.

"Ah. Jonathon. I wanted to introduce you to Miss Smith. Eleanor, I'd like you to meet Mr. Jonathon Kinsale."

She wanted nothing more than to disappear, or at least to run away home where she belonged. How could she help but feel humiliated? Mr. Kinsale would probably think that she was nothing more than some cheap female James had brought along for an illicit assignation, and why should he not think that? She was surely one of many.

But as she was unable to vanish at will, she curtsied instead. It happened automatically, since such manners had been drilled into her from a young age. At least it gave her the chance to bow her head gracefully and hide her red face.

Her polite response seemed to startle Jonathon, and he was actually bemused enough by her curtsey to redden slightly himself. "Pleasure to meet you, Miss Smith."

"You'll be delighted to learn, Miss Smith, that Jon used to be an actor himself. Miss Smith is a great admirer of the theater, Jon."

"You are an actor?" she said dumbly, feeling as if she ought to say something. Considering that she'd always dreamed of meeting a real actor, her vocabulary was proving surprisingly limited.

Jonathon raised an eyebrow slightly at her upper-class accent. "Yes, but I haven't actually acted for a few years, Miss Smith. I hope you enjoyed the play."

She nodded, still not feeling particularly at ease. "Yes. Yes, indeed." Her voice sounded dry and scratchy.

James looked slightly worried. "I'll fetch you a glass of water." And before she could protest about being left alone with Jonathon, he'd gone.

"So, Miss Smith, you're not an actress yourself, are you?"

She paused before answering, thinking of the performance she'd been putting on since meeting James. "Not in an official capacity."

He raised an eyebrow, inviting her to explain her cryptic words.

"I mean, not at all. I'm a governess."

"Ah, yes, I remember now that James mentioned that." He was still looking at her curiously, seeming to believe her no more than if she'd said she was the Empress of China, and she started to worry that he'd somehow seen through her disguise. But she'd easily convinced James—how could Jonathon determine the truth in such a short time?

Before she could elaborate on her lie, an attractive black-haired woman approached them, smiling broadly. Eleanor immediately recognized her as the lead actress from the play. She exuded confidence and potent perfume, and made Eleanor feel like a small and insignificant worm in the presence of a butterfly.

She fixed her superior gaze on Eleanor. "And who would this be, Jonathon?"

"This is Miss Smith, Liz. She's James's friend." He looked very uncomfortable with the situation. "Elizabeth Potter is, er, an actress, Miss Smith."

Liz raised her brows archly at the word friend. "And where is our *friend?*"

"Getting water. Perhaps you should go see what's taking him so long."

Eleanor wondered if he was trying to make the awful woman go away.

"She'll need more than water if she's spending her time with him," Liz said unhelpfully. "I've also been his friend, if you recall, so I speak from experience. Here, Miss Smith." She offered her own glass. "I haven't touched that yet—you have it. I'll get another."

"Liz—" Jonathon warned.

But she ignored him and breezed off.

Eleanor silently wondered what kind of friend Liz had been. Not a particularly pleasant one.

"I suggest you pay no attention to her," Jonathon said.

She shrugged, eyeing the glass of amber liquid dubiously. Drinking a glass of spirits was comparable to climbing an Alpine mountain from her perspective, but it obviously wasn't much of a challenge for a woman like Elizabeth Potter.

"That's whiskey, m'dear," Jonathon pointed out cheerfully. "You needn't drink it."

She had always thought whiskey was an exclusively male drink. Her gaze followed Liz across the room, where she now stood next to James with her hand resting on his back in a most familiar way.

She looked forlornly at her glass. She'd have to drink

it. She didn't know why, but she felt that she had to prove something.

"I'm familiar with it, Mr. Kinsale," she lied.

"You've had it before, then?" he asked, clearly amused.

"Yes…once or twice, thank you." To demonstrate, she raised the glass to her lips and took a confident swig. And when her throat caught fire, she tried not to cry.

Jonathon smiled gently in sympathy. "Maybe I should see about that water?"

She nodded, her gaze traveling once more across the room. James had lowered his head to hear something that Liz was whispering into his ear. He'd obviously forgotten about getting the water himself. He'd forgotten about her.

Jonathon left, and she was, for the moment, alone. She sipped the whiskey again, more cautiously this time, feeling miserable. The second sip went down easier, and so did the third. Her head felt light.

Standing around with no one to talk to made her feel like a gooseberry, so she walked to the side of the room to examine a series of framed engravings. *A Harlot's Progress,* by Hogarth. She frowned at the scenes of gaudy debauchery, in no mood for moralizing.

Next to the prints, an open door led into a smaller room, and she entered warily. The second room was empty, except for three large wardrobes, a well-worn chair and a cheval glass. She walked over to the mirror to examine her reflection. She looked nothing like the glamorous Liz. She was, she thought, the human incarnation of a field mouse. How truly disappointing. She sank down into the chair and had a bit more whiskey, once again feeling completely out of her element. Why had she agreed to go there in the first place? Why had he asked her, if he'd clearly rather spend his evening with someone else? For several minutes she was miserable and alone, which was better, at least, than being miserable in a room full of people.

"Eleanor? I've been looking for you."

She turned to look at James. He stood in the doorway, his athletic frame silhouetted by the light that shone behind him. She ached with wanting to touch him, and with having neither the confidence nor the experience to do so.

"Jonathon was supposed to be watching you," he said as he entered the room more fully. There was a trace of accusation in his voice.

She rose from her seat, swaying slightly. "He went to get a glass of water since you were busy. I...I wandered off."

"Are you all right?" He was next to her by now. He'd seen her sway, and his arm was around her shoulders. His mouth was close to her ear, and she could feel his breath on her neck. She didn't even try to shake off his arm. She felt cold, and she wasn't at all sure that her feet would go where she wanted them without assistance. She was drunk.

"I think, perhaps, I just need some air."

He eyed her nearly empty glass and began walking her back to the main room. "I think that'd be a good idea."

"Um...how do you know her?"

"Who?"

"That, um, Liz woman."

He stopped walking. "Are you jealous?"

"No." *Yes!*

"I was rather hoping you would be. She's jealous of you."

"Why would anyone be jealous of me?"

"Because you're clever and beautiful. I knew Liz in Ireland, actually, many years ago. We were friends, but we aren't any longer. Not in…that sense."

Friends again. What a ridiculous euphemism. "She was your mistress, you mean?"

He started walking with her again, slowly. "And what do you know about mistresses?"

She blushed, wishing she'd held her tongue. "Nothing."

"Well, for your edification, our relationship wasn't as official as that. A mistress is typically compensated for her services. It's a business arrangement."

"*We* have a business arrangement. You said so yourself."

"Not like that, unfortunately."

"Oh." She went quiet. "Am I your friend?"

They'd just entered the main room, but he stopped to look at her. "Yes," he said slowly, allowing his fingers to trace a path along her cheekbone. "God, I hope so."

His gaze was so deliberate, so sensual that she swayed once more, and it had nothing to do with the whiskey. He held on tighter. "Here, here…we'll just step back out the door we came in, and I'll take you outside." But they took only a few steps before he stopped once more. His body went rigid. "Oh, damn."

She felt too pleasantly warm all over to be offended by his oath. "What?"

He didn't answer right away so she turned to look at

him. His eyes were dark with anger, and his expression hard. He looked…furious, in a way she'd never seen him before, and he was staring in the direction of the main door. A man had just entered. He had a familiar appearance, but she couldn't imagine why.

"Who is that?"

He forced his gaze back to her face, and she could see he was battling to keep his response in check. "It doesn't matter. We'll go through another door."

"James? What's wrong?"

"It's nothing, Eleanor. That man was a friend of my brother's, and I'm afraid I've got some unresolved business with him." He sighed, looking down at her. "But I don't want to deal with him while you're here. Do you think he's seen me?"

She was still looking at the man, wondering what this business could be and why he seemed so familiar. He was elegantly clad in evening dress, and would once have been handsome, but now the signs of dissipation had ravaged his face. She could only assume that like several other gentlemen there he'd come for the actresses rather than the play itself. He'd definitely seen James, and he was staring at them with a look of disdain and, oddly, nervousness, as well. He began walking in their direction. Who was he?

And then she remembered, or at least she thought she did. She'd met him once before—had danced with him at a ball, actually. He'd been condescending and rude, and she hadn't liked him one bit. He'd hardly bothered to look at her the whole time, but that didn't ensure he wouldn't remember her now….

He was just a few yards away, and though he hadn't noticed her yet, he might at any second. She had to do something.

So she stood on tiptoe, put her arms around James's neck, and she kissed him.

Only the most tactless person would interrupt a couple in the midst of an embrace. That was what Eleanor figured, anyway, and out of the corner of her eye she could see the man turn and walk off in the other direction. Sober, she'd have come up with a different solution, but it did work.

And so there it was, her first kiss. Sort of.

She didn't know what she'd expected. She'd seen Charles kiss Beatrice before, when they didn't know she was looking. He'd held her tightly to his chest and had made a mess of her hair. But none of that happened in this case. In fact, James wasn't kissing her back, wasn't even touching her. It occurred to her suddenly that she might be doing it all wrong.

She pulled away slowly, feeling insecure and horribly conscious of the fact that several people were now staring at her. His expression didn't help. He looked… well, rather perplexed.

"Where did you learn to kiss?" he asked.

She felt heat rush to her face. "I…well…"

"It's an unusual technique."

She turned on her heel and began to walk. But before she got very far his hand snaked out to catch her. "I don't think we're finished yet," he whispered in her ear.

"I think so. I think I will go home now."

She pulled away, not really looking where she was going, too ashamed to lift her head and all too aware that she'd made herself conspicuous. There was another door, closed this time, at the far end of the room, and she opened it, hoping it would lead her outside. But she wasn't that lucky. It was an office, a dead end. She turned around, but James was already there, leaning nonchalantly against the door frame, his hands in his pockets. There was no way out…not without walking past him.

"It occurs to me, Smith, that somehow, in between your French lessons, you neglected kissing entirely," he said, entering the room and closing the door behind him.

"Thank you for pointing that out. I will be going now."

"It would be cruel of me to let you go without a lesson." He began walking toward her. She should have run, but instead she raised her chin, too proud to let him intimidate her.

"Thank you, I don't need a lesson, Mr. Bentley."

"Oh, but I think you do."

He'd reached her at this point, but still she held her ground. His dark gaze roamed boldly over her face.

"First, we'll have to take that ridiculous thing off your head."

She stayed very still as he gently lifted the wig from her head, desperately trying to tamp down the now-familiar feelings churning inside her.

"Now, that's much better," he said, lowering his head slowly, brushing his lips against hers while expertly removing the last few pins that held her hair in place. Thick coils of brown hair fell around her shoulders and down her back, and she held her breath as his gaze skimmed across her face like a caress. His eyes still smoldered, but his anger had been replaced by passion.

"Do you know how long I've wanted to kiss you?"

She hadn't the faintest idea, about the answer to his question or about anything else at that very moment. She felt dizzy and weak, and then his lips touched hers once more. She'd wondered what kissing him would be like since she'd first seen him, but her imagination hadn't prepared her for the bolt of electricity she felt all the way to her toes. His kiss was tender and demanding at the same time. Teasing her lips, her cheeks, her neck. She reached for his jacket to steady herself, but instead she pulled him closer, melting into him.

"Open your mouth. Just a little," he whispered hoarsely.

Tentatively, she did as he instructed. She'd have jumped off a bridge if he'd told her to at that moment. And slowly, carefully, his tongue met hers. She gasped in surprise, but she didn't pull away. At first it felt playful, gentle, but not for long. His kiss deepened, and he drew her closer, his hands roaming through her hair. This kiss was so different from her own lame attempt. It was exquisite, sublime, and she hoped it never ended. Her hands gripped the back of his neck, marveling at the heat of his skin, the contrasting coolness of his fine linen shirt. She wanted something more, only she didn't know what it was she wanted.

But he seemed to understand. Her body was pressed to his, and his hands wandered down her back, tracing a path along her spine to cup her bottom and pull her closer, so that she could feel his hardness against her belly. That was a shock, almost enough of a shock to break through the warm bubble of pleasure that enveloped her. But then, well, it also felt very nice. So nice that she pressed back. With a groan, his kiss deepened, his tongue thrusting, driving her wild. Eleanor forgot where they were. For the moment, all she was aware of was his lips on hers, his hands on her body, his heat.

Next thing she knew, he'd lifted her as if she weighed nothing at all and was carrying her across the room to the desk. He pushed the inkstand and piles of papers out of the way with his free arm, and then lowered her slowly, letting her slide down the front of his body until she was seated on the desk, facing him, straddling his hips. In the dim light, his eyes were dark and dangerous. She felt suddenly nervous once again.

"James, I…" She started to straighten, but he was too close and she couldn't do so without pressing her body against his. So she leaned back instead, only then he leaned forward so that he was almost on top of her.

"What, darling?"

"Hmm?" *What?* She'd been about to protest, but his lips had already begun to move down her throat, and she'd no idea what she'd planned to say. Every thought she'd ever possessed slipped away. And his wicked eyes told her he knew.

"Hold on to me, sweetheart, or you'll fall."

She did as he told her, wrapping her arms around his neck just to keep herself from becoming completely horizontal. His lips moved farther still, across the drab fabric that covered the swell of her breast.

"I'm starting to hate this dress, Smith," he said as his

hands began to work their way up her thighs, pulling her gown with them.

She hated it, too, but she couldn't manage the words to tell him so. She nodded, but he wasn't looking at her face.

"Shall I buy you a new one? I'll buy you as many as you want."

She didn't nod this time; she didn't do anything. The warm wave that she'd been floating on cooled suddenly. Buy her a new one? That was a jarring note. An awful, sudden reminder of their balance of power, of who he thought she was. Reason forced its way into her mind and she started to struggle to sit up.

"What's wrong?"

"You cannot buy me anything, James." She sounded breathless, but firm.

"Don't be stubborn, Eleanor. Let me take care of you." He leaned in to kiss her again, but she ducked to the side and his kiss landed by her ear.

"Please let me up."

With a quiet curse he stepped away.

She climbed off the desk and backed up several paces, needing to put distance between them in order to regain her composure. She looked down at the floor, not wanting to meet his eyes. If he hadn't made that remark, where would this have led? The embarrassment. What must he think of her?

Finally, she looked at him. "I'm sorry."

He ran his hand through his hair, looking no more composed than she felt. "You've no need to apologize. Good God, we can do this anytime you want."

That made her frown. Why had he pursued her? He

should have just let her run away, as she'd clearly wanted to do. He was the experienced one; this was his fault. "We won't be doing that again."

His expression became inscrutable. "Ah, now you're angry."

"You should not have done that."

"You seem to forget that you kissed me first."

She colored, realizing that he was, of course, right. Unfortunately, he was too perceptive to let this observation pass without comment. He took a step in her direction.

"Why *did* you kiss me?"

"I didn't mean to."

"It was an…accident?"

He sounded so dubious that she knew that now was her chance to tell him—everything, from the beginning. She'd been wanting to for so many weeks. Her mouth opened, and she willed the truth to come out. But nothing. She couldn't tell him now, not *right* now. Not after what had just happened—kissing might be a routine business for him, but she felt as though the earth itself had changed. Maybe she could meet him tomorrow. Maybe she could write…

She wished her voice sounded stronger. "I was trying to prevent that man from approaching. I was afraid I might recognize him from somewhere…perhaps he knew my employers. I thought he was looking at me. I have to go."

She turned, but he stepped in front of her. "Don't go."

"I must. I have been gone too long already."

"Eleanor." There was a pleading note to his voice. "Please stay."

She looked up at his face, wishing she really were Miss Smith, wishing she could give herself to him without having to fear the consequences. She shook her head. "I can't."

"Then come later tonight. Come to my house."

"Your house?" she repeated slowly.

He'd already moved to the desk and was jotting something on a piece of paper. He folded it and slipped it into her pocket. "That's my address, Eleanor. Please come."

She was shaking her head. His eyes were so dark, so intense, and she was feeling so confused. "I don't know what you want from me."

He cupped the back of her head and kissed her again, so tenderly that her body ached for more when he pulled away to speak. "I want to love you, Eleanor. I want to kiss you whenever I please. I want you in my bed, when I wake, when I go to sleep. I don't want to see you secretly, once a week. I want you every day."

She still didn't understand, not at all. Was he asking her to…? There was nothing she could imagine wanting more, but it couldn't be possible.

Hesitantly, she said, "Are you asking me to marry you?"

His startled expression was answer enough. Obviously he was not.

He recovered quickly, but she'd seen the look of guilt that passed across his face for just a fraction of a second. "Be my mistress, Eleanor. Let me take care of you. Come live with me."

She remained very still, absorbing his words. Mistress. How stupid of her to think he'd ask her to be anything else.

She stood there for just a few seconds, but they were the longest, most humiliating seconds of her life. And then she did something she'd never even contemplated doing before. She slapped him.

The impact sent needles through her hand, but he was clearly more startled than injured. In his brief instant of surprise, she turned and ran. He watched her go without trying to stop her. He felt, in that rare moment, too damned remorseful to do otherwise. He'd hurt her, embarrassed her, and he knew that she wouldn't be coming back soon, not of her own volition, anyway.

Chapter Nine

Eleanor had arrived home from the theater with little time to spare. Just as she slipped into bed, she'd heard Charles return from his evening out. She heard the front door close quietly, the shuffle of his feet walking up the staircase. And then she'd lain in bed until it was nearly dawn, too humiliated to sleep.

Now, one day on, the Jerseys' masquerade awaited her unwilling presence. It was the last social event of her disastrous season. She'd be leaving London in the morning, and she didn't think tomorrow would come fast enough.

Dusk was gradually taking over the sky, and subdued, violet light filtered through her bedroom curtains. Soon, she'd have to light a candle. Right now it seemed like too much effort.

She was lying supine on the small sofa at the foot of her bed, her feet propped up on its arm in a most unlady-like fashion. She wore a white embroidered chemise, stays and stockings. Green-striped silk slippers completed the unfinished look. A book lay neglected on her stomach. Discarded clothes were strewn about the room.

"Eleanor?" Beatrice entered without waiting for permission. Framed by the doorway, she looked elegant even at eight months pregnant. "Good heavens, but you're the picture of melancholy. Would you like tea?"

"Oh. Yes, please." Eleanor sat up and rearranged her legs.

Beatrice crossed the room, a worried frown slightly marring her otherwise perfect visage. She carried just one dainty teacup, and she handed it to Eleanor as she sat down next to her. "Better have it quickly because Aunt Louisa will be here in half an hour to take you to the ball. You're not even dressed yet. Are you certain you're feeling well?"

"Yes, I'm fine. I'm looking forward to it," she lied.

"I do wish I could come with you, but the prospect of standing all night in my condition—"

"I understand."

"I was actually hoping that we could talk before you went out. Do you have a moment?"

Eleanor didn't like the sound of that. Tea was obviously just a pretext. "Well, I do have to get dressed…. What do you want to talk about?"

"Nothing in particular. It's just I feel I've seen very little of you the past few months, even though we've been sharing the same roof. The summer seems to have sped by, and I've been so absorbed with my own concerns. And, well, you've been rather reticent."

Now guilt, heaped on top of humiliation. Eleanor already felt bad enough about neglecting her familial duties all season—things like being obedient, getting married and doing her best not to arouse general opprobrium. She'd been selfish, not to mention dishonest. "I don't mind at all, Bea. You've no need to apologize."

"I hope not. I've been worrying that since we're to leave in the morning you might feel as if you're being forced to forfeit the rest of your season on my account. Are you sad to be going?"

Eleanor wished she knew the answer to that question, but she hadn't the faintest idea how she felt. Sad, yes, to be walking away from the only whiff of romance she'd ever experienced—she was devastated, in fact. And sad and embarrassed that it had ended so badly. She'd allowed herself to fall in love, while he'd wanted nothing more than to toss her governess's skirts over her head. And, God forgive her, he'd almost succeeded.

She was desperately sad, but she didn't have a choice. She *had* to leave.

"I think I will manage," she said slowly, not wanting to look directly at Beatrice.

"You're *truly* fine, then?"

If fine was nearly allowing herself to be made love to by a man, and then being stupid enough to feel brokenhearted about it.

"Yes, Bea."

"Really? Because we've all been worried about you. I suppose I was hoping that you might bring me up to date a bit. We can finally have that chat we've been meaning to have all summer." She paused. "Have you... Have you met anyone yet?"

"Surely you're not that uninformed."

"I know, I know, you've told me *many* times that no one's taken a fancy to you, but I thought perhaps that might have changed recently."

Eleanor sipped her tea. She was beginning to have the awful feeling that her sister suspected something. "No, nothing has changed."

"Then perhaps Lady Jersey's masquerade will help move things along. It's the principal event of the late season—it's actually rather exciting, as far as these things go. *Everyone* comes, and a number of undesirables manage to sneak in each year, which gives it…a certain fillip of intrigue, I suppose."

"Oh?"

"Yes, and it's always expected that any gentlemen who've not yet proposed marriage will do so there. It's all due to the masks, I think."

"The masks?"

"I imagine so. Nothing to make one bolder than a disguise, don't you think? Honestly, the *Times* is always full of engagements the next day."

Eleanor was having a hard time taking this in. "Engagements? Surely you're not suggesting that someone is going to…*propose* to me."

"Louisa tells me she thinks you're in love."

Eleanor paled. "Then you're both mad. Why would she think that?"

"Well, you *have* been acting very strangely. And also, apparently, there has been a bit of talk."

"Talk?" The room felt as if it was beginning to spin around her. How on earth had they found out…?

"Well, I haven't heard this gossip myself, but apparently you've been linked to Lord Lennox."

The room halted abruptly. "Lord Lennox?"

"Yes. Who did you think I was talking about?"

"I...I had no idea." She realized she was sputtering and took a deep breath. "I've only met him a few times."

"Well, according to Louisa, he seems rather fond of you. And he's apparently quite the catch, although I must admit I only know him by sight."

Eleanor had heard few things more preposterous. "I suppose he is fond of me, Bea. We've become...friends, in a manner. But literally, I've done nothing more than dance with him, probably not more than four or five times. He has made no indication that he might want to...marry me."

Beatrice sighed. "Oh, well. Louisa is already annoyed at me for being too lenient with you all season, and she's certain that his proposal is imminent. It seems Lord Lennox is rumored to be seriously looking for a wife, and you're the only girl he's shown any interest in."

Eleanor looked down at the swirly Persian carpet, wishing once more she could spend a quiet evening at home with a cup of poison hemlock. The weight of her family's expectations would make the ball even worse.

Beatrice put a comforting arm on her shoulder. "I know it's not much fun—remember how much I hated my first season? But by tomorrow morning it'll all be over. I'll send Meg in to help you with your dress." She rose to leave her alone.

Eleanor sat very still for a minute and then lay back

down. If her family thought she was going to marry Lord Lennox, then they were headed for disappointment.

But it wasn't he who worried her.

It was James.

She'd never managed to tell him the truth. Obviously they'd made no arrangements to meet again before she'd fled, and after a week or two passed he might start to wonder what had happened to her. She didn't *think* he'd try to contact her at Beatrice's house, but such an event wasn't impossible, either, given how persistent he was. If he did come…oh, God…what would he think when Cummings informed him that Eleanor Smith didn't exist? That the only Eleanor living at the house wasn't an employee after all? And that she'd left London for the immediate future?

She wondered if he'd care. She hoped he would. But she also knew that he might not bother to seek her out in the first place. By next week, he might have replaced her with some other fool.

And she'd be miles away, unable to forget him. She knew she wouldn't, even if, at the moment, she wanted to very much. She certainly couldn't imagine ever finding a husband now. Compared to James, everyone else would come up short.

She closed her eyes and saw a desert of spinsterhood stretched out inexorably before her. She really would be just like Aunt Louisa.

When the invitation to Lady Jersey's masquerade had arrived many weeks ago, James had promptly thrown it in a silver bowl along with all the others he'd received. But then Will had stumbled onto his doorstep late that evening, announcing that not only had he finally decided who he'd ask to marry him, but also that he was going to do it that very night. Certain his brother was going to do something he'd later regret, and also make an ass of himself in the process, James had seen no alternative but to come along.

At least it was better than how he'd been spending his evening so far. Brooding over Eleanor and feeling sorry for himself.

En route to the ball, James had tried to talk Will out of his plan. "Perhaps you should wait until tomorrow. You're foxed."

"Oh, God, can you tell?" His eyes had a glassy appearance, and he stopped to find strength in a lamppost. "I've been wandering around for an hour trying to walk it off."

James put his arm around his shoulders and steered him down the street. "Is your intended so awful that you required fortification?"

"She's not awful at all," Will said defensively, but then his voice turned thoughtful. "Wouldn't contemplate asking her if it weren't for needing an heir, of course. I suppose a man requires something different in a wife than he would in another woman."

"What do you require?" James asked, playing along. "Watch that puddle."

"Oh, damn." Will sat on a nearby set of front steps and frowned at his shoe. "I don't know. Someone who's pretty and good-natured, from a good family. Good-natured is essential because I don't see myself ever being faithful. Someone who wouldn't mind if I carried on my affairs. Someone practical, without any over-blown romantic notions. Not going to fall in love with her, so someone I can be friends with."

"I don't think such a saint exists."

"Put a fiver on it then. I know just the girl. I'll intro-duce you to her once we get there. When will we get there? Blasted long way to walk."

They arrived at the Jerseys' extravagantly large house a few minutes later, and Will immediately went off to locate the unfortunate girl. James merely hoped to get the introduction over with soon, so he could return home. He was already regretting his decision to attend. His brother was a grown man and could take care of himself, wet shoe and all.

Tall windows lined one wall of the ballroom, and he strolled over to them, hoping to catch a breeze. He could also see the entire room from this position, and he scanned the crowd, looking for his brother. There must have been hundreds of guests, each person costumed to a different degree. There were the usual van Dyke costumes, shepherdesses and Marie Antoinettes, but most, like him, had opted for normal evening clothes and a mask. Will seemed to have been completely absorbed in the crush.

A door at the end of the ballroom led out to the large garden. The warm night beckoned, and James picked his way through the crowd and out the door, preferring to be alone. Misery, at least in his case, didn't like company. And he was definitely miserable. He wondered if Will would notice if he left, but brotherly duty won out.

Outside, the Jerseys had created a raised, paved terrace, demarcated from the rest of the garden by a flight of stone steps and a pair of flowering urns. Several wrought-iron benches lined its edge, and James sat. Through the door and windows, he could still see inside the brightly lit ballroom, but no one, thankfully, would be able to see him in the dark.

He'd never really had any difficulties with women before. His romantic relationships to date had been straightforward affairs, without any emotions thrown in to complicate matters. But Eleanor was different. Before she'd arrived in his life he'd felt bored, lost and aimless—hell, he'd probably felt that way for years. He hadn't realized, until he'd faced the threat of never seeing her again, just how much he'd looked forward to each of their meetings. It wasn't just the thrill of the conquest that caused his anticipation, either. Seeing her had given shape to his weeks, and making her smile had given him a purpose. He couldn't simply let her walk out of his life. She *had* to forgive him. He'd just give her a few more days to sulk.

He supposed he might have fallen in love with her. That could be the only explanation for the hollow pain he now felt, for the sense that he'd lost the only good thing his life had offered in many years. He knew he'd be damned lucky if he could convince her to forgive him, or to trust him again. He couldn't excuse his behavior, other than that he'd been so disarmed by her kiss that he'd been rendered temporarily insane. His strategy all along had been to practice patience, seducing her slowly, but instead he'd practically jumped on her and had then insulted her for good measure. He'd asked her to be his mistress the first time he'd met her, too, and the suggestion hadn't been greeted favorably then, either. Only this time she'd punctuated her departure with a slap across the face. Never again, full stop. Experience should have taught him something.

The only problem was, he really did want her to be his mistress. He wanted everything he'd told her: to see her during the day, to be able to walk down the street with her on his arm, to buy her all the pretty things she wanted, and to have her in his bed each night. He was sick to death of pretending he didn't want these things, and he was tired of waiting. He didn't think she'd mind being his mistress that much, either, at least once she got over her initial objections.

Of course, he could have asked her to be his wife instead. That would have achieved the same objectives, and was what she'd initially thought he was proposing. The embarrassed, crestfallen look on her face when she realized what he'd really meant had haunted him all day. In fact, he'd never really contemplated marriage before, other than assuming it to be something intended for other people. She'd probably reject him if he asked her, anyway.

But then, maybe…he could at least try?

The thought should have sent a cold shiver of alarm down his back, but instead it felt welcome, comforting and good. There was no reason why he shouldn't marry her; there was absolutely nothing wrong with her. She was his superior in every way, as far as he was concerned. She was pretty and clever and modest—sure, she had neither fortune nor a prominent family, and Will might object to having a former governess for a sister-in-law, but James didn't care one whit about these things. She was perfect. So why not? If marriage was the only way to keep her in his life, then he would ask her. He would do whatever it took to convince her.

He looked at his watch and rose, suddenly anxious to leave. He wanted to find her, before he talked himself out of the only sensible decision he'd made in years. He couldn't contact her tonight—she'd lose her position if he went to her place of employment at such an hour, and she wouldn't be too happy about that. But then again, she wouldn't be working there much longer anyway, at least not if he got his way.

He reentered the ballroom halfway, standing in the doorway and glancing across the crowd to locate his brother. He wanted to get the introduction over with. Will was usually easy enough to locate, given his height, but he wondered what his partner would look like. He knew his usual type fairly well: petite, vacantly pretty blond women with curvaceous figures.

But when he finally found his brother moving through the crowd, he was surprised. His partner wasn't what he'd expected at all. She was quietly beautiful, with her brown hair pulled back to reveal tiny, delicate ears, and soft curls teasing her slender neck. And her face—half concealed by a powder-blue mask—was sensitive, intelligent and flawless, to his eyes, anyway. Pert little nose, generous lips. James knew her face as well as he knew his own. He just didn't know why she was dancing with his brother.

He watched them for several minutes, unable to move, unable even to be certain that his eyes did not betray him. This was the girl that Will intended to marry? Eleanor? It didn't make sense. What the hell was she doing there? He could hardly even believe it was her. Perhaps the eyes that looked out from her mask were green, not blue, and it wasn't really her after all. Or perhaps it *was* Eleanor, and she was, for some inexplicable reason, playing an elaborate charade on everyone in the room.

Or perhaps she'd been playing it on him.

He immediately knew the answer. She looked far more at home in these surroundings, in these clothes, than she ever had when he'd seen her before. He'd never felt like such a fool.

She looked so beautiful, and suddenly so unlike the girl he'd come to know. She tilted her head back to laugh at something Will said, revealing perfect white teeth. James unconsciously clenched his fists. He'd always known how lovely she was, but he'd thought he was the only one, with her beauty hidden by her awful wig and her dowdy gray dress. Now she was the very picture of a spoiled debutante, of the sort of girl he'd assiduously avoided since he was sixteen. Her gown was expensive, obviously so, and tailored to emphasize her subtle curves. A single strand of pearls hung from her neck, a neck that had been too poor for such finery only yesterday. A neck he'd kissed only yesterday. Now he could wring it.

He could easily ascertain the gentle rise of her breasts, and so could everyone else, his brother included. He was sure he'd seen Will cast his gaze downward to sneak a glimpse of creamy flesh. He held her closer than was necessary, closer than was proper, and James wanted to smash his face in with a tightly closed fist. He wanted to hurt him.

And Eleanor…he wanted to drag her home—to his home—and…he didn't know what. Make love to her until she cried out his name again and again, until she forgot his brother existed. He wanted to claim her as his even though she clearly was not.

Chapter Ten

The music ended, and Eleanor and Will walked to the side of the room to enjoy the cooling breeze that wafted in from the garden.

She wondered what time it was. She hadn't seen her aunt since soon after they'd arrived. After she'd introduced her to Lord Lennox, Louisa had sought shelter in the ladies' retiring room. Strangely enough, she'd seemed fairly unimpressed by him, even though just a few hours earlier she'd been adamant that Eleanor do everything in her power to extract a proposal. Eleanor suspected that, once she'd been confronted with his open rakishness, she had a sudden change of heart. That was a good thing, she supposed; the pressure eased considerably.

"You're woolgathering again, Miss Sinclair."

She forced a smile to her lips for his benefit. Normally she enjoyed the camaraderie she felt around him, but he was in a strange mood tonight. "I'm sorry, my lord. It's a nasty habit."

"What are you thinking about? Me?"

She answered with a dismissive snort, but his words made her uneasy. Was it possible…? He couldn't *really* plan to ask her to marry him, could he? Surely she was the last person he'd think of.

"Shall I lie and answer yes, my lord?"

"You wound me."

She thought she smelled the traces of brandy and smiled back indulgently, realizing the cause of his behavior. He'd simply imbibed too much. "I merely jest, my lord."

"No, lit'rally. You must have stepped on my foot three times while we were dancing."

Her eyes widened. "Oh! Forgive me. I'm so clumsy."

"Must be why one must always queue to dance with you, hmm?"

She frowned at his sarcasm, good-natured though it might have been. "How very observant you are."

He quickly realized he'd offended her. "Look, sorry, didn't mean for it to come out that way. Can't seem to help teasing you sometimes. It's like you're my sister."

"But you don't have a sister, Lord Lennox."

"Well, no… If I did, though…"

Eleanor sighed. Actually, she felt relieved that he thought of her in such patently unromantic terms—here she'd been, starting to worry that Louisa might have been right about his intentions. "You don't need to explain. That's always the way of it, to tell you the truth. It's not my reputation for toe stomping that keeps gentlemen away—*everyone* seems to think of me as their sister. If I'm thought of at all, that is."

"Maybe that's what some gentlemen want."

"You needn't try to console me, my lord. I'm quite used to it."

"No, really. Maybe some gentlemen want someone like a sister."

She cocked her head. "What a funny thing to say. What on earth do you mean?"

His face was pallid. "What I mean is…let's start anew. What I *don't* mean is that any man wants to marry his sister—I hope that's clear, Miss Sinclair. I do not approve of…um, *that*. What I intended to say was…" He stopped dead with a sigh. His eyes pleaded with her to put him out of his misery. "I don't know what I'm talking about. Shall we forget about it?"

She was happy to forget about it. His command of the English language was deteriorating, and the mention of marriage made her want to run home more than ever. She leaned forward slightly to ask in a low voice, as politely as possible, "Are you tight, my lord?"

He straightened with dignity. "No, Miss Sinclair, I am not. A lady should not ask a gentleman such a question."

"I am sorry."

"In fact, I think I will have another drink."

"Do, please."

With a brief bow, he walked purposefully across the dance floor, leaving her alone. She just watched him depart, utterly perplexed by his unaccountable behavior, not that he was ever conventional. She certainly wouldn't wait for him to return. She'd find her aunt and go home. For once even Louisa wouldn't insist on remaining at the ball until the bitter end.

But she only managed to take one step in the direction of the ladies' retiring room before a light tug on the back of her gown prevented her from going any farther. The voice that whispered in her ear was rich, caressing and familiar.

"Miss Smith. What an unexpected…pleasure."

A few steps, and they'd walked out the garden door into the balmy evening. Her feet moved against her will, impelled by the pressure on her back. He didn't take her the whole way into the garden. They'd gone only a few feet onto the terrace when he pulled her to the side and turned her around so her back pressed against the stuccoed side of the house. For the first time that night, she faced him. He'd removed his mask, and it hung loosely around his neck. In the shadows, he looked sinful, dangerous, so handsome that she held her breath. And he was furious. Furious with her. Eyes dark, mouth a hard line.

He leaned forward, his arms braced on either side of her shoulders so she couldn't escape. She wouldn't have dared. Any sound of struggle might have brought other guests out to the terrace, and her reputation would be in tatters. She didn't think he'd care if he ruined her.

"What are you doing here?" she finally ventured, her voice a mere whisper even though that hadn't been her intention. She wanted to sound strong.

His gaze wandered insolently over her face. "I should be asking you the same question, Smith. If I recall, this isn't your night off."

Her face burned at the reminder. "You needn't be nasty."

He finally took a step back, running a hand through his hair in frustration. "I don't know how else to be. I don't even know your name."

"Please listen, James, I can explain—"

The cutting, bitter anger returned. "Better tell me soon, sweet, or I'll think of something else to call you. Several phrases come to mind."

She narrowed her eyes. "My name *is* Eleanor."

"Eleanor Smith, right? And you're a governess?"

"Sinclair," she amended quietly. "I'm not a governess, as I think you know."

"Ah, I see. And the lady you claimed to work for? The marchioness?"

She closed her eyes, knowing the entire truth had to come out. This wasn't how she'd planned it at all. "She is my sister, Beatrice."

He leaned forward again, bracing his arms, making her feel pinned to the wall. "And I'll guess the rest. Your father sent you to London for the season so you could find a suitable husband. A rich lord perhaps. Someone with impeccable bloodlines."

She couldn't deny his words, so she looked at the ground and said nothing.

He tilted her chin up, forcing her to meet his pitiless gaze. "So that makes me wonder, what are you doing with me?"

His words were quiet, so quiet that they scared her more than any amount of blustering. "James, you don't understand. Please let me explain—"

"I think I understand exactly."

"I don't think you do!"

"I could have made love to you last night, Eleanor. You enjoy my touch, but still you intend to marry someone else. You think I'm beneath you."

She didn't think that. She didn't at all. But his words hurt, worse than any injury she could imagine, and her own words matched his venom. "Perhaps I do, James. How on earth were you even allowed in tonight? Had the butler fallen asleep?"

She wished she could take it back. In a few short seconds she'd made him despise her. She could see it in his eyes, in the way he moved slightly away as if his proximity to her made him ill.

"He doesn't love you, you know."

She didn't care about anyone but him, but she was guided by pride at the moment, not reason. "Who? Lord Lennox? And what have you heard?"

He leaned in close again, his face only inches from hers. "That he's looking for a brood mare and thinks you'll suffice. Although I'm not so sure what he'd think if he ever learned about your…activities."

She blanched at his bluntness, but she had to defend herself. She tried to push him away, but he was solid and unmovable. "I am not marrying anyone. But if I were, what business would it be of yours? You certainly didn't ask me to be your wife."

"No, I asked you to be my mistress. The position is still open."

"And am I supposed to be flattered?"

He lowered his head even more, his lips so close to hers she could feel his breath. "I think you'd rather enjoy it."

His kiss was different this time. It was an onslaught,

all tenderness and patience replaced by toe-curling urgency. Hard. Demanding. He took from her without asking for permission, and she, smitten fool, parted her lips and gave. She should have been offended. She should have been scared by his intensity. But instead she wrapped her arms around his neck, and ran her hands through his soft, black hair. She pressed her body wantonly to his, not caring what was right, or proper, or dignified, and he pulled her closer. His hands wandered up her arms to stroke her face, her neck, her breast. He teased her nipple through her silk gown—not playfully, but mercilessly, making her groan with frustrated pleasure. It felt wonderful, and yet like punishment at the same time.

And then he stopped, so suddenly she was left breathless and trembling. She clung to his arms to steady herself, but he removed her hands and stepped away.

"Surely your beau must be looking for you, Eleanor. We mustn't keep him waiting."

She shook her head, unable to think about Lord Lennox, Louisa or anyone in the ballroom, just a few feet away, who might discover her in this compromising position.

"Do you still think you'd hate being my mistress?" His voice was a whisper, a caress, but his words were so cruel she could only close her eyes against them.

And when she'd opened her eyes, he'd walked away. She saw only his tall, black-clad back as he entered the ballroom. She leaned back against the wall, welcoming its coldness on her skin.

* * *

Louisa had been pleased to leave, and she'd spent the entire journey home expressing her doubts about Lord Lennox. *He is obviously a wastrel, a rake, and can you believe, Eleanor, that he would turn up tonight foxed....*

Eleanor had barely paid attention. Her aunt's words sounded muffled, as if she'd stuffed cotton in her ears, and all she'd done was nod in agreement when it seemed appropriate. She didn't care about Lord Lennox. When Louisa's carriage stopped at Beatrice's house for Eleanor to alight, she managed little more than a mumbled goodbye before walking dazedly up the steps to the front door.

She let herself in with a key, since Cummings would have retired hours earlier. Louisa's driver whipped her horses into a trot, and the clop of their hooves echoed down the empty street.

She closed the door behind her as quietly as possible. Her soft dancing slippers barely made a sound on the polished marble floor. The hall clock ticked soothingly. It read quarter past one. The house and its occupants slept.

Eleanor peeked out the window. The street was clear and covered in a protective veil of darkness. She opened the door to Charles's study, located a pen and paper and spent several minutes writing a note, not wasting time to worry about misspellings and blots of ink. She waved it dry, folded it and then tucked it into her pocket.

Then back into the hall. She silently opened the front door.

Chapter Eleven

Eleanor had no trouble finding James's house, since he'd given her his address just the day before. He didn't live far from Beatrice, and the walk there took her less than ten minutes. The shadows of lampposts and gate-posts seemed to come alive, to leer at her and to follow her down the street as she went; she glanced over her shoulder every twelve paces or so until she arrived. She mounted his steps and stopped in front of the door. His house was large and imposing—not as large as her sister's house, but hers was a family home, meant to house a whole brood of children. He was just a bachelor. Why—*how*—did he live here? It didn't make sense.

She took a deep breath, held it for a few seconds, and then knocked so lightly that no one was likely to hear her. She hoped he wouldn't be in, although she didn't like to contemplate what he might be doing at a quarter to two in the morning other than sleeping, alone, in his bed.

She'd written the note just in case he didn't answer, and she retrieved it from her pocket. It explained everything, as best she could. It even contained an apology, which she felt she owed him. Although she'd been humiliated when he'd asked her to be his mistress, she didn't think he'd intended to offend her. He was a rake; such was habit, and she'd been foolish to hope otherwise. She *was* angry about the callous way he'd treated her at the ball, but he'd been understandably shocked to see her there. Her own words had been spiteful, too, and she had to tell him she didn't mean what she'd said.

She just wanted him to know that her intentions had always been good. It hurt her that he could honestly believe she thought she was better than him, and yet she couldn't understand why such an idea would even cross his mind. Why should he feel inferior, if he were as rich as his house suggested? Perhaps his wealth really *did* come from criminal means. Beatrice *had* said something about undesirables turning up at the Jerseys' masquerade....

She slid the note through the slot in the door. The night was so quiet that she could hear the muffled sound it made as it hit the floor on the other side.

She turned to leave, not actually feeling any better. She felt worse, in fact, because it was over. She'd said her bit, silent words, on paper, and she'd never know his response. The end. Dawn was just a few hours away, and Beatrice and Charles wanted to leave London by midday.

But then the door opened behind her.

"Eleanor?"

She turned slowly. James had answered the door himself. He'd removed his jacket, waistcoat, cravat and shoes, although he still wore his dark evening trousers and white linen shirt. The shirt was open at the neck. For a moment, she just stared, mesmerized by his beauty.

And he stared back.

"I—I'm leaving."

He stepped outside in his stockinged feet. "But why did you come in the first place?"

"I left you a note."

"Why leave a note when you can tell me yourself?"

He opened the front door wider and motioned for her to enter. After a moment's hesitation, Eleanor reluctantly went in, collecting her note on the way. She definitely didn't want him to read it now. It spoke too candidly of her feelings, and, face-to-face, she wasn't yet ready to be so frank.

He followed, closing the door behind them.

The hall was dark, so dark she could hardly make out his form. She immediately regretted her decision to come inside. "I should leave."

"Maybe you should sit down to tell me?" He crossed the hall, opened a door and entered another room. She followed nervously. His voice sounded completely neutral, and she'd no idea what he was thinking. Maybe he'd calmed down, started to forgive her….

The room appeared to be a study. A single lamp burned on a small table, and a fire smoldered in the grate, for light more than warmth. It was a dark, masculine room—rather cluttered, but homely. Still, it didn't put her at ease.

She hovered in the doorway and swallowed. "I…I…"

"Have a drink?" He poured her a glass of brandy and water without waiting for her to answer. He handed it to her, and his fingers brushed against hers. She closed her eyes against the wave of sensation.

He didn't seem too affected, though. He motioned for her to sit in a comfortable chair by the fire. She smoothed her skirts and sat, and he took the chair across from her.

Then it was quiet. She sipped her brandy, rallying for strength, and glanced around the room, trying to find some way to begin.

"You have a lovely house," she said rather lamely. "Who is in that portrait?"

James turned around to look at the picture behind his desk. "That's my maternal grandfather."

"He looks rather roguish."

"He was, I suppose. He started life as a pickpocket, but when he'd saved enough money—"

"Stolen money?"

"Yes, stolen. When he saved enough, he bought a decent suit of secondhand clothes and decided to try his luck as an actor. Then he went on to spawn seven illegitimate children, my mother among them. With the exception of two aunts, they also ended up on the stage."

"How have you managed to pay for this house, James?" She didn't mean for her question to come out so bluntly.

"You have an obsession with this topic. I don't find it particularly endearing."

"No, I do not. I just don't know anything about you. You don't make any sense." She blushed, realizing that without even meaning to she'd managed to get round to the topic she'd come there to discuss in the first place. "You don't know much about me, either."

"I know enough." His tone suggested he didn't like what he knew.

"I didn't intend to lie to you, James."

"Didn't you?"

She felt her lower lip start to fold. He wasn't making it easy. "All right, I did mean to lie, but I had no choice. When I first told you my name and about being a governess I was only trying to protect myself. I didn't know who you were, and I couldn't trust you."

He just looked at her, but his expression gave nothing away. He *had* to understand the point she was making. She'd been under no obligation to tell him the truth at first. It was only later…

"And then I wanted to tell you the truth, but I didn't know how. I wanted to very much."

"Why would it matter if you told me or not?" he asked.

Because she'd fallen hopelessly in love with him. She just couldn't tell him so. "Because I am not a natural liar. I had no desire to deceive you. That is why it mattered."

"Because of honor, then? That's it?"

"More than that. I—" She felt as though she was standing on the brink of a chasm, with the truth on the other side. She took a deep breath for courage and prepared to leap, but then balked at the end. How could she explain that she'd continued to lie to him because she'd known that telling him the truth would have changed everything? If he'd known who she really was she would never have been able to see him again. But admitting as much would be admitting how vulnerable she was to him, and she wasn't willing to do that, not while he was sitting there, regarding her so coolly.

"I don't know why it mattered." That was the best she could come up with.

"Come here, Eleanor," he said finally, his voice quiet.

She didn't rise from her seat. She was too wary. She wished she knew what he was thinking, but his face was completely inscrutable.

"I said come here." His voice was soft, but the words serious.

"No."

"Shall I come get you?" He rose.

She rose, too. Like a bolt. And she dropped her glass in the process, creating a dark, blooming stain on the Savonnerie carpet.

"I don't know what you're so scared of," he said, taking a step in her direction.

"I'm not scared." She contradicted herself by taking a clumsy step backward.

"Then why are you running away?"

Their chairs had been separated by only a few feet, and she didn't think running would get her very far, anyway. "I've told you everything I wanted. Why should I stay any longer?"

"Don't I get a turn to speak?" He took another step.

"Fine. What do you want to say?"

"I want to know why you really came tonight."

"I've already told you." She was starting to recognize the look in his eye. It meant he was about to kiss her.

"I was rather hoping you might want to finish what we started earlier."

She didn't react quickly enough. With little effort, he caught her.

The next thing she knew, she was in his arms, pressed hard against his chest, his lips on hers, demanding, hungry. His kiss was too urgent for her to do anything more than hold on to him tightly, but it didn't even cross her mind to resist. She welcomed his mouth, his hands. Kissing was easier than speaking. It was the only way she could tell him how she felt, and she could convince herself, with his strong arms wrapped around her, that he felt the same way.

She closed her eyes, surrendering herself completely. She felt something hard pressing against her lower back…a table, and she held on to it to steady herself. She heard the thump of something fall over and roll off the table and onto the floor, but she didn't care what it was, if it was broken, and neither did he, not while his fingers were working on the front of her spencer, opening buttons, pushing it off her shoulders. Underneath, she still wore her ball gown. Champagne silk cut high at the waist, and very short, slightly puffed sleeves that revealed almost her whole length of arm. Her stays pushed her breasts high so they swelled above her bodice. She hadn't realized until then, with his green, exploratory gaze roaming over her, just how much bare flesh it showed.

"Stay with me tonight."

Now his eyes met hers, so intense, so hot that she felt sapped of the ability to speak or disagree. Instead, she just nodded. His words scared her. She knew what they meant: he wanted to make love to her. But no matter how nervous it made her, no matter how life-changing this decision would be, she knew there was nothing she'd ever wanted more. When she returned home to her father's house, as she inevitably would, when she returned again to the narrow limits of obedience and duty, she knew she'd regret not making love to him—she'd regret it every bit as much as she would if she did. But she had the rest of her life to reflect on her mistakes, and that life seemed pallid and dull compared to this one night.

With little effort, he lifted her into his arms and carried her to the door. He shifted her into one arm to open it, and they were in the dark hall again. He headed straight for the wide staircase, his lips never leaving hers.

At the foot of the stairs, though, he did pause. "Tell me to stop, Eleanor. Tell me you don't want this." His voice was harsh, ragged. "Tell me and I'll open the door and send you on your way."

She shook her head. " I...I don't want to stop."

His lips found hers once again, and she was kissing him back, holding his face. He took the steps two at a time, and soon they'd reached his bedroom door. The doorknob rattled with his impatience, but then they were inside. The room was completely dark at first. The curtains had long since been drawn for the night, but her eyes quickly adjusted to the gloom. She could just make out her surroundings: the outline of a chest of drawers, a table, a chair, a bed.

He lowered her with painstaking slowness, every inch of her body brushing against his. His lips traveled along her neck, and she let her head loll back to give him full access. His hands moved agilely down her back, opening buttons as they went. Her gown loosened, and with a gentle tug he pulled it to her waist, and then the rest of the way to the floor. The feeling of cool air touching her skin was a dose of reality, but even knowing that she really was in his bedroom, half-undressed—even knowing that once she'd made love to him she couldn't *un*make it—didn't change her mind. James was otherwise unobtainable; he wasn't going to marry her, and if all he offered was one night, she would accept it. She needed this memory. So she just stood there in her shift and her stays, and she waited.

He was unbuttoning his shirt. She thought she saw his hand shake, but it was too dark to tell. His shirt parted to reveal skin. Darker than his crisp white linen. Golden, she imagined, and taut. Boldly she reached out to touch him, needing to confirm with her hands what her eyes couldn't see. First his chest, then his hard stomach. Hot skin. Smooth. She heard him draw his breath, and he captured her wandering hand in his. He held it behind her back, kissing her at the same time. With his other hand, he nimbly untied her stays. They joined her gown on the floor. Her shift came next, over her head in one fluid motion. And she, oh dear, became achingly aware of her slender body, naked but for her stockings.

He didn't allow her the time to have second thoughts, though. She didn't know how they'd reached the bed, but suddenly it was right behind her and he was easing her onto it. James stood above her, and she imagined he could probably see her pale limbs quite well, even in the dark. And her small, round breasts. And the chestnut triangle at the junction of her thighs.

She yanked the damask bedcovering over herself and sat up.

"James?"

He was unbuttoning the last button on his shirt. Her eyes were fully adjusted now, and she thought he looked amused. "Yes?"

"You're going to make love to me?"

He nodded.

She was quiet before answering, feeling horribly insecure. "I've never done this before."

Off with his shirt. He sat on the bed, right next to her. "I don't mind teaching you."

She closed her eyes and lay back down as he began unfastening his trousers. She just couldn't watch, although she was curious. His thigh touched hers, his hip touched her hip, and then he was leaning over, covering her with his chest. So broad, and warm, and strong, pressing her into the bed. And then suddenly he rolled over, taking her with him, so she was on top, looking down.

"Hello." He smiled wickedly up at her, teasing her.

She wasn't comfortable enough to smile back. "Hello."

He kissed her on the nose. "Making love should be fun, Eleanor. That's why people do it, you know."

"Fun?"

He nodded. "For example, when I kiss you here—" he demonstrated, just below her ear "—do you enjoy it?"

She nodded, as little ripples of pleasure danced across her body, leaving goose bumps in their wake. His lips didn't leave her as he rolled over to be on the top again.

"And here?" Her nipple this time. Embarrassingly, it hardened and grew in welcome as his tongue gently lapped it. She tried to sit up again, but he drew it into his mouth and, oh, the sensations. Feelings unlike any she'd experienced before. Relentless pleasure as his fingers teased her other breast, and then moved lower, lightly stroked her stomach, her leg. Down her hip, then up her soft inner thigh. Then in between, the most intimate part of her body. She went rigid, and his mouth returned to hers, absorbing any protest she might have made. And soon she forgot what had ever been wrong. It felt so right. The most exquisite sensation imaginable, expanding inside her like a bubble close to bursting. Her hands wandered up his firm arms, his neck, and into his hair, gripping him, holding him close. One hand roamed over his powerful shoulders and down his back, reveling in his warmth and his strength.

But then, something felt wrong. An unexpected ridge, and then another. It felt like a series of scars, some small, some bigger, slanting across his back.

"James?"

He had gone very still, then slowly pulled her hand away, holding it above her head.

"No more talking, sweetheart." The pressure from his fingers increased. She closed her eyes as the unfamiliar feelings grew. And then, just as she thought she was going to explode, he drew away his fingers and entered her fully with one smooth motion.

She went stiff. She hadn't expected that. She'd known that entering her was part of the process, but she hadn't expected it just then, and she hadn't expected the pain. She heard him curse quietly.

"James?"

"Shh, darling, it won't hurt much longer." He rained

kisses on her face, her neck, her breasts, and she tried to relax. The pain had already eased. It just felt strange, and when he began to move slowly, the friction did funny things to her insides. Good funny things. He kissed her again, teasing her tongue into play with his, and suddenly good started to become too good—wonderful, in fact. Like a ball of pleasure growing inside her, intense, insistent, finally bursting in hot vibrations. Her nails dug into his back, and she cried out in ecstasy. He matched her cry, swept over the brink by her release.

Eleanor lay quietly in his arms until his breathing became deep and even. Her life had just changed forever, and now that the physical pleasure had subsided, she was terrified. She didn't know what to do, didn't know what she'd just done. He'd told her that his offer of mistress still stood—is that what she'd become? She'd made love to him, and he'd said nothing of marriage. But mistresses were dirty secrets, and that wasn't what she wanted to be. She wanted to be a wife. Her family would be horrified if they ever found out what had happened.

She carefully extracted herself from his embrace and sat up, her eyes traveling over his body as it lay sleeping next to her. He'd rolled onto his side. His back was broad and strong, and she could just make out the faint scars in the darkness, just as she'd suspected. She reached out her hand to touch them, but then thought better of it, not wanting to wake him. They looked as if they'd occurred over a period of years, rather than in a single accident, and it scared her. How had this happened? Who was he? Now that he knew her real identity, she felt even more confused about his. He was hiding something, she knew it, and she was afraid it was something sinister.

She slowly rose from the bed, making sure not to disturb him. Her thighs felt sticky, and her clothes were strewn across the floor. She collected them quickly, and put them on as best she could, although she couldn't reach the top buttons of her gown. If anyone saw her walking home, they would know what she'd been doing, but at least that wasn't likely to happen. The city still slept peacefully, but it wouldn't for much longer. Dawn would soon break and her sister's servants would rise; Beatrice planned to leave London by noon.

Chapter Twelve

When James awoke, he'd stared for several minutes at the empty spot next to him in bed, at the depression in the pillow where she'd slept. He should have been relieved that she'd left early—seeing her, after the night they had shared, might have made him rethink his feelings, and he was determined that nothing had changed. He wanted nothing to do with her. One night. That was all it was.

But he hadn't felt relieved. He'd felt like a cad of the worst sort, and like a coward, too. He hadn't really meant for it to happen, not like that. He'd planned to pleasure her while keeping her virginity intact. But when he'd felt her hand tracing the scars on his back he'd been overcome by long-suppressed memories: of Richard, who'd made each of those scars with horse-whip, cane or hot fire poker, and of Will, for whom life had been easy. Will had no secrets, no problems, and he'd have so much more to offer Eleanor, even if he didn't love her. Blind with that thought, he'd suddenly found himself making love to her properly, needing to claim her as his. He should have pulled out once he'd realized what he was doing, but he needed to give her some pleasure after hurting her. As for himself, he'd had the most powerful climax of his experience, and he'd loathed himself as it happened.

That was why now, several hours into the afternoon, he was easing his pain with a steady stream of whiskey.

He was in his study, the room where last night he'd taken her into his arms and kissed her as if his life depended on it. Her spencer still lay crumpled on his demilune side table, and the candlestick she'd knocked off the table lay broken in half by its feet. Her tumbler remained overturned on the carpet. There was so much *her* there, and he wished his useless maid would hurry up and clean the room. She'd poked her head in a few hours ago, noted the evidence of what her timid mind perceived to be a Roman-style orgy, and she'd backed out of the room posthaste.

His butler knocked on the door and then entered after a discreet ten seconds. "Mr. Kinsale has arrived, sir. Will you see him?"

Bloody hell. He'd forgotten he'd promised to meet with Jonathon today. He nodded curtly. "Send him in."

Jonathon walked in a few seconds later, carrying a large ledger and humming cheerfully. "Good afternoon."

He sat across from him and opened the ledger on the desk. "Figures have worked out for once. *The Country Cousin* did well, in the end, and Colin Boyle has agreed to write another, but I don't think we can afford to stage something original again until next year. Shakespeare is always popular, and we don't have to pay the chap for his efforts." He finally looked up. "What's wrong with you? Not still brooding about the fair Miss Smith, are you?"

"There is no Miss Smith."

Jonathon cocked his head. "No? Who'd I meet the other night, then?"

"I saw Miss Smith at a ball yesterday, dancing with my brother. Her name's Eleanor Sinclair. Father's a viscount, or something, and Will plans to marry her."

Jonathon sat back in his seat. He pondered this information for a long minute. "I've little problem believing your Miss Smith is a viscount's daughter, but your brother getting married? How the hell did that happen?"

James shrugged. He should never have mentioned it. "Guess he met her at some social event. Will had told me he was looking for a wife, although I didn't think he was serious. He's no idea I know her…just wants a vessel to produce his heir."

"I see. A biddable virgin to bear the future earl. Except she's not exactly biddable, is she?" He paused, suddenly looking worried as a new possibility entered his head. "Please tell me she's at least still a virgin."

James said nothing. Silence was a sufficient answer.

Jonathon swiveled in his seat to look at the study door as if she would magically appear, before leaning forward to hiss, "Good God, you're an ass. She's not still here, is she?"

"She left this morning before I awoke."

"So you decided that since you can't marry her, you might as well ruin her for everyone else? Bloody hell, James, that was a selfish thing to do."

James suspected his friend was right. Perhaps that

was why he'd done it, but he didn't care at the moment. The thought of her marrying Will—of Will *touching* her—made him feel sick, and so angry…at least it was no longer a threat. "Since when did you become a champion of the female sex?"

"Bloody hell, the female sex has nothing to do with it. Don't want my best friend called out by some irate father."

"I'm going to strangle you if you don't shut up."

Jonathon duly grew quiet, although his fidgeting suggested it wouldn't last. James rose to look out the window, wishing he'd never met her. If he'd known she'd turn him into such a maudlin, vindictive fool then he certainly wouldn't have bothered to seek her out in the first place. Never, in his nine and twenty years, had he seduced a virgin. Especially the young, pampered daughter of a peer. He didn't know why she had to be different.

Jonathon offered his next words very carefully. "You know, there is a solution to this problem."

James continued to stare out the window, trying to ignore him.

"You *could* ask her to marry you. You bloody well should, in fact."

"No."

"Why?"

"Because I don't want to."

"Are you so sure?"

James finally turned to face him. "Nor does she want to marry me."

"So you've proposed already?" Jonathon rose to pour himself a glass of whiskey. "You should have said so in the first place."

"Look, Jon, in case you've forgotten, I never had any intention of marrying anyone, particularly someone like her. She hasn't changed anything. No, I didn't ask her."

"I think you might be surprised by her answer."

James sat on the worn sofa. He wondered what she'd say, but he didn't think it'd be yes. He knew she felt some affection for him, though, or at least she had. She'd certainly liked kissing him well enough, and she hadn't minded sharing his bed, either. But that made things even worse: that she could care for him and still be prepared to marry someone else. "It doesn't matter because she's no intention of marrying someone like me. Someone like my brother, perhaps. Some bloody earl—"

Jonathon rolled his eyes. "What a completely fallacious argument. You're not a turnip farmer, you know."

"As far as she's concerned, I'm not much better. Never told her about my illustrious forebears."

"Then maybe you could enlighten her."

"Why should I have to do that?"

"Well—"

James shook his head. "I wouldn't change her mind that way."

"Look, James, all I'm suggesting is that you are, or at least should be, exactly the sort of chap a girl like that would want to marry. And even though seeing her at a ball came as a nasty shock, she's still the same girl."

"Oh? And what girl would that be? I don't know who the hell she is anymore. Didn't even know her real name until last night."

Jonathon snorted. "Well, you're a fool for not suspecting something. I only spoke to her for a few minutes and I was having a hard time believing she was who she claimed to be."

"Then perhaps you could have shared your concerns," James said stiffly. "She told me she was a governess, and I saw no reason not to believe her."

"Really?" Jonathon looked truly surprised. "I never had a governess myself, but you probably had a few when you were very young. Were any of them like Miss Smith?"

No, they were plain, long in the tooth women without an ounce of Eleanor's charm, intelligence and beauty. "Are you trying to prove that I'm gullible?" he asked angrily. "I don't need to be convinced."

"No, not gullible. Maybe just optimistic."

"What do you mean by that?"

"I mean perhaps you were ignoring the obvious signs? Perhaps it suited you that she was just a governess. You'd never have approached her if you'd known who she really was."

James knew that was probably true. He should have questioned her tony accent, her education, her manners. Hell, even her clothes should have given her away—the supposed castoffs he'd seen her wear, the frivolous reticule she'd left behind at the theater the first time he'd spoken to her. There'd been so many clues, and he'd ignored each one.

"And anyway, how much does she know about you?" Jonathon asked.

"That's different, Jon." James knew he hadn't been completely honest with Eleanor, but it *was* different. That was his official policy; unlike Eleanor, he didn't lead some sort of separate life. He kept quiet about his background because he detested the value people put on titles and birth. Because he'd seen his own mother excluded by society. Because Richard's treatment of him had amounted to torture, simply because he shared his mother's blood.

"It's not so different," Jonathon argued. "Tell her the truth and I'm sure she'll admit everything. It's obvious she cares for you. Why else would she have come to the theater with you week after week?"

"It's called slumming, Jon."

"Then aren't you slumming, too?"

James rose. He'd had enough. "Stay as long as you like. I'm leaving."

Jonathon nodded. "I'll show myself out."

James closed the study door louder than was necessary, crossed the hall, and then, outside, into the mid-August afternoon heat. He started walking briskly north toward Hyde Park.

He reached it in fifteen minutes. Then he kept walking, straight through the park, stopping when he reached the placid waters of the Serpentine. The park was crowded on such a warm day. Happy couples strolled around the lake's perimeter, while children tossed bits of stale bread to the eager swans. He stayed for only a few minutes before turning around and heading back through the park the way he came.

For all his protestations, he knew what he had to do.

Thirty minutes later he stood in front of Eleanor's sister's house, staring at the imposing, black-painted door. He wondered if he was completely daft. For all he knew, her father was inside, planning his demise. But he took a deep breath and raised the polished brass knocker.

After a long minute, an ancient butler opened the door.

"Mr. James Bentley, for Miss Sinclair."

The butler cleared his throat before wheezing out, "You've just missed her, sir. She left for the country two hours ago."

James said nothing. This was a shock. Perhaps he'd scared her off. Perhaps her family had learned what had happened and they'd whisked her away.

"When did she decide to leave?" he asked finally, trying hard to keep his voice even.

"They've all left, sir, and have been planning to do so all season. Would you like to leave a note for Miss Sinclair?"

All season. She'd known she was leaving for months and hadn't bothered to tell him. "When will they return?"

"I am not at liberty to say, sir."

"Where in the country have they gone?"

"Would you like to leave a note?" the butler repeated.

No, he didn't want to leave a bloody note. What had he expected? That she'd be waiting for him to turn up on her doorstep, pleading for her hand? One night. That was all he'd expected from her, and all, apparently, she wanted from him.

He turned and walked away without thanking the man.

Chapter Thirteen

Six weeks later

"Don't know why you wanted to come," Will complained. "You always leave these things early."

"Nothing else to do tonight," James replied distractedly, his gaze drifting over every head in the Marchioness of Pelham's airy drawing room. His brother's question was fair enough. He didn't want to be there, except...

"Nothing to do? Haven't seen you sober in weeks. Can't be getting bored of that already. Haven't you any more money to lose?"

James ignored his sarcasm. He hadn't actually been invited to the party, but it hadn't been difficult getting past the footman at the door, considering the great number of guests. Will had merely produced his own invitation, and since they'd come together it had been assumed that they both belonged. Perhaps Eleanor would be there, too....

He hadn't even known that her family was back in town until Will had mentioned his plans for the evening. He didn't know if Eleanor would have come back with them, and he didn't know what he planned to do if he saw her. Kiss her or strangle her. It was a toss.

Every day since she'd left, he'd debated going to find her. It had been easy enough to discover the location of her family's countryseat in Hampshire. But, damn it, he'd been fully prepared to marry her, and *she'd* left *him*, not the other way round. He wasn't going to swallow his self-respect and follow her around all of England like some pathetic swain. Shouldn't have even come tonight. Wouldn't have, except…except he didn't know what. Except even though she'd wounded his pride, he still cared about her. And he was worried about her.

"There's Eloise Harman," Will was saying, changing the subject to something less confrontational. "Rather uninspiring, isn't she? But apparently old Mrs. Harman produced nine healthy boys in addition to her."

"How do you know all this?" James asked, returning to the present.

"Henny and Venny sent me a list of girls they wouldn't mind being related to. Eloise Harman was in a column labeled Breeders. Awfully vulgar of them."

"You're not still seriously considering marriage, are you?" How it pained him to bring this subject up. He hadn't told Will about his relationship with Eleanor, but he'd been thankful that, so far, his brother seemed to have forgotten about her entirely. He'd barely noticed she'd left to begin with.

"No, just pretending to be considering it for their

sake. Dashed inconvenient for Miss Sinclair to disappear like that, but I suppose I didn't really want to marry her, anyway. I should pick someone new, but it's *such* a bore."

James didn't like the way Eleanor's name sounded on his brother's lips. The now-familiar urge to pummel him into the ground returned. "I'll find us a drink."

"For a change," he said drily.

Will's nose looked temptingly breakable, but James put his hands in his pockets instead. So what if he'd been drowning his sorrows recently? So what if he'd lost a bit of money?

He crossed the room, in search of refreshments.

It was a large gathering, so he wasn't too worried that anyone would realize he was uninvited, although he didn't plan to stay any longer than was necessary. It would probably be best if he didn't talk to anyone, either, except the footman who was passing out drinks. He'd definitely have to speak to him several times if he was going to last much longer.

He hadn't quite reached the footman, however, when a female voice burst into his pleasant reverie. Actually, it sounded rather like Eleanor's voice, perhaps just a bit more excitable.

"Lucy! I am so delighted you came!"

But it was only her sister, now much diminished in size. Blast. He'd been hoping to avoid her. If there were anyone who'd realize that he wasn't supposed to be there, then it would be she, the one who'd compiled the guest list. He turned quickly so that his back was facing her, and he fixed his gaze on the damask-covered wall, waiting for a moment when he could walk away without being noticed.

But then again, perhaps she'd say something useful. There were other guests gathered nearby, so he wouldn't look *too* conspicuous standing around....

He pretended to inspect a Dutch genre scene that hung nearby in a gilt-wood frame.

"I simply adore your dress, Lucy. Who made it?"

"Mrs. Hamnett—she has a shop on Regent Street... next to Mr. Blade's, where you bought those lamps for the sitting room."

James rolled his eyes, wishing they'd get round to discussing something pertinent. He couldn't feign interest in this dreary painting indefinitely. But they continued to discuss the merits of Mrs. Hamnett, followed by a Mme Lidelle and a shop known as Foubert's which seemed to specialize—as if he needed such information—in ribbon.

Ribbon. There was no explaining women. His attention began to fade. But then—

"Eleanor was particularly fond of Mme Lidelle," the sister said. James was once again listening closely.

"She always wears her clothes so beautifully." The voices were hushed now, and he had to strain a bit to hear them. "Where is she tonight?"

"Miles away, Lucy—she returned to my father's house after Violet was born."

"You mean she hasn't come? But I was so hoping to see her."

"I'm afraid she refused outright. You wouldn't think she was so stubborn, but when she doesn't want to do something she's a perfect mule. *Father* even came to London with us, and you know how much he hates it here. But she simply wouldn't hear of it."

"She'll come back next season, of course?"

"Well, I did manage to get her to promise, but I wouldn't wager on it."

These words were followed by an uncomfortable silence. Even James, unable to see their faces, could tell that something rather unpleasant was about to be broached.

"You don't suppose," Lucy began carefully, "that her reluctance could have something to do with—"

"Do not mention his name," Beatrice whispered. "He's here tonight, and I wouldn't want any of this to be overheard. In fact, she professed complete disinterest in the man, but I'm not so sure. She said she wanted to stay at Father's because she wasn't feeling well, and that certainly seems to be true. I'm actually getting rather worried about her. She was spending a lot of time with a consumptive during the season. Someone called Jane Pilkington. Do you know of her?"

"No, not at all."

There was another awkward silence, then Lucy spoke, "You…you have heard the rumors, haven't you?"

"What rumors?"

The conversation stopped abruptly, and James turned his head just enough to realize that they were walking away. Perhaps they'd realized they had an audience.

It didn't matter. He didn't care if he'd aroused their suspicions. He could leave now. He'd heard everything he'd needed.

Eleanor was in the country, at her father's house. And her father was in London. That meant she was…

Alone.

* * *

"Blast it all, James, don't know why you always decide to leave so suddenly. Every time I take you anywhere, you immediately insist on going. D'you have something to do in the morning?"

Actually, James planned to rise early to drive to Hampshire and find Eleanor. Having decided on this course of action, he wasn't going to waste another minute at this blasted affair. They were standing in the large hall. He'd already put on his coat and was waiting for Will to follow suit. It was taking too long, and he was growing impatient.

"You could stay."

Will sighed, frowning at his coat. "No. I don't enjoy these things. Can't find my…blasted sleeve's inside out. Useless butler they've got here, not to sort these things out." After a bit more struggling and swearing, he finally brought his coat to order. But just as he began to pull it on, a heavy hand landed not so gently on his shoulder.

"A word, Lord Lennox."

Both James and Will turned around. Two men stood waiting. The one who'd spoken was tall and about sixty, with silvering brown hair and blue eyes. The other looked to be in his early thirties, and was taller still, although not quite as tall as either Stanton.

"Do I know you, sir?" Will said, looking down his nose at the hand.

"David Sinclair, Viscount Carlisle. My son-in-law, Charles Summerson, Marquess of Pelham."

"And?" Will asked arrogantly.

"And I believe you're acquainted with my daughter."

A look of unhappy understanding passed across Will's face.

"What's this about?" James asked. Neither his tone nor his body betrayed his emotions, but every fiber of his being felt suddenly tense.

"There's a blasted rumor circulating," Will explained, speaking to the room at large. "It's utter rubbish, and I refuted it to anyone who dared mention it in my presence."

"I believe my son-in-law's study would be a better place to have this conversation."

Eleanor's father and brother-in-law crossed the hall and opened a door. David Sinclair motioned for Will to enter.

"Oh, bloody hell," Will muttered, doing as bidden. "This is the last thing I need."

James and Charles Summerson followed, looking at each other suspiciously.

"So I understand you know what this is about," Eleanor's father said, once they'd all entered. He stood behind the desk, forcing everyone else to stand, as well.

"I think so."

James didn't have the faintest idea. "I don't know. What rumor?"

"My brother, your lordship. James, er, Stanton," Will said awkwardly.

David Sinclair ignored the introduction and kept his gaze on Will. "I returned from the country just yesterday, and already I have been confronted by the most pernicious gossip."

"I'm sorry—*what* rumor?" James repeated. Eleanor's father raised an eyebrow at the heat in his tone, but Will hardly noticed.

"Someone has been spreading the word that Miss Sinclair was seen leaving my house early in the morning after Lady Jersey's ball. You wouldn't have heard it since you rarely bother going out in polite company, but I tell you it's been damned difficult to deflect."

"Any idea how it got started?" David Sinclair asked.

"None at all." Will meant it.

James walked over to the mahogany side table and began pouring a brandy. His hand shook slightly, but he needed to occupy himself somehow, needed to turn his back to everyone to hide any emotions that might cross his face. How could this have happened? Gossip was notoriously unreliable, but bloody hell, the rumormongers had cocked up their tales this time. Eleanor leaving Will's house? It made sense, though, since not many people even knew James Stanton existed. *And* Will was the one who'd been linked to her earlier in the season. The gossips had gotten them confused.

He took a large sip of brandy and turned to face the rest of the room. Eleanor's father was now seated at the desk.

"There was also a rumor that you wanted to marry her, Lord Lennox."

"There was," Will said. The room was silent for several seconds. "I hope you're not suggesting I started this rumor in order to precipitate such an event."

"Did you?" he asked boldly.

Will drew himself up. "I don't need to coerce anyone into marrying me. It's malicious gossip, and I've done nothing but try to quell it."

David Sinclair sighed heavily. "God preserve me

from daughters. I don't know how a rumor like this would attach itself to Eleanor, of all my children."

Will sat, too, with an air of resignation. Finally, he said, "The rumor that I was considering asking your daughter to marry me is true. Was actually planning on doing so at Lady Jersey's that night, only she left before I could get round to it."

Her father frowned at that rather thin excuse. It suggested a lack of persistence undesirable in a potential son-in-law. But still…

"Do you think my daughter returned your feelings?"

"I think she liked me," Will said. "That is sufficient sentiment in most cases."

"I would not force Eleanor into marriage under even the worst scandal, but if your esteem for her remains, and if she feels any fondness for you…"

James had heard enough. He could see Will mulling over David Sinclair's words, could see his mouth opening to speak. James didn't know what was going to come out, but there wasn't a chance in hell he'd allow his brother to agree to marry Eleanor.

"Perhaps the gossips have somehow confused you with another Stanton."

The three men turned around to stare at him.

"That's hardly possible," Will said. "There aren't any more male Stantons, except some obscure second cousins. That's the very reason Venetia and Henrietta have been plaguing me and I've got into this ruddy mess."

"That isn't true."

"'Tis." Will paused. "What—you don't mean *you?* I appreciate the gallant effort to preserve my bachelordom, old boy, but you needn't sacrifice yourself. You don't even know Miss Sinclair."

"I beg to differ. I know her well."

Silence. James counted the mantel clock tick six seconds.

Eleanor's father rose. "Are you suggesting my daughter might have been seen leaving your house, sir?"

"I am saying it outright."

Will put his head in his hand and groaned, knowing what was about to happen. Charles Summerson had been quiet throughout the whole conversation, so there had to be some other reason David Sinclair had asked his powerfully built son-in-law to attend.

A fist like a rock connected with James's cheek. He let it happen once; he figured he deserved it. But when Charles tried again, he ducked and pushed him backward into a carved mahogany pedestal. The door flew open and Beatrice rushed in, just in time to see the early Qing vase that had lived on that pedestal for many years topple off and shatter on the floor. She looked horrified.

"Charles!" she shouted.

He looked at her guiltily, knowing she didn't approve of fisticuffs, giving James enough time to return the favor of a black eye.

By the end of the night, it had been agreed: James would be leaving in the morning for Hampshire after all, only now he would be accompanied by Eleanor's father.

Will had practically glowed with relief.

Chapter Fourteen

Eleanor had been happy for Beatrice and Charles; their new daughter, Violet, was healthy and beautiful. And she'd enjoyed seeing Ben and his wife, Kate, and their own small son. They lived most of the year in Dorset, but had come all the way to Pelham House in Kent to celebrate the birth. She'd also been happy to see her father, who'd traveled there from his own house in Hampshire, bringing Helen with him.

After three weeks, with the baby deemed suitably heralded, Ben and Kate had retreated back to Dorset, while Beatrice, Charles, both children and their proud grandfather had gone to London, where Beatrice had a large party planned. They'd tried to bring Eleanor with them, but she'd insisted on going home to her father's house instead. After a series of debates, they'd given up trying to coerce her. As happy as she was for everyone, she much preferred being alone. All that happiness was only drawing attention to how comparatively glum she was—and had been, since leaving London less than two months ago. Eventually, she'd have to tell her family what was wrong; they weren't blind, and they'd figure it out on their own, anyway. But for now she preferred to keep her secret.

Unfortunately, she wasn't entirely alone at her father's house. Helen had been sent back with her, having been judged too young and intractable to be brought to London quite yet. At the moment, they were sitting at a mahogany and parcel gilt games table in the drawing room, playing backgammon. Helen had been losing steadily. Her best friend, George Gregson, was there, as well, reclining lazily in a bergère by the large bow window, reading a book. He was the local vicar's son, and a year older than Helen. They'd been friends for as long as Eleanor could remember. Eleanor didn't know if Helen yet realized how handsome George had become.

"You've lost again, Helen."

"Blast."

"Helen—"

"Sorry, Eleanor, but that's the last of my allowance. You'll have to give it back, or I won't be able to buy you a birthday present."

Eleanor frowned at the coins as she slid them across the table. "Am I to expect half a loaf of bread?"

"Obviously. Do you think they're having a good time in London?"

Eleanor shrugged. "I suppose. Beatrice had her party two nights ago. She would have enjoyed it, but Father and Charles would have spent the whole time in the library, smoking and overindulging themselves with the other refugees. I can hardly believe Father agreed to go there in the first place, but I suppose he wanted to show off Violet."

"Why didn't you go back?"

"I preferred to be with you, you charming creature."

"I don't believe you," Helen snorted.

"You expecting anyone?" George spoke up.

"Hmm?" Eleanor asked, tidying the checkers. She'd almost forgotten he was there, he'd been so absorbed in his reading.

He looked up from his book. "There's a carriage coming up the drive."

"Maybe it's Mrs. Stratfield," Helen suggested. She rose from her seat and walked over to the window, pleased to have the spell of boredom broken by the arrival of an unexpected guest. "She's supposed to be stopping by once a day to check on us. Silly old thing."

Eleanor hid her smile at the accurate description of their widowed neighbor. "If she hadn't agreed to check on us occasionally, then Father would not have let us stay here alone, Helen. He doesn't trust you not to burn the house down."

"I suppose," she said reluctantly. "It's not Mrs. Stratfield, though."

"Is it your father, George?"

"No, though I wish we had that carriage. Awfully smart."

"A smart carriage coming up our drive? Who can it be?"

"Don't know," Helen said. "It's dark green with… looks like claret-colored trim. Two grays. And then Father's carriage behind it. Oh, *how* disappointing. He shouldn't be back so soon."

Eleanor stopped organizing the checkers and went very still. "Green? With claret trim? Surely you can't see the color of the trim from this distance."

"I can, too. It's just stopping out front now."

"Can you not see who's inside it?" Her heart was racing.

"One minute...he's just getting out. Hmm...no, never seen him before. He's dashed handsome, though. Wonder what he's doing here?"

Eleanor remained alone in the drawing room, anxiously drumming her fingers on the games table. She expected her father to open the door at any second. If he knew what she suspected he knew, then he would be very angry indeed.

But when he did finally enter the room, he didn't shout, or even look cross. He just closed the door quietly behind him, looking very tired and disappointed.

"Hello, Father," she said meekly. "We were not expecting you."

He pulled out a chair and sat across from her. She folded her hands to keep them still, but she couldn't meet his gaze. Disappointment was far worse than anger.

"I imagine you have at least some idea why I've returned."

She wished she didn't. Somehow her father knew what she'd done. And where was James? "How did you find out?" she asked very quietly.

"The wheels of gossip always prevail, Eleanor. I'm afraid you were seen leaving his house early in the morning. He's refused to provide me with any details of how he met you, but I trust you know him."

She nodded miserably.

"I don't want to know how this came about—"

"I can explain, Father."

"I'd really rather you didn't. If what he says is true, then you should marry him."

She wondered what exactly he had said. That she'd made love to him? Please, not that. Or perhaps he'd lied diplomatically, and said they'd merely been having a late-night conversation, one so interesting that it lasted until dawn.

She couldn't bring herself to ask. "He tells the truth."

"I see."

Eleanor rose from her seat, too uncomfortable to sit facing her father. She supposed she should be thankful that James hadn't told him how they'd met, since she didn't think he'd describe her activities with much sympathy, but, oh dear, it did leave the awful task up to her....

She turned around abruptly. "Did Beatrice ever mention my friend Jane?"

By the time she'd finished her story, her father's face was in his hands.

Without even looking up, he asked, "Will you marry him?"

"No."

He met her gaze, and she finally realized just how angry he was underneath his layer of imperturbable patience. But she held her ground. She repented her actions sorely, but she still had some pride left. "He's not asked me. He does not want to marry me."

"I can make him want to marry you. I'd quite enjoy it."

She wouldn't be cowed. "Well, I would not. This

isn't his fault. I…I should never even have met him if I hadn't been so foolish, and if I'd told him the truth from the beginning, then he might have acted differently. I will not have him forced."

"Be reasonable, Eleanor. In fact, the gentleman waiting in my sitting room is perfectly willing to do the honorable. He even volunteered."

"He's not a gentleman."

"I agree. He's a scoundrel. But my other son-in-law is a scoundrel, too, and I've managed to—"

"No, what I meant was he really isn't a gentleman." She said this hesitatingly. She didn't care one jot about James's murky background, but learning about it would only increase her father's disappointment in her.

Only he looked rather more confused than disappointed. "Girls these days have terribly high standards. The son of an earl—even the youngest son—was considered a catch in my youth."

She furrowed her brow. "I'm not sure we're talking about the same person."

"There's not more than one, is there?"

"Father!"

He rose, wanting to end their discussion. "Listen, Eleanor, he's told me next to nothing, and maybe you know more than I do. Perhaps you should go speak to him? He's been uncommunicative from the start, but at least he came forward willingly to admit his fault—the gossip was actually pointing the blame at his brother."

"His brother?" She was so confused.

"Lord Lennox. Good God, am I to understand that

you visited a gentleman at his house, late at night, without even knowing who he was?"

She rose. "He's in the sitting room?"

The butler had shown James into the bright sitting room nearly half an hour ago, and the amount of time that had passed was beginning to make him nervous. Several family portraits hung from the walls, although a picture of Sinclair's favorite racehorse took pride of place above the chimneypiece. Most interesting to James, though, was a group of portrait miniatures, arranged higgledy-piggledy in between two windows. Four were children, identically framed. All were blond except for one, a brown-haired girl with serious blue eyes.

He heard the door open behind him and knew it was Eleanor without turning around. "Is this you?"

"And Beatrice, Helen and Ben," she said quietly. "They were painted about ten years ago."

James finally looked at her. She stood in the doorway, dwarfed by her surroundings. She'd lost weight, he thought, and dark shadows rimmed her eyes. She was trying to give the impression of being composed, but he could see her worrying her dress. She noticed the direction of his gaze and stilled her hands. She entered the room fully and closed the door behind her for privacy.

"You have a black eye," she said.

So did her brother-in-law, although he thought it would be best not to mention it. "I've suffered worse."

"My father would like me to marry you."

"You have no other choice, Eleanor."

She met his gaze then, and he saw that she was truly angry. "You've left me no choice."

He wished she'd continued to look fragile and scared. Her anger only sparked his own. "Is that so? I don't recall inviting you to come to me that night."

"I went to your house because of guilt. I felt I owed you an explanation for my lies, despite your outrageous behavior."

"What is your point?"

"I should not have done so if I'd known you'd lied to me, too."

"But I never lied to you, *Miss Smith.*"

She put her hands on her hips. "No, *Mr. Bentley?* Then how do you explain that I hadn't the faintest idea who you were when my father told me just now?"

"Did I put on a wig and invent some ludicrous profession?"

"You told me your mother was an actress and the illegitimate daughter of a minor criminal—"

"Indeed, she was," he interrupted her, "and then she married my father. I cannot help what conclusions you drew."

She sat down on the sofa, feeling exhausted. "But why didn't you tell me?"

"But why—" he mimicked her words cruelly "—should you care?"

She flushed with anger. "I *don't* care. I'm merely pointing out that you are a hypocrite!"

"Is that so?"

"If you won't admit to having lied, then you must admit to deliberately withholding the truth. And what about your name? You cannot claim you were honest about that."

"Bentley was my mother's maiden name. I have used it—with everyone, not just you—for the past decade."

"I don't understand. Are you illegitimate?" She immediately blushed again, knowing he'd misinterpret her words for snobbery. "I wouldn't care if you were."

He shook his head. "I'm not illegitimate."

Why wouldn't he explain? It made no sense at all. She remembered Lady Barbara Markham's gossipy words from weeks ago: he ruined a girl, stole from his own family, was disowned… "But then why have you taken your mother's name? Were you disowned?"

"It isn't an official change, Eleanor. Merely a preference. If we marry, you may call yourself Stanton, as I'm certain you'll prefer."

"If I marry at all, I will use the name of my husband."

"Fine," he said shortly.

"Fine!" She rose from her seat and walked back to stand by the door. But she had one thing to say before she left. "You accused me of thinking you were beneath me. Surely it was really the other way round?"

"How so, Smith?" He took a step closer.

"If you'd loved me, *if* you'd thought I was your equal, then you would have asked me to marry you months ago. Only you thought it wasn't necessary, so you asked me to be your mistress instead. I was just a governess, after all, and that was the best I could expect."

The anger and mistrust in her voice hurt James more than he would admit. Of course he'd never have dreamed of asking her to be his mistress if he'd known who she really was. But then, he *had* planned to ask her to marry him, she just didn't know it. And he remembered how he'd felt when he'd come to that decision: elated, relieved, content. That feeling had lasted all of two minutes.

"What is your answer?" He walked toward her.

"What, sir," she bit out, "is your question?"

"Will you marry me?" he repeated, speaking quietly now. He stood next to her, looking down at her beautiful, angry face.

She raised her chin. "I suppose I have to."

"You needn't sound so delighted about it."

"Neither do you."

He looked as though he wanted to say something else, but he held back in the end. "Then I will see you in London. Tell your father I will arrange the necessary license." He brushed past her on the way out the door.

Chapter Fifteen

London, two weeks later

They'd be marrying in the morning, and tonight: a party, at Louisa's large house. Her objective was to invite the entire ton, pretend that everyone was really very happy, and thus dispel any further rumors of improper behavior or an unwilling groom. If the impression could be given that the wedding had actually been planned all along…

Well, Eleanor didn't think even Louisa was capable of a miracle on that scale. She'd only arrived from her father's house the previous afternoon, and she hadn't experienced the gossip personally, but even the loyal staff at their London home seemed to be giving her disapproving looks. She didn't think anyone would believe this was a love match. Especially since she hadn't yet ventured out of her aunt's sitting room and into the bright, noisy fray of the ballroom. The sitting room was closed to guests, and with the door just slightly ajar it was a perfect spot for her to survey the party.

Nearly everyone Louisa had invited had come— Eleanor would have preferred fewer guests, frankly— and although many faces were familiar from earlier in the season, quite a few she'd never seen in her life. She imagined they'd merely come out of vile curiosity.

She assumed that James was there, too, even though she hadn't seen him yet, or since he'd left her father's house two weeks ago, for that matter. His brother would also be present, and she hoped to avoid him if possible. She didn't think he'd harbor any ill feelings toward her, but…well, how awkward.

"Come away from the door."

Eleanor turned around to frown at Louisa's bossy tone. Both she and Beatrice were in the sitting room, too. They'd apparently come to torment her. "Auntie, your guests will miss your company. Perhaps you should join them."

"They will manage without me."

"Do you love him?"

Beatrice now. Agony. Eleanor blushed and finally moved from her post at the door. Obviously she wasn't going to answer her sister's question, so why bother asking? Maybe she had loved him once, maybe she still did. But that didn't mean she wanted to discuss it.

So she just shrugged. "I don't know, Bea. Perhaps things will improve once we've left London. At the moment, there's too much pressure for me to think about such things."

"Must you really travel to Norfolk straight after the wedding? Could you not stay a few days so we could all become better acquainted with Mr. Bentley?"

"It will take us several days to reach Wentwich Castle as it is." She hadn't been asked if she minded traveling immediately. James had informed her in a terse and irritating letter, and her belongings had already been sent ahead. She didn't relish the idea of being alone with him in his family's ancestral home, in the northernmost bulge of Norfolk, but London didn't seem particularly friendly at the moment, either.

"I hear the Lennox earldom is one of the richest, and that the house is positively massive. It is in the Gothic taste, is it not?" Beatrice asked.

Eleanor nodded, imagining the ghost of a dead butler rattling his keys through the corridors late at night, and storms rolling off the North Sea to pound the walls and windows. She sank down onto the sofa next to her sister. "That is what I've been told. The house really belongs to Lord Lennox, of course, but he has offered it to us as long as we like."

"Until the gossip dissipates?"

"Thank you, Bea, for the reminder. That is, of course, what I meant."

Louisa spoke up. "I am not letting you go to the country alone with Mr. Bentley. I do not trust that man."

"Well, you certainly can't come with me."

"I have done a bit of research, Eleanor. He is a rake, through and through, without any honorable qualities to redeem him."

"Oh, he is not."

Louisa raised an elegant silver brow. "His actions toward you completely support everything I've learned. *I am coming.*"

"Honestly, Auntie—"

"Don't scold me, Beatrice. Someone must protect her, and you didn't do much of a job."

Beatrice turned pink, but Eleanor sighed, knowing it was futile to argue when Louisa used that voice. "Very well, but please…I accept the lion's share of blame for what happened…um, to me. He's already been forced to do enough, and forcing your company on him on top of everything else is almost unpardonable."

Louisa rose, her skin too thick for her to be offended. "I will come in my own carriage, so you won't have to bear my uninterrupted company."

"Don't come right after the wedding," Eleanor pleaded. She didn't know *what* he'd think of this new development, and she'd need time to explain. "Give me at least a day alone with him."

"You've had your wedding night already. Why should you need privacy?"

"Auntie!" Beatrice said sharply. "Please."

Louisa remained composed. "Fine, Eleanor, I concede. I will return to my guests now. Do not stay late tonight. You must be fresh for tomorrow."

She sailed from the room.

"I know it's uncharitable, but sometimes I really don't like her."

"You handle her beautifully. I'd be in tears by now." Beatrice regarded her curiously. "You *do* seem inclined to defend Mr. Bentley. That's a promising start."

"It's nothing more than my natural tendency to contradict everything Auntie says."

Beatrice took her hand and squeezed it reassuringly. "I think we should join the guests now. You're the reason they've all come."

"I'd really rather not, but I suppose I must." With a good deal of reluctance, she rose.

As they walked from the sanctuary of the sitting room, Beatrice remarked, "We should also find Mr. Bentley—you'll have to dance with him. I'll ask that a waltz be played. And you must try to look a little more pleased to be here."

Eleanor forced her lips into a tight smile. "Very well."

"Why *is* he called Bentley, by the way? If his brother is named Stanton."

Her smile disappeared. She'd tried to get him to explain, but still she hadn't the faintest idea. "I don't know. It… He isn't officially. I think he simply prefers it. It was his mother's name."

"Oh. Well, soon enough you will understand more. Many marriages begin unhappily. Mine certainly wasn't blessed from the— Eleanor? Are you all right?"

No, she wasn't. Her step had faltered, and she was beginning to panic. She'd just seen James for the first time that night. Her gaze had collided with his—it felt like a physical impact. He stood directly across from her on the other side of the room and looked so heart-stoppingly handsome that she wanted to melt to a puddle on the floor. That, or run away and hide again. His eyes didn't betray his feelings, however. He just stared back levelly.

Beatrice didn't notice the direction of her gaze. She

was too busy looking at her ashen face. "Eleanor? You are feeling fully recovered, are you not?"

She tore her gaze away. "I'm fine. It's rather hot in here."

"I should not have asked, except you looked quite unwell this morning, too. And, of course, you were ill when I was in my confinement with Violet. I…it's a rather delicate question, but I…I wondered if it were possible you were—"

With child? Terribly, frighteningly possible. She'd expected her monthly flow a fortnight after making love to James, and two months after that portentous night she was still waiting. But this wasn't the time to discuss her fears. "I'm getting married tomorrow, Bea. It's nothing but a severe case of nerves."

Beatrice nodded and squeezed her hand. "I should not have asked."

James was steadily making his way across the dance floor. Eleanor could see him out of the corner of her eye, but she refused to look at him. She could feel his gaze, though, leaving her hot and flushed where it wandered. Her face, her shoulders….

"I say, Eleanor, he *is* good-looking," Beatrice said, finally noticing him. "I was never introduced to him properly, you know."

"I'll introduce you now," she said desperately. She did not want to be left alone with him, and she gripped her sister's hand.

Beatrice pried it away. "No, no, it will have to wait. I just saw Lucy, and there was some bit of gossip she promised to tell me. And I must see about that waltz."

Eleanor watched her walk off, making a direct path to the musicians, who were quietly tuning their instruments. She wished she'd come back. The thought of facing him... She knew she had to do it sometime, but she was rather hoping to put it off until they were standing next to each other in the church tomorrow morning, under the watchful eye of God.

She turned around slowly. James was a mere few feet away.

"Eleanor." She tried to read his expression. He didn't smile, but he didn't look angry or resentful, either.

"James." His name sounded like an exhalation of breath, rather than stiff and formal, as she'd intended.

And then, as Beatrice had promised, a waltz was struck up.

"Dance with me?" His voice was soft, like a caress.

A few curious stares had been cast in their direction. She knew that she didn't have any option but to dance with him. She'd only cause more gossip if she refused. And, in about seven months' time, if what she suspected was true, there would be another flurry....

She nodded hesitantly, forcing a smile and trying to appear relaxed for their audience. He led her through the crowd to the center of the floor. They were the first there, as if the dance were being reserved for them.

Formalities: he bowed, she curtsied. And then, something unexpected. He kissed her lightly on the lips, for everybody to see.

She was so surprised, she started. "Why did you do that?"

"You looked like you were being led to the guillotine, my dear. We're supposed to be convincing everyone that we're desperately in love, remember?"

Her cheeks infused with color. She wished he hadn't phrased it like that. She wished he'd just said that he wanted to kiss her. His gaze was warm, now, even tender, and she would have readily believed him. Their last words to each other may have been hissed in anger, but she still couldn't hate him.

"We travel to Norfolk tomorrow?" she asked as they started to dance. It was a dull comment, since she knew the answer, but she needed to say something.

He nodded. "I see you received my letter. I hope you don't mind, but I think it would be best if we avoided London for a while."

"I understand. Um, when were you last there?" This seemed like a safe topic.

"At Wentwich Castle? I was there about a year ago, just after my brother died, but before then I hadn't been since I left at sixteen."

She wondered what could have been so awful to keep him away that long, or to make him leave in the first place. Suddenly, she was relieved that Louisa had insisted on coming with her, although how on earth was she going to tell him? How horribly embarrassing.

"My great-aunt will be coming with us," she said rather bluntly, hoping he wouldn't protest too audibly.

His face did not brighten with joy, although he didn't look openly hostile to the idea, either. He chose his words diplomatically. "I'm sure she's charming."

"She's unspeakable, actually. I...I'm sorry, but I could not dissuade her. She's just very protective of my sisters and me, since our mother died when Helen was born. But I have made her promise to wait a day or two before coming."

"I suppose she's reason not to trust me."

"Or me," she assured him. "I'm afraid I've declined greatly in her estimation."

"Then I guess we're mutually untrustworthy. At least we're well matched in one respect."

She wanted to dispute his barbed words, his jab at her perceived dishonesty. Now was her chance to try to explain once more. They were dancing, everyone was watching, and he would be forced to listen to her.

"James, I—" She broke off and started again. "You must know that I would have told you the truth eventually. I was just working up the courage. And I *never* had feelings for your brother. I had no idea that he planned to propose. I...I don't even believe he would have in the end. He's not...interested in me in that way."

James shrugged. He'd already realized that he'd overreacted, although he saw no immediate need to admit as much. It wasn't that he'd thought she'd had feelings for Will, or the other way round. Will was delighted they were getting married, not least because it meant the pressure on him to produce an heir had suddenly eased. The problem was just that, damn it, she *had* been dancing with him, and if it hadn't been Will, it would have been someone else. Was it jealousy? He didn't know, since he'd never been plagued by that emotion before. But he'd felt like an out-and-out fool at the time, and he still rather did. And he couldn't help wondering how she would have responded had he asked her to marry him as he'd originally intended, when he'd still thought she was a humble governess and she'd thought he was no one at all.

"It doesn't matter now. I don't expect you to love me, Eleanor—"

"James—"

"—but we are where we are, and I hope we can still be friends. Do you think we can manage?"

Not love him but still be his friend? She thought precisely the opposite. She was so afraid that she was hopelessly in love with him already, and that they might never be friends again.

"Answer me, or I'll have to kiss you again."

She nodded reluctantly.

"There, that wasn't so hard. Now, it's getting late and your father keeps glowering at me. Would you mind terribly if I left?"

She wouldn't blame him at all. Being the object of everyone's curiosity wasn't exactly fun. "I wish I could leave."

His eyes again: warm, intense. And then he was leaning in to whisper, "You might come with me."

By heavens, she wanted to. Had she no fortitude at all? "I think I've distressed my family enough already."

"Just as far as the door, then."

She allowed him to guide her through the stuffy room by the merest pressure on the small of her back. The hall was cooler, quieter, and occupied only by Louisa's butler, who opened the front door in anticipation.

But James didn't step away from her and say goodbye. "Come outside with me."

She didn't resist as he led her into the clear night. The butler closed the door gently behind them, and they stood in silence on the dark portico.

She tried humor; it was either that, or melt helplessly. "You're not going to abscond with me, are you?"

"You've already turned down my offer."

"Oh."

She shivered, and he placed his arm around her waist, dangerously close to the miniscule bump that was so small she almost didn't believe it was there. She stiffened and glanced at him sideways, wondering if he'd any idea. But his face showed nothing, and she relaxed. It felt nice. She didn't know why he was being friendly, but if he'd decided they were going to get along, then she wouldn't complain.

"It's a pleasant change, being able to put my arm around you and be seen with you in public. Never liked that business of having to pretend I was your chaperone."

"You were not very good at it," she pointed out.

"Don't suppose I was, though it doesn't matter anymore. As of tomorrow I can ravish you whenever I like."

She colored and glanced at the door. Surely the butler had heard that. "Be serious, James."

"I am. Shall I kiss you now to prove it?"

"Here?" she squeaked. "What if someone comes outside?"

"Good. Then our task for the evening would be complete. Can't keep my hands off you, remember? We're madly in love." He demonstrated by trailing his finger up her neck and along her cheek.

She swallowed and glanced at the door again. She

knew he didn't mean it, but his words still made her knees weak. "Just one kiss would be all right, I suppose."

His head dipped. It was the gentlest, most wonderful kiss, so tender and yet she could feel it all the way to the tips of her silk slippers. He pulled away slowly, and she wanted more.

His voice was rough and soft at the same time. "No one came outside. Maybe I should try again?"

She didn't protest as he lowered his head once more. His kiss was deeper this time, and she unconsciously stepped closer and put her arms around his neck. She was quite dazed when he stepped back.

But when he leaned in to continue, the door really did open. She pushed him away quickly and immediately started straightening her clothes. A middle-aged couple stepped outside a second later. After a brief, interested glance, they lowered their eyes discreetly and continued walking down the steps to the street.

"I should go inside," Eleanor said shyly once they were out of earshot. "My family will wonder…"

"You're not going to run away in the middle of the night and leave me at the altar, are you?" he asked teasingly.

"Not if you promise to be there."

He kissed her again. On the cheek. Just a goodbye kiss, but it caused a swell of heat. "Until tomorrow, then."

She watched him walk down the street to where his carriage waited. Tomorrow. She didn't know what to expect, then or every day after. For the rest of her life.

They were married in the morning at St. George's, in Hanover Square. Although the circumstances weren't exactly ideal, the ceremony was nonetheless beautiful. Louisa and Beatrice had arranged everything, from the garlands of ivy draped down the aisle and around the church door, to the choice of hymns. Eleanor had been too fretful to make any decisions beyond the length of her train. She just wanted to get it over with.

They'd limited their guests to close family and friends, but for Eleanor, at least, that still amounted to nearly one hundred people: her entire family, including assorted cousins, aunts and uncles, and also friends and servants she'd known for her entire life. James had invited just a few friends, including Jonathon, but none of his family members came except for Will. She wondered why he hadn't wanted more people to be there. She knew his family must be bigger—he'd mentioned family in Ireland, and he surely had cousins, aunts and uncles in England, too—but obviously they weren't close. She tried to justify it: as a man he simply wouldn't be that interested in his wedding and wouldn't need everyone he'd ever known to witness it. And he was fairly unwilling to be going through with it to begin with. But it *did* look very odd.

She supposed, though, that it didn't really matter who came in the end. The entire ceremony was a haze to her, and probably to James, as well. It seemed like nothing more than a long walk down the aisle on her father's arm, followed by too many solemn words and references to duty and procreation, and then a return procession—only this time with her father's arm replaced by her husband's.

Then, into the carriage she and James went, bound north for Wentwich Castle.

Everyone else had lunch.

Chapter Sixteen

They'd been driving for most of the day, and the sky was beginning to darken with the coming of night and gathering storm clouds. Eleanor had said little during their journey, and James had tried unsuccessfully to sleep. Instead, he watched her through partly closed eyes. She looked tired and nervous and cold. A trail of tiny goose bumps marched up her arms, and he was tempted to pull her into his lap and assure her that everything would be all right. But he held back. They'd only been married for a few hours, and if he succumbed so soon, then it wouldn't be much longer before he was declaring his love. That would be a mistake. She'd married him for necessity alone, and he'd have to keep reminding himself of that fact.

The first fat raindrop hit the roof of the carriage just then, soon followed by another. It was just a pitter-patter at first, but the rain steadily increased, streaming down the windows.

Eleanor cleared her throat anxiously. "Your poor

driver must be wet through. Perhaps he should pull up under a tree to wait the storm out?"

James stretched, relieved to break the silence. "We'll stop for the night in just a few more minutes. There's an inn not far from here. Stayed there a few times when I was traveling to and from London with my parents. Many, many years ago."

"Oh. How far are we from Wentwich Castle?"

"We'll have a whole day's driving tomorrow. We should arrive after dark."

"Did you grow up there?"

He nodded, sensing she needed to talk about something—anything—especially since the prospect of spending the night at an inn with him had suddenly become imminent. His childhood wasn't a topic he'd pick himself. "We spent almost all our time there, except for the occasional excursion into town. My mother didn't like London."

"Really?"

He nodded again but left it at that. How could he explain to her that the reason his mother didn't like London was that no one there was ever very nice to her? Despite her beauty, intelligence and grace she'd never been fully accepted. Those merits hadn't mattered one whit in polite society, not while her birth was common and her reputation was touched by the scandal of having been his father's mistress before she was his wife.

"My parents both died when I was nine, as I've told you. I lived there for another seven years."

"You were not sent off to school?" She sounded surprised.

"Will was sent to Eton, as was Richard before him, but I had a tutor from the time of my parents' deaths." Tutor. That was a grand title for spiteful Mr. North, who conducted his French lessons in broad Glaswegian and punished every mistake James made with the heavy rap of his cane. Richard had hired him precisely because he was both inadequate and mean.

"You preferred being educated at home?"

No, he'd wanted nothing more than to join Will at school, if only to escape his brother's brutality. But Richard had insisted he have a tutor instead; he said James would only embarrass their family if he were sent off to school, where all the boys would be his social superiors. James had even wished that Will would be forced to stay home, too—not because he wanted him to share his fate, but because he didn't want to bear Richard's cruelty alone. As it was, no one save himself and Richard fully knew what he'd had to endure.

He shrugged. He wanted to change the subject. "I did not want to leave. It is a lovely house. I hope you'll like it."

"But then why *did* you leave?"

"All young men want a bit of adventure."

"And you simply stayed away for ten years?" She looked quite incredulous, and he supposed it made sense considering how attached she was to her own family.

"It was twelve years, actually. I was in the service for two, and then Ireland for ten."

"Did you not see William during all that time?"

"No."

"I don't understand you, James."

So much for light conversation. She looked truly worried and confounded. "That's perfectly all right."

He had missed Will, but by the time he left home he resented him, too, for his optimism and his easy charm. Although Will hadn't been completely unaware of Richard's unkindness, he was usually away at school and therefore witnessed almost none of his abuse. James hadn't wanted him to know; it was humiliating. He'd always downplayed the physical violence he'd had to endure, and he'd slowly withdrawn into his own sullen world. By the time he left home he felt numb enough that he didn't think he'd miss anything. It had taken over a decade and his brother's death for that to change. If it even had changed.

Eleanor looked as though she wanted to ask more questions, but the coach began to slow as they neared the inn. A stable hand ran out to meet the horses.

The rain was coming down hard, beating the roof like a drum.

"It's pouring," she said woefully, eyeing the distance between the carriage and the beckoning inn.

The driver opened the door, looking cold and wet. Rain streamed from his hat.

"Oh, dear," she said.

James began shrugging out of his waistcoat, having removed his jacket at lunch for comfort; it was now packed away in a valise. "Here, take this."

"Oh, no, but you'll get drenched—"

He ignored her protests and draped it across her shoulders. "We'll have to run for it. Quickly now."

She stepped into the downpour with the driver's help,

and then tried to avoid puddles in her dash for the inn's door. The vestibule inside was warm and dry, and she held the door for James, who entered right behind her. She couldn't help smiling at his wet face, but then she blushed when she realized the rain had made his fine linen shirt quite transparent.

"Here," she said shyly, handing back his waistcoat.

"You keep it. It's cold."

"No, I'm perfectly dry underneath. You take it. You look…rather indecent."

James looked down at his wet shirt. "Suppose we don't want to shock the innkeeper."

He pulled it back on just in time for the gray-haired innkeeper to open the inner door and greet them warmly. "Good evening, Mr. Stanton. Do come in."

He held the door wide as they entered.

"I think you haven't been here since you were a small child," the innkeeper continued.

"My wife, Mrs. Stanton."

"It is a pleasure, my lady. Will you dine downstairs tonight?" the innkeeper asked.

James glanced at Eleanor. She looked exhausted. "Better have a tray sent to our room."

"I understand, of course. It is a long journey. My grandson, Chester, will show you up, and I'll see to your belongings"

They followed the boy up a rather narrow, creaking staircase. Their room was at the end of a long hallway, and was surprisingly bright, warm and well-appointed with its restful, cream-painted walls. Chester left them, promising to return soon with their supper and baggage.

"I'm sure this isn't how you always imagined your wedding night, Eleanor," James said once they were alone.

"Will we be sharing this room?"

"It is customary to do so."

She blushed. "Of course. I'm sorry."

He felt immediately contrite. "No, I'm sorry. I shouldn't tease you. It's not as if we've done anything in the customary fashion so far."

He hung his waistcoat on the back of a chair and removed his sodden shoes and socks while she warmed herself by the fire, trying not to look at him.

"The man called you Stanton."

"He remembers me from a long time ago. I didn't feel like explaining."

"Oh."

"Will you not take off your wet clothes?" he asked.

"I'm not too wet."

"Your hat is dripping. Here." She held very still while he untied the ribbon at her chin and carefully removed her hat.

"Thank you," she said awkwardly. She stepped from her soggy shoes.

His gaze traveled over the rest of her. "Perhaps I should remove your spencer, as well. It looks wet."

His hand playfully grazed her buttons, but she swatted it away. "Your waistcoat kept me perfectly dry, sir. Well, mostly, anyway."

A knock on the door announced the arrival of supper, saving her for the time being. Chester entered discreetly, followed by the innkeeper, bearing their valises. The former left a lidded tray on a table by the door, and his grandfather left the bags on a stand at the foot of the bed. Both left quietly.

Eleanor didn't think she could eat, although she peeked under the covers to examine the steaming, hearty fare. Potatoes, meat of some sort… She realized that she was a wife, now, and that she should probably offer her husband food. That was the correct, expected thing to do, wasn't it?

"James? Would you like…" She turned around, but her words died instantly. He was unbuttoning his shirt before the fire. She fixed her gaze on the wall. "Oh."

"What's wrong, Smith?"

"You're undressing."

"I'm wet."

"Yes, you are."

Yes, he was. His wet shirt still clung to his back, but he'd already opened it in the front, revealing golden, dewy skin. His black hair curled temptingly. She wondered if there was a cloth somewhere to dry him with.

Dry him? Good heavens, what a thought. What a thought she mustn't think again.

But she *could* look. It had been too dark the night they'd made love for her to see his body particularly clearly, and academic interest allowed her gaze to wander over every hard plane of his form…well, at least as it was reflected in the dressing mirror that sat on the table in front of her. That was about as bold as she could get for now. The flicker of candlelight and the fire in the grate made his skin glow like warm honey. And muscles: he had plenty of them, and not an ounce of fat. He removed his damp linen shirt and turned around to take a clean, dry one from his valise. She caught a full view of his back: broad, lean and strong, tapering at his waist.

She could also see the scars. Faint, pale flecks, some hardly perceptible, some not, and all covered almost immediately in clean, white linen.

She turned around as he buttoned his shirt. "What happened to your back, James?"

"I thought you'd modestly averted your gaze, my sweet governess."

"I…I had, of course. But I just happened to see…"

"You needn't apologize. They're just a few childhood injuries."

She frowned. "But so many?"

"All right, more than a few."

"How?" she asked suspiciously.

"Well…" He paused. "For example, how did you get that scar on your nose?"

Eleanor unconsciously touched the small and barely visible mark. "I fell out of a tree. Beatrice had been reading to me from *Grimm's Tales,* and I was pretending to be Rapunzel in her tower."

"I wasn't pretending to be Rapunzel, but it's pretty much the same thing."

"But why all in the same place?"

"They're not."

"No?"

He stepped closer. His fresh shirt was only halfway buttoned, and he parted it at the top. Suddenly all that golden skin was close enough to touch. She swallowed, but focused her attention on the jagged scar, about two inches long.

"This is the worst of them."

She frowned. "It looks almost too bad for childhood."

"It's not from childhood. It's from my stint in His Majesty's Service."

"Good heavens, you were shot!"

"I'd have shown you months ago if I'd known it would inspire your sympathy."

"I... But, why? Who shot you?"

"He didn't leave a calling card," he said. "Your food will get cold."

She didn't think she could manage a bite, not with him standing so close. She was too nervous. They'd be sharing a bed, and she'd been thinking about it since she'd woken that morning. "I don't want to eat."

"What do you want to do instead?"

She knew what she wanted to do, but she was too bashful to suggest it. She forced herself to meet his gaze. "What would you like to do?"

"Distract you from your silly questions."

"Distract how?"

"That's another one."

"Another what?"

"I feel like I'm talking to a parrot. I'm going to extract one item of clothing for every question you ask." He started with a hairpin. A fat curl fell to her shoulder.

"Maybe you should ask another," he said, his eyes darkening. "Just to test my word."

"Um..."

"No hesitating, either." He untied the ribbon at the back of her neck, letting her simple strand of pearls fall to the floor.

"You're making up the rules as you go along."

"Do you mind?"

"That's a question."

He gave her a look, challenging her to remove anything of his.

She didn't know where the courage came from, but her fingers shyly found the buttons on his shirt. He'd only managed to fasten three—the bottom three, starting around the middle of his flat stomach and ending…oh dear, she mustn't think about the direction her fingers were headed in. She must think about, well, gardening, maybe.

With her mind focused on the many varieties of roses, she made short work of his shirt.

"There." She felt rather satisfied with her work.

"There? You're supposed to remove it, not just unbutton it. Have you forgotten the rules already?"

"No." She certainly hadn't, although she wasn't about to point out that he'd just asked two more questions. But removing his shirt seemed so intimate. It meant touching him, while he was just watching her.

"Shall I help you?"

She nodded, although she didn't know what form that help would take. He took her hands in his and placed them on his shoulders, just underneath his shirt. She couldn't imagine how red her face must be, or how unsophisticated he must think her, but she carefully pushed his shirt back. It slid easily down his shoulders, and he pulled it off the rest of the way himself.

"Is it my turn, now?" he asked.

"You're the one who keeps asking the questions."

"Darling, all that's left is my trousers, and quite frankly I don't think I can manage you fumbling around down there."

"Oh."

He tilted her chin up, so she was looking at him. "That was a compliment, you know."

She hadn't known, and she didn't quite understand how it could be, but now he'd taken control and she was relieved. His hands began on her buttons, first on the front of her tightly fitting spencer. And when he'd dispatched that item, he moved to the back of her dress. His lips brushed against her neck as her dress fell to her hips and he pushed it the rest of the way to the floor. It pooled around her feet, followed by her stays. And then any games were over. His lips hungrily found hers, and she kissed him back. They were moving, never breaking their embrace, but fumbling across the room, clumsily falling into bed. Somehow along the way he'd pulled her chemise over her head, and she was too intoxicated to object. He sat back to roll down her stockings, pausing to look his fill. *Now* she blushed.

"James—"

He ignored her protests and started working on her stockings, carefully untying her garters and peeling each one down to her toes; at least that meant he was no longer looking at her breasts. She forgot about her shyness entirely as he kissed her ankles on the way back up, stopping at her knees, her thighs, her hip, her breasts. She also forgot what he'd said about his trousers, since somehow her hands ended up ineffectually trying to unfasten them, anyway. He came to her rescue, making short work of them, and then his fingers found her, hot and moist. As he touched and teased, she felt herself rushing toward ecstasy, moving against him to hasten her release. She gripped his shoulders as pleasure surged around her and lapped her body like waves. She cried out his name, but his own mouth absorbed the sound. And then, too impatient to wait any longer, he plunged inside her, finding his pleasure almost immediately on the crest of hers.

For several minutes, they lay quietly in each other's arms, too shattered to speak. Sleep was beginning to call her name, and she floated toward happy unconsciousness.

"Eleanor?"

But that was James.

"Eleanor, I—" He stopped.

"Hmm?" she asked drowsily, rolling over to snuggle up against his chest.

But he didn't answer. Lying there, with her calm and sated in his arms, he felt so full of love that he thought it would spill over if he opened his mouth. Unable to put his feelings into words, he told her with gentle caresses, with soft kisses on her nose, behind her ear. He stroked her hair until she slept.

James didn't sleep for a long time. His eyes looked into the darkness as the fire died, and his mind worked restlessly.

So much for trying to resist temptation. He could try all he liked, but the moment she actually looked hurt, or scared, or angry he found himself powerless to do anything but tease her into good humor, to do anything he could to make her happy. It made him happy to do so, and he'd had blessed few things to feel good about in a long time. He could devote the rest of his life to making her smile, and he didn't think he'd grow bored. He'd been very close to telling her he loved her.

But that would have been disastrous. It was too soon to make such declarations, and the subject too charged. There was so much she didn't know about him, so much he didn't want her to know. She made him vulnerable, a foreign feeling that threatened the hard, bored exterior he'd cultivated for so long. He had to remind himself that she hadn't actually wanted to marry him. She did not return his feelings.

He carefully extracted himself from her arms and gently pushed her toward the other side of the bed, putting necessary inches between them. He rolled onto his side, facing away from her.

Chapter Seventeen

They arrived late the next night. All Eleanor could see of the house as they approached it was a crenellated silhouette, black and forbidding against the cloudy sky. Perhaps it would be more cheerful in the morning, at least if the rain that had hovered over them like a bad omen finally passed. She certainly hoped so. She wanted to hold his hand as they approached the massive front door, but he didn't offer it, and she was too shy to ask. He'd been quiet in the carriage again and had spent much of the time reading or just looking out the window. She supposed they *had* been up very late, and on top of that, they'd woken at dawn. He would be tired. But she also suspected he was trying to avoid talking to her. He seemed distant, as if he'd forgotten their closeness the night before.

The butler opened the door, and the housekeeper came out to greet them. Eleanor was surprised when they introduced themselves not only to her, but to James, as well. She'd expected them to be old retainers, but they seemed instead to have been hired since James had left the house so many years ago, presumably by one of his brothers. They were perfectly friendly, just…not at all familiar. It didn't seem like much of a homecoming for James, and it was so very different from the reception she'd received when she arrived back at Sudley after her unfortunate season. Many of their servants had known her since before she could walk, and everyone had waited in the hall to greet her, genuinely happy that she had returned.

"Mr. Leonard will show you to your room, Eleanor. I just have a few things to discuss with Mrs. Glynde."

She wanted him to come with her, but all she could do was nod uncertainly. It was late and…well, no doubt the servants were eager to return to their beds, and she wouldn't endear herself to them by wasting their time with her protests. She followed the butler up the main staircase, down a long, dark hallway and past a series of closed doors—he explained the function of each room as they went, but she knew she'd never remember. And then, finally, her bedroom, at the end of the corridor. He opened the door and checked that the fire still burned cheerfully in the grate.

"Shall I have a maid sent up to assist you, my lady?"

She shook her head. She didn't want anyone roused unnecessarily, and James could help her when he arrived. "Thank you, but I think I can manage."

"The bell is by the door, if you should need anything. Good night, my lady."

And then he was gone, and she was alone. She stood

in the doorway for several seconds, feeling rather hopeless and lost.

Then she removed her hat and gloves, tossed them onto the bed, and started to explore the room. Her clothes, sent ahead several days earlier, had been neatly put away inside a linen press and a chest of drawers. The room was large—larger than any she'd ever occupied before—and it also contained a cheval glass, two comfortable chairs and a sewing table. Three porcelain Chinamen, their dainty umbrellas raised against an imagined Eastern sun, grinned at her from the mantelpiece. It felt most definitely like a woman's room.

She opened the sewing table's slender drawer. The room had probably been unoccupied for many years, but it still contained silver thimbles and brightly colored thread. She closed it, feeling like an intruder, and examined instead the pastel portrait that hung next to the bed. A beautiful young woman, with black hair and brilliant green eyes. She could only be James's mother, Eleanor thought; this room must have been hers.

She sat gingerly on the mahogany four-poster bed that dominated the room, not wanting to crumple the yellow silk coverlet and make too lasting an impression. It didn't feel like her room. She felt like a guest, which she supposed was true enough. She wondered how long they would stay there.

Then she wondered if James would come at all. He'd called this "her" room, but presumably they would share it, at least for sleeping? And what would he need to discuss with the housekeeper at such a late hour, anyway? Was he just trying to get away from her? When they were in the carriage, he'd promised to show her the grounds tomorrow, but he'd said nothing about tonight. In fact, other than that vague promise he'd said little at all.

After sitting there for half an hour, she finally accepted that he wouldn't come. She considered trying to find him herself, but she hadn't the faintest idea where his room might be, and she'd passed so many doors—and that was just down a single corridor. The house must have thirty bedrooms, and he could be in any one of them.

She lay back onto the bed, resting her head on the pillow. She didn't even bother trying to remove her gown. She'd dressed simply that morning, knowing she'd be in a carriage all day, but the contortions required to remove it on her own would burst her seams. So she just closed her eyes and concentrated on sleep, allowing the lamps to burn down and gradually extinguish.

And after many minutes, just as unconsciousness was about to claim her, the bedroom door opened with a soft, reluctant sigh. She sat up slightly as James entered, but neither she nor he said a word. He eased into bed next to her, wrapping his arms around her and pulling her close. That was all she was waiting for, and finally she slept.

Eleanor felt she could have dreamed it. When she awoke, she was alone again, still fully clothed and now quite uncomfortable, with her stays biting into her rib cage. But she knew he really had been there.

She rose from bed and pulled the bell by the door. It would be rather awkward to explain to a maid why she was still wearing yesterday's dress, but there was little to be done. Just hope the maid didn't like to gossip.

While she waited, she stood at the tall window. The sky had cleared, and the view that rolled out before her—cleansed by the deluge, and left soft, and fresh and dewy—was enough to make her optimistic again. She'd noticed as they'd traveled that the surrounding land was fairly flat, but the house itself sat atop a gentle rise that sloped down to a large ornamental lake, enshrouded by mist. And then, in the distance, another hill rose, this one crowned by a folly—she could barely see what shape it took, but when she squinted it seemed to be a mock medieval ruin made of rustic stone. Whoever had designed Wentwich Castle certainly possessed great imagination.

The maid knocked and entered.

"I fell asleep in my dress," Eleanor said, obviating any uncomfortable questions. "We arrived very late."

The maid, a shy girl of about twenty, merely nodded, as if it were perfectly normal for a wife to sleep fully clothed on her second night of marriage. Eleanor silently appreciated her tactfulness as she went to work on her buttons.

Twenty minutes later, she was dressed and feeling considerably better. She didn't know why James had come to her so late, but he'd probably just had things to attend to. And undoubtedly he'd left her so early in the morning in order to give her ample privacy. He was merely being considerate. Her smile, when she finally located him in the breakfast room, was genuine. He was finishing an egg and reading.

"Is that a newspaper?" she asked.

He looked up. "Just a provincial one, I'm afraid. We're mentioned."

"We are?" She sat across from him. So far, this was very nice. Polite conversation at the breakfast table.

"Here. 'The Honorable James Stanton'—that's me—'married to one Miss Eleanor Sinclair, daughter of the Viscount Carlisle'."

"Is there not more?"

"I think we're fortunate to be included at all. The new window at Norwich Cathedral was obviously deemed more important—takes up most of the page. Shall I show you the park now?"

"But my breakfast."

"I've had a basket packed for you."

"Really?" That seemed promisingly thoughtful. She nodded and rose.

They bundled into warmer clothes in the hall, and Mr. Leonard opened the door.

Eleanor stepped out eagerly into the sunshine, but was immediately buffeted by a cold gust of wind.

"Steady there," James said, putting his arm around her. She snuggled in closer, but he stepped away as they walked down the path. She felt rather wounded, but she suppressed the feeling. She was determined to have a pleasant morning; perhaps he simply found it easier to walk without her clinging to him.

"The house isn't as old as it pretends to be," he explained, turning around to look at it. "We've lived on this spot since the sixteenth century, but the old house was razed about fifty years ago to make way for this monstrosity. My grandfather thought battlements, towers and a few pointed windows would improve it. Not so sure m'self."

"I'm starting to like it. Oh-—this is the view from my bedroom!" she exclaimed, realizing that they were standing at the top of the descent to the lake.

He nodded. "How do you find your room?"

"Perfect. Was it your mother's?"

"Yes. She's the lady in the portrait."

"She was very beautiful."

"Oh? Do you think she looks like me?" There was a welcome hint of devilry in his eyes.

She couldn't help grinning back. "I will not be tricked into saying I think you're beautiful."

He took her hand and started walking with her down the slope. "Well, I think you're beautiful. Have no problem saying so, either."

"James—"

"You can't scold me, Smith. I'm permitted to say that kind of thing now."

She put her free hand on her hip, trying to think of a retort. Only just as her mouth opened he leaned down to kiss her. Her eyelids fluttered closed.

"Suppose I can kiss you whenever I like now, too," he said, slowly pulling away. "Maybe I should kiss you again?"

She would have liked that, but she yawned playfully instead. "How large is the estate?"

"Typical girl. You only care about one thing," he

teased, and they started walking down the hill once more. "We have about two thousand hectares, I think. Most is let to farmers."

"I would not have thought the grounds would be so hilly."

"It's entirely artificial, I'm afraid. My grandfather also had large quantities of earth moved to create these hills. Should be completely flat and featureless."

Eleanor was having such a nice time she had already forgotten about the chilly weather. They'd reached the lake, and it sparkled merrily in the sun. "Perhaps we could stop here while I have my breakfast?"

"Of course."

She sat on a large, smooth rock, and he sat next to her, handing her the basket. Two apples, fresh bread and butter. "It's a lovely house, as you promised. I was rather worried by the aspect I saw when we first arrived."

"Yes, well I don't recommend wandering around the east wing alone after dark. And I definitely wouldn't go searching in the kitchen for food late at night."

"What's in the kitchen?"

"You mean who. Maggie Kettle, the late scullery maid."

"Her name can't really have been Kettle."

"Upon my honor, it was. She died in 1772 of unrequited love."

"Love for whom?"

"My mad grandfather."

Eleanor giggled. "I do not believe you."

"I dare you, then. Go into the kitchen after midnight. Will did it once when he was twelve, and he came out pale as death."

"You must have enjoyed growing up here." The words came out suddenly, because at that moment he really did seem to love the house, and to be happy talking about his childhood. But she immediately wished she could take her words back. His expression changed, subtly but perceptibly. He obviously hadn't enjoyed living there, although she couldn't imagine why.

"I did enjoy it, I suppose. I often forget, having spent so much time away."

"I've always preferred the city," she said, wanting to change the subject to something he was more comfortable with. She hated the guarded look that had clouded over his eyes. She wanted him to tease her again, to kiss her and make her laugh.

"I, as well," he said.

"My father has always despaired of me, since he cares for nothing but dogs and horses. Ben also hates London, and I suspect Helen will, too, since she's a complete hoyden. I'd not be at all surprised if she refused to have a London season at all, and after my experience, I half expect Father to let her. Far less trouble in the end."

He nodded, but didn't seem to be entirely paying attention. After a few seconds, he remarked, "I rather envy your closeness to your family, Eleanor."

"Do you?" she asked with surprise. "Well, it's fine, I suppose. But you won't envy me when Aunt Louisa arrives tomorrow. She's close like a leech, and she's meddlesome, too. And hardly a day passes when I don't get into some argument with Helen, at least when I'm at home."

He nodded, and they settled into silence. It started to make her nervous.

"What are you thinking about?" she asked hesitantly.

"Nothing, Eleanor—I suppose just how very different your life has been from mine."

"Why—because I have a large, irritating family?"

"Yes, and other things. Anyway, it was a stupid comment. I didn't really mean it."

"Oh." She broke off a bite-size piece of bread and chewed it slowly, trying to look unconcerned. But she thought he probably *was* bothered by her closeness to her family—although she hadn't the faintest idea why that should be—and she wasn't ready to let the subject drop. "You're close to Will."

"Yes," James said slowly. "He wasn't at home much, though, when we were children. He was sent to school at nine, so from that point I only saw him at holidays. And then, of course, I left."

"But what about your family in Ireland?"

"My grandfather—he died six years ago—three aunts, three uncles and seventeen cousins. Almost all actors, or employed somehow in the theater, as I think I've told you. All loud and affectionate, and it took me a very long time to get used to them."

"Why did they not come to the wedding?"

"It happened rather suddenly, if you remember."

She wondered if he'd even informed them. "I should love to meet them someday."

He shrugged as if he didn't believe her.

"Is that why you stopped using your own name?"

He raised an eyebrow. "Is what why?"

She wished she hadn't asked, but it was too late now. "Because you felt like they were your real family.

Since Will was never at home and Richard was so much older—"

"Don't sentimentalize, please. You're far too intelligent."

His impatient tone brought her up short. "I'm sorry."

He looked away. "No, I'm sorry. You said nothing wrong."

But she had. Obviously, she had.

"It wasn't that I felt I belonged more to that side of the family," he explained slowly. "I've got a lot more in common with Will than I have with any of them."

"Then why?"

"I first used my mother's name when I was in the service. For the first six months, I was James Stanton, the son of the Earl of Lennox, but no one actually believed me since people like me don't join on as common soldiers. And the few who could be convinced just asked questions I didn't want to answer. So gradually I became someone else."

"Why did Richard not pay your commission?"

"I ran away, Eleanor. Remember?"

"Of course." The impatience had returned to his tone, making her feel stupid for asking. Still, she wanted to ask another stupid question: why run away? But before she had a chance, he spoke again.

"I don't know if I can give you what you're used to." He didn't look at her.

She paused uncertainly, but she had to ask, "What do you think I'm used to?"

"A large, happy family. You'd have been better off marrying someone like Will."

She shook her head. "He would not have made me happy."

"I've never even considered having a family before."

"Well, I am your family, now, and I'm afraid there's little you can do about it. You get the lot of us Sinclairs—my father, two sisters and a brother. You didn't speak to Ben at the wedding, and I'm afraid it *will* take him a while to warm to you, but I promise he will eventually. He was beastly to Charles for almost a year—"

"You're being deliberately obtuse. I meant children, Eleanor."

"Oh." But she didn't understand. What *did* that mean? That he simply hadn't thought of being a father before, or that he categorically did not want children? Unfortunately, he didn't have a choice in the matter. Not anymore.

Only now seemed like a bad time to tell him about the baby, when he was already annoyed with her. Perhaps he was simply feeling overwhelmed by everything that had happened in the past few days. The sudden addition of a wife in his life must be enough change for him to cope with at the moment. She would wait until he was a little more accustomed to his new circumstances, and then she would tell him.

She knew she was making excuses.

"There is no rush, James. We can talk about these things later. Shall we keep walking? There must be a wonderful view from the next hill."

He shook his head. "I just remembered that I should visit our old housekeeper in the village this afternoon. She'll have heard that I'm back and will be put out if I don't stop by her cottage to say hello."

Eleanor would have liked to go with him, to see the village in the daylight and to meet the housekeeper, who'd obviously known James when he was a child. But he didn't ask her.

She felt crushed. "Shall I come with you?" she offered, knowing it was pathetic to invite herself along. But she didn't want to end their morning like this, so suddenly and on such an awkward note.

He was already rising from the rock. "You won't enjoy it. Mrs. Deacon has lost most of her senses, and I'll be back in a couple hours, anyway. I'll walk back to the house now, to have my horse readied—will you come with me?"

She shook her head no, and watched him walk away, up the hill to the house. Then she turned around and stared out over the lake, feeling the cold wind slice through her pelisse once again. Her morning had started with such promise. Her appetite had faded, so she broke her bread and tossed it to the ducks.

Unfortunately, the rest of her day was no better. She'd assumed he'd at least return for supper, but he didn't even come home at all. He sent a note instead; it arrived while she was eating her soup, alone in the silent dining room. The note said that in his brother's absence, James felt responsible for their various tenants, and when he'd arrived at the village, he'd been confronted with leaking roofs and broken windows, all in need of immediate attention. By the time he'd finished seeing to everyone, it was too dark to ride home safely. He would spend the night at the village inn and see her in the morning.

She didn't believe him. Obviously it wasn't too dark

to send a messenger with the note, so surely he could have safely ridden the few miles.

He was trying to avoid her.

Chapter Eighteen

Mrs. Glynde was arranging flowers in the hall when
Eleanor finally made her way downstairs the next
morning. She'd slept badly during the night, and she'd
been inclined to stay abed all day—and would have, too,
if she hadn't worried that doing so would let James
believe she'd been upset by his callousness.

"Good morning, Mrs. Glynde," she said, trying to
sound cheerful.

"Well, good morning, my lady," the housekeeper
replied warmly.

"Those are lovely."

She wiped her hands on her apron and smiled.
"Thank you. It is my favorite task, although there's not
much growing at this time of year. Would you like a tour
of the house?"

Eleanor wasn't sure a tour would even be necessary,
since she'd no idea if they'd be staying a week, a month
or longer. Still, she smiled gratefully, pleased to have

someone to talk to. "I don't imagine I'll ever find my way around otherwise."

"Hmm. Well, you saw the dining room last night. Not sure where to start."

"You could show it to me again. I've honestly no idea how to find it again on my own, even though I had my supper there. And I should love to hear about some of the pictures in it."

"It's just across the hall."

Eleanor dutifully followed her through a generous set of double doors and into the large dining room. A long table stretched down its middle, surrounded by twenty chairs, nineteen of which had been superfluous during her solitary meal. The walls were lined with paintings, mostly nautical subjects depicting scenes of British maritime success. But there were also three portraits. They interested Eleanor most.

"The first earl, I think," Mrs. Glynde said, motioning to a man wearing the sort of full wig popular during the time of Charles II. A Garter star beamed proudly on his blue silk doublet.

"And the next gentleman?" Eleanor asked.

"I'm not sure about that one, but the lady in the next portrait is the fifth earl's first countess, I believe. Lord Lennox's mother."

Eleanor stared at the woman. Her hair was teased into a frothy, cottony confection, as was fashionable about thirty years earlier.

"But you're not certain?"

"I've been here less than a year, my lady. The present Lord Lennox hired me when he came into his inheritance."

"Which servants have been here a long time?" Eleanor asked, hoping she would find someone who'd known James for many years.

Mrs. Glynde shook her head. "None, except for a few of the gardeners and Molly Jones, the dumb scullery maid. Many left soon after the fifth earl and his countess died."

Eleanor frowned slightly, thinking that was very odd. "I suppose there's not much you can tell me, then," she said, her words a thinly veiled invitation to gossip. She knew she shouldn't indulge in this activity with servants—she could practically hear Aunt Louisa scolding her for doing so—but she didn't care. James was so evasive, and she couldn't help wondering what he was trying to conceal.

"Well, my lady," Mrs. Glynde said slowly, as if waiting for approval, "I can only tell you what I've heard in the village."

"What have you heard?"

She nodded back in the direction of the countess. "That she was very beautiful, but the earl did not love her. It was little more than an arranged marriage. His true love was his second wife—her portrait is in your room. It caused a scandal when he married her."

"Really?"

"So I've heard. There are more pictures in the long gallery, if you'd like to follow me."

They walked from the dining room, back into the hall, and through another set of doors.

"Most of the other portraits hang here, or at least the good ones. The lesser pictures are dispersed throughout the bedrooms."

"That is Lord Lennox," Eleanor said. William appeared to be about eighteen in the portrait, and he was every bit as handsome and arrogant in appearance then as now.

"Yes. And here, his father, the fifth earl."

"What about the sixth earl?" She wanted to see what the mysterious Richard looked like.

"That, I don't know. I don't think there are any pictures of your husband, either. Perhaps because their parents died so unexpectedly, few arrangements were ever made to have the children painted."

"Except for the present Lord Lennox?"

"Well, I suspect he's vain enough about his looks he insisted on it!" Mrs. Glynde blushed, realizing she was being far too familiar. "I apologize."

"You needn't be at all contrite, Mrs. Glynde. You may be candid with me. I am not your employer, and how else will I ever learn anything?"

A knowing look passed across her face. "No one much cared for the eldest son."

"You mean servants? Is that why they all left?"

"I'm not certain. You…you know how people will gossip, especially about a handsome, rich young man—and by all accounts, your husband's eldest brother was that."

"What kind of gossip?"

"That is enough, Mrs. Glynde."

The cold voice made them both jump. Eleanor turned around with dread. James stood in the doorway, only a few feet away. His face was emotionless, but it was a studied indifference, and she could tell he was actually furious. His mouth was hard and his hand gripped the doorknob tightly.

"Excuse us, please, Mrs. Glynde."

The housekeeper walked away quickly with her head down, keenly aware that she might have lost her shortly held position.

"It is not her fault," Eleanor said. "She was just giving me a tour, and I was encouraging her to gossip. If you are to be angry with anyone, then it should be me."

His expression remained unemotional. "You should know better."

"I know. I do. I'm sorry."

He crossed the room to stand by her, forcing her to tilt her chin up to see his face. "Mrs. Glynde has been here just a few months, and she's not a reliable source. If there's something you feel you need to know, why don't you ask me?"

"I don't think you'll tell me," she said quietly.

He brushed a loose strand of hair from her cheek. "What are you trying to discover?"

"I don't know."

"Come to the library with me. We'll finish your tour."

She shook her head. She didn't want to go anywhere with him when he was in this mood. "No."

James leaned down, about to lose all patience. "Eleanor, you can either come with me, or I will carry you there."

She didn't doubt his words. She raised her chin and followed at a distance.

Like the other rooms she'd been in that morning, the library radiated off the entrance hall. Leather-bound books lined three of its oak-paneled walls, and light flooded in from a large bow window on the fourth. An upholstered sofa faced the fireplace, flanked by two armchairs. Additional books, overflowing from the shelves, were stacked squatly atop scattered tables.

He closed the door behind them. She waited anxiously for him to say something. Why had he brought her there? She was expecting him to speak to her sternly about the dangers of being too intimate with servants, but he said nothing. She crossed the room to the bow window and looked out over the lawn, before turning around to face him.

"I *am* sorry, James. I will not be so familiar again."

"I know."

He didn't elaborate. She couldn't tell from his words or his tone whether he forgave her, or if his terse "I know" was a threat. She opted to believe the former and tried to change the subject. "It's a lovely room. Thank you for showing me. I will spend more time here."

"I had my lessons in this room."

"Oh?" She sat down on the built-in window seat in front of the bow window. "It's wonderfully atmospheric. I should have loved to have my lessons in a room like this. Mine were in the nursery, with Helen poking me in the ribs the whole time. I was always so jealous of Ben, especially when I visited him when he was at Magdalene. I can't imagine a more ideal place for study. But all he seems to have done is nap by the river and drink too much."

"Was that Oxford or Cambridge?"

"Oxford. Based on my short visit, and on what paltry evidence I've observed in my brother and his friends, very little learning actually seems to occur there. You're far better educated for not going at all, I think."

"Is that so?"

His tone was completely neutral, but she sensed she'd said the wrong thing again. "I think so."

"The window seat opens."

"It does?" She rose, turned around to look. "That's clever. One could put…uh, dirty teacups in there. To tidy up quickly." She had to cease this nervous chatter.

"I'm sure Mrs. Glynde has explored the possibilities."

"Perhaps…it's locked, actually. How strange—"

"My tutor put the lock on. He locked me inside it when I forgot to do my lessons, at least until I was big enough to prevent him."

She snorted. "I will not be gulled by any more of your gothic tales, James. Most likely this is where he hid his sherry."

"He would, though," James said. "When I forgot to do my lessons, which was often enough. Or as the whim struck."

She went very still, realizing that this time he might actually be serious. "But you must have told Richard. He was your guardian, was he not? Why was your tutor not dismissed?"

"He fully approved. Mr. North would lock me in there until Richard was ready to deal with me. It took hours, sometimes. Then Richard would beat me. Or, if he was in London, then North would do the job himself."

"You should not jest about such things." But she knew he wasn't. It made horrible sense. The scars on his back, his reluctance to speak of his childhood. A wave of revulsion forced her to step away from the window seat. He'd finally explained everything; just a few words had painted a frightening picture of his early life. And she wished to God she was still ignorant.

"I am in total earnest, Eleanor. I could tell you worse stories. Would you like that?"

She flinched. "No."

"Isn't that the sort of information you were trying to discover?"

"I…no, of course not."

"You look shocked."

"I am shocked." She took a step forward, wanting to touch him, to reassure him that everything would be fine. But the look on his face, the tension in his body made her stop. He didn't want her near him.

And then it was over. He walked out the door, slamming it behind him. She just stood for a moment, wondering if she should go after him. But no, she knew he didn't want that. She'd felt, when he'd left, that he wouldn't want to see her again. He was too angry, and she was so appalled, so horrified by what she'd learned, that she felt she'd been rendered impotent and dumb. *What* could she offer him but platitudes?

She sank down onto her knees on the Aubusson carpet, too stunned to cry for many minutes.

Louisa arrived late that afternoon, demanding tea and cake. Eleanor showed her into the sitting room, which she gave a critical glance. She ran her finger across a rosewood table, frowning at the dust particles that dared cling to her glove. "Where shall I sit, niece?"

"Oh…" Eleanor was trying to combine *just* the right amount of milk and tea in Louisa's cup without allowing her hand to shake too apparently. She couldn't quite concentrate. "On the sofa. I'll sit there, too."

She sat, and Eleanor joined her, sloshing tea all over the saucer on the way. Louisa accepted her teacup wordlessly.

"Did you have a pleasant journey, Auntie?"

"Why are your eyes so puffy?"

"Are they? I just slept poorly."

"Humph. The journey was pleasant enough, until I happened across your brother-in-law en route. He will arrive soon. Infuriating man."

Eleanor frowned, wondering why James's brother would have decided to come. "We were not expecting him."

"Announced that as his intention at the luncheon I gave after the wedding. I'm pleased your husband doesn't own this house. It is so cold, and so unfortunately situated. I should never be able to visit you if you lived all the way out here. Now, where do you plan to settle?"

"What?"

"Where will you and your husband live permanently? Surely you don't plan to stay in your brother-in-law's house forever."

"Oh. Um…" She faltered. She hadn't thought that far in advance. "We'll live at James's house in London, I suppose. We haven't discussed it yet."

"That's a funny thing not to discuss. Are you even speaking to each other?"

Eleanor flushed. They had been, sort of, until that morning. Now, she'd no idea. "Well, I…of course we—"

The door opened at just that moment, saving her from drowning in her own speechlessness. Will entered, dropping his gloves on the table by the door. He looked worn-out from travel.

Louisa acknowledged his presence with a single, unfriendly nod of her distinguished head. "Lord Lennox."

He responded with a pinched, rather challenging smile. "Madam." Eleanor, though, received a smile with real affection. "Sister, dear."

"We did not know you were coming," she said, feeling embarrassed.

"It was a spontaneous decision. Your dear aunt must possess exceptionally fleet horses, Eleanor. We stayed at the same inn last night, and I suggested she follow me this morning, since I'd know the route blindfolded. But then, while I was thanking the innkeeper, she sped off into the dawn. One would almost think she was trying to get away from me. Or perhaps conceal her broomstick in the cloud of dust."

Louisa gave him one of her feline smiles, which always made her look as if she was baring her teeth for second helpings of a wounded pigeon. "Have you been rehearsing these insults all day, my lord?"

"Tut, madam, you won't convince me you're not pleased as punch by your recent aggrandizement."

"I've no idea what you're talking about."

"But you're now related to the Earl of Lennox, of course. How marvelous that must be."

Louisa's nostrils flared, her patience clearly at an end. "He was behaving like this last night, Eleanor. I *tried* to be civil."

"There's no need to lose your temper, Auntie."

She rose from her seat. "I am not your auntie, Lord Lennox."

And she left without even a nod of goodbye.

"You've made yourself a dangerous enemy," Eleanor said. She tried to inject a bit of humor into her voice, but she failed miserably. She could barely manage a smile.

Luckily, he didn't seem to notice. "It's all bravado. I'm actually terrified of her. I'd no plans to come, but then I overheard your aunt stridently declaring that she planned to inflict her company on my brother. I'm sorry to intrude, but I could hardly let him face her alone. Where is he?"

Eleanor didn't know. She hadn't seen him since he'd left her that morning.

"I'm not sure. Maybe he's gone for a ride?" she offered.

Will nodded, but there was perhaps a trace of worry in his eyes. If there had been, however, he quickly disguised it. "Ah. Well, he'll be back. Supper at eight?"

She nodded, hoping that James would reappear by then. She didn't think she could handle Louisa's knowing expression or Will's sympathy if he didn't.

He left her to oversee the unloading of his carriage, and she walked back to her room, feeling defeated and alone. Supper was going to call for another performance.

Only she was sick to death of pretending.

Chapter Nineteen

It rained for most of a week. Louisa colonized the drawing room, where she sat from morning till teatime, embroidering handkerchiefs and making disapproving noises to anyone who had the courage to enter. Will slept late, and then spent his afternoons riding around the estate and calling on his tenant farmers. Eleanor slept late, too; she did so hoping to give the impression that she did not sleep alone. She then spent the remainder of her days hiding in one of the numerous bedrooms with a book, feeling thankful that the house was big enough for her simply to disappear.

She didn't know how James spent his days, although he always made an appearance at eight o'clock each night, as they all sat down to eat. He didn't speak to her then, except politely and formally, just for the sake of appearances. Under different circumstances, she might have put great effort into searching him out during the day, into forcing him to listen to her. But the truth was, she had nothing to say to him and no meaningful comfort to give. She simply could not fathom what his life had been like, and he obviously regretted giving her that brief glimpse. The humiliation of having told her his secret, the pain of reliving those dark memories, wouldn't simply disappear; she was now, somehow, a part of it.

"It looks like a lovely day, my lady, at last. Will you be venturing outside?"

Eleanor turned around to smile at Mrs. Glynde, who'd been eager to make amends since their shared indiscretion. She realized she'd been staring out the breakfast room window for many minutes now, watching as a clear blue sky had bullied the gray storm clouds into quiet submission along the western horizon. Now, the clouds had almost disappeared.

"Yes, finally. You have read my mind perfectly."

"Not a bit. I saw you gazing out the window. I brought your Indian shawl just in case."

Five minutes later Eleanor was stepping lightly across the lawn, carrying a wool blanket and a book. The sun had warmed the air only slightly, but it had softened the frozen ground enough to create patches of slippery mud. She had to put her arms out to steady herself against falling as she made her way down the gentle slope to the lake. The damp penetrated her boots, and playful gusts of icy wind romped around her, nearly sending her flying onto her backside and stealing her hat in the process. She wrapped her arms around her body and quickened her pace again. It was too cold to move any way but briskly.

Her destination was the folly that overlooked the

lake. James had promised to take her there on her first morning at Wentwich Castle, before he'd so suddenly abandoned her to go to the village. She passed the lake and started the gentle ascent up the next hill, almost losing her footing again as she went.

She was considerably warmer and slightly out of breath when she arrived at the top of the hill. Although she knew the folly to be the product of James's grandfather's building campaign fifty or so years ago, it really *did* look like a neglected, miniature medieval ruin. Mosses and ferns grew randomly from its rocky crevices, which she suspected might be part of the intended effect. Wentwich Castle itself, from this vantage point, looked misty and majestic.

The folly's craggy stone wall provided shelter against the wind, and she spread her blanket on the ground before it and sat, carefully arranging her limbs so as to avoid the bedraggled hem of her skirt. She opened her book but only managed to read the first paragraph—three times in a row, uncomprehendingly—before giving up. She lay back on the blanket instead, watching puffs of cloud rush across the sky above her.

She'd been pretending that everything was fine all week, and she wondered if she'd actually convinced anyone. Perhaps they were all just indulging her. Louisa certainly seemed to suspect she was unhappy. Eleanor could tell by the worried looks she kept giving her, whenever she thought she wasn't paying attention. At the same time, Louisa seemed to have accepted that Eleanor's personal safety was under no threat, even if the same could not be said of her heart. She'd even hinted that she might return to London in the next week or two, and Eleanor almost wished she could go with her. Why shouldn't she, if her husband wasn't going to speak to her and the house itself wasn't even hers? She was not obliged to stay there.

But she knew that wasn't really what she wanted. Even if she weren't having his baby, she wouldn't consider leaving James, even temporarily. His demons might be far more powerful than her meager frame, but she wouldn't give up.

She closed her eyes and took a deep, relaxing breath, enjoying the sun's warmth.

"Eleanor?"

She opened her eyes and sat up slowly. James stood before her, his jacket collar turned up against the cold. The wind had blown his hair and cravat into disarray, and he looked as if he'd been walking for a long time. As always, the sight of him made her heart flutter and her fingers ache to touch him, to trace a line along his firm jaw, where the faint trace of growth suggested he hadn't yet shaved.

"I didn't know you were out," he said

"I thought to enjoy the sunshine. Will you sit?"

He looked reluctant, but he sat down, and then leaned back on the blanket, propping himself on his elbows. She wanted to hide herself in his arms, and a week ago she might have been bold enough to attempt it. Only now she didn't think he'd welcome her.

"Where are you coming from?" she asked. She didn't like to make such inane talk, but she was happy to skirt the more serious issue that had come between them.

He didn't answer right away. He just lay down fully, so that he was flat on his back with his arms crossed behind his head. "There's a path that runs several miles north from here, through the forest. It's called the Duchess's Walk."

"Who was the duchess?"

"My…great-great-great-aunt? Something like that. She married the Duke of Comeragh, but when he died and she was reduced to dowager duchess she moved back to Wentwich Castle, which is where she would have grown up."

"And she liked to walk."

"One can only assume."

She leaned over and kissed him then, lightly on the lips. She didn't plan to do it. It just sort of happened.

He raised an eyebrow. "Surely I don't deserve kisses, do I?"

"James, I—"

He didn't let her finish. He put an arm around her and pulled her close. She rested her head on his chest, feeling better than she had all week. Feeling as good as she could imagine feeling ever, warm and secure.

"I'm sorry of I've made you unhappy, Eleanor. It was never my intention."

"I'm not unhappy," she said, sitting up to rest on her elbow and look at his face. At that moment, she wasn't, not really.

"Of course you are. Everyone can see. You just toy with your food at supper and you're getting very thin."

Eleanor shrugged as if she wasn't bothered by his observation. She knew she'd lost weight. It was just that every time she ate a full meal, it threatened to reappear a few hours later. Beatrice had been the same with both her pregnancies, losing weight before she'd finally gained it. "My appetite's diminished for some reason. It will return."

"You're not happy," he insisted, his eyes searching her face. She knew she couldn't lie to him anymore.

"No, I haven't been. But I feel happier right now."

"I wonder if you'd like to return to London, to be closer to your sister."

She sat up all the way and looked out at the horizon, not wanting him to see the moisture in her eyes. He was asking her to leave; it was as if he'd known what she'd been thinking earlier. "Would you come with me?" she asked.

"In a few weeks…in time for your birthday, if you'd deign to spend it with me."

"How did you know about my birthday?"

"Your aunt told me. I could take you to the opera. You could even wear your wig, if you like. I still have it, you know…you left it behind when you last dashed from the theater that night. Feeling nostalgic for Miss Smith already."

"I miss her, too." She smiled, wishing it could always be like this with him. Warm, and comfortable, and teasing…

But there was something she had to know.

"I should love to go to London, if you'll come with me, but I…"

She broke off, and he patiently waited for her to continue.

"I…"

"Yes?"

"Would you like children?" The dreaded words came in a burst.

He digested them slowly. "Why are you asking this now?"

"We should speak about it sometime, James. We *must* speak about it."

He sighed and was silent for a minute. She was so nervous she almost prompted him to speak, but then he asked, "Does this have anything to do with going to London?"

Did it? She supposed so—she couldn't contemplate going anywhere without telling him first, and since he had brought up the subject of leaving…

And she supposed she hoped, deep down, that if she told him about the child he'd insist she stay with him forever. "Possibly."

"I see. Is it that you're worried that if you go without me you would not be doing your duty? I *am* inviting you to go, Eleanor. I want you to be happy."

"My duty?" What was he talking about? That wasn't what she'd meant at all.

"Living with your husband. Producing children. They are, after all, the usual outcome of marriage," he explained.

"No, no, what I meant was—"

He sat up, too, and put his hand on hers, sensing her nervousness. "I am not some kind of monster, Eleanor. I don't expect you to spend the rest of your days heavy with child. You're young. We needn't have children at all. You said yourself that there was no hurry."

She *had* said that, but she'd been trying to make him

feel better. She wanted children with all her heart, and would be having them, or at least one, whether he liked it or not. How on earth could such an occurrence be prevented if they made love, anyway? Was his aversion to children so strong that he proposed never to do so again? Was that why he hadn't been visiting her at night?

"Do you think I don't want children?" She spoke slowly to try and preserve her self-possession, but her anger showed through her level tone.

He began cautiously. "You didn't want to marry me, and although I think you've resigned yourself to it I imagined you wouldn't want to have children with me, either. Or at least not so soon, Eleanor. There are measures we can take to limit the chances."

"Like not coming to my bedroom?"

"Well, that would be one solution, but that's not what I meant. There are other precautions."

"Oh." She felt a tear roll down her cheek and turned her head. She didn't want him to see her like this. But seeing her face didn't matter, since her shoulders shook and her breath came in ragged sobs.

"Why are you crying?"

She wiped at her face. He put his hand on her shoulder, but she shrugged it away as if it had burned her. She rose.

"What's wrong?"

"I'm afraid your measures come too late."

She started walking back down the hill toward the lake, her back straight and rigid, trying to maintain some semblance of dignity.

"Eleanor, wait—"

She heard him rise to follow her, and her walk turned into a run. The grass was wet, and her feet were numb with cold. Her mind was numb, too, and her body frantic and clumsy.

And she slipped. She landed hard on her hip, with her feet facing down the hill. Her hands absorbed some of her fall, but not enough. The wind was knocked out of her, her hip throbbed, and her chin was scratched raw where it had grazed the ground. She'd bitten her tongue when she landed, and she tasted blood, sickly and metallic. Her stomach threatened to empty itself.

He sounded as though he was just a few feet away. "Eleanor—Eleanor, wait!"

Without pausing to look, she rose, wiping her muddy, abraded hands on her skirt. But she walked this time, feeling suddenly weak, weary and unable to run. And then, after a few strides, she felt unable to move at all. She stopped and sank to the ground, crouching and holding her knees close to her chest, helpless against the pain.

"Eleanor? What's wrong?"

He was at her side, his arm around her back, holding her close. His touch was firm, but his voice sounded remote. She didn't know what was wrong. A sharp cramp twisted through her stomach, and she felt a liquid warmth between her thighs. Warm like a poultice, and then more warmth, creeping up her spine and down her arms, all the way to her fingertips, tingling. Warm like sleep, anesthetized and black.

That was the last thing she remembered.

* * *

It was an unbearable feeling, discovering and losing a child at the same time.

James had been standing before her bedroom door for many minutes, trying to work up the courage to enter. Eleanor had been inside for a very long time. He had carried her limp body back to the house and held her hand while Mr. Leonard fetched the doctor; he'd watched her eyes gradually open and her body stiffen with consciousness, with the memory of what had happened. She hadn't spoken, and he hadn't asked her to. He just kept holding her hand, wishing he could do something to ease her pain. And then Doctor Bushell arrived, and he'd been ushered from the room. He didn't want to leave, but he didn't protest, either. He didn't feel that he'd belonged there, with Eleanor so pale, and the doctor prodding her stomach gently through her shift, and Louisa looking grim. There was nothing he could do to comfort her. This was entirely his fault, and he knew that if she had the strength to say so, she would insist he leave.

So he'd just waited in a chair by the door and tried to think of nothing more than the present moment and the immediate future, of Eleanor sleeping comfortably through the night and waking tomorrow without any pain. He didn't want to dwell for one moment on what might have been.

But as the hours passed he couldn't help it. He wondered if their child would have been a boy or a girl, and if it would have been fair like their siblings, or darker, like themselves. He knew he would have wanted a girl, which was a revelation, since he hadn't known he'd wanted anyone.

When the doctor finally emerged, he explained what had happened. She'd been about two months pregnant. The baby would have been no longer than his thumb, he said. He'd assured him that Eleanor would be fine; she was young and strong and healthy. The bleeding had stopped, and she should sleep, sedated, until tomorrow morning. He'd also assured him that although her fall had precipitated the miscarriage, she might have lost the baby anyway. It happened all the time, and there was no reason that they should not try again. James had nothing to feel responsible for.

But he did feel responsible. He wished she'd told him— he could have prepared himself for the loss. He supposed she'd been trying to do so, and her hemming and hawing was entirely his fault, since he'd already told her he didn't want children. It was only now that he realized that having a family might have been just what he'd needed. He didn't know why he hadn't guessed that she was pregnant right away, when she'd first started asking him how he felt about children. Stupidity seemed to have become his strong suit.

Finally, he carefully opened the door. It was nearly five o'clock, and the late-October sun hung low in the sky, filling her bedroom with shadows. Louisa, looking severe and angular in the dusk, kept watch beside the bed. She glanced up at him as he entered.

He expected her to address him in a cold, accusatory tone, if she even bothered to speak to him at all, but instead she just said, "She's sleeping. Dr. Bushell gave her laudanum."

He nodded. He felt his throat constrict, and his lip threaten to crumble, something that hadn't happened since he was a small child. He would not break down in front of this fearsome woman, and he put every ounce of control he'd ever possessed into standing upright and looking strong, when all he wanted to do was beg her forgiveness for being such a bastard and so unworthy of Eleanor, who he knew she loved like her own child.

"I did not know," he said finally, his voice thick and broken.

"I don't think anyone did."

"I…I am so sorry."

She rose. "I know you are. You needn't be, though— not for my sake. I'm sorry. I'm sorry for your loss. And I—" She broke off suddenly, as if she realized she was unfamiliarly close to exposing her buttoned-up emotions. "I will leave you alone."

She walked from the room, closing the door behind her with a soft click. James lit a lamp, but he didn't sit by Eleanor right away. He still felt like an uninvited guest, and he stood at the side of the room for several minutes, listening to the faint, regular sound of her breathing. Finally, he took Louisa's seat by the bed. Eleanor slept quietly, her slender hand lightly fisted on her pillow. He wanted to lie down beside her and wrap her in his arms, and whisper in her ear how wonderful she was and how wrong he'd been to push her away. But he was afraid he'd wake her, and she wouldn't want to see him.

Her hair was loose, and the lamplight picked up red and blond strands that he'd never seen before. She wore a virginal white cotton nightdress and looked, he thought, angelic. It was a sobering thought, since there'd been an awful moment earlier that afternoon when he'd feared she would die. She was pale, and she looked so vulnerable and young, younger even than her nineteen years. No, he corrected himself, not quite nineteen. She'd be eighteen for a few more weeks. And he'd done this to her. He took a deep breath and slowly exhaled.

If he'd set out to ruin her life, he could hardly have done a better job. Jonathon had called him selfish, and he'd been entirely right. He should never have touched her, not if he knew that he could never deserve her kindness, that he could never give her the comfort and stability that any wife would want. He was too damaged himself.

He pulled the chair as close to the bed as possible and lifted her hand in his. He needed to touch her, to satisfy himself that life still circulated through her veins, even though she looked cold and still like alabaster. Her hand was warm, and he kissed it gently.

Her eyes slowly opened, disorientated and so blue that he found himself fascinated. It took her several seconds to focus on his face. "Hello."

"Hello, yourself." He caressed her cheek, wishing he could do something to change what had happened. Anything just to travel back in time by several hours and do the right thing, for once, rather than the wrong. Like telling her he loved her instead of inviting her to leave. He'd thought he was being considerate at the time, but he could no longer quite understand his reasoning.

"I love you, Eleanor." His voice was hoarse and foreign. He'd known that he loved her for months, but this was the first time he'd been able to say it. He longed to hear her return his words, but her eyes closed and she drifted drowsily back into the arms of oblivion. She slept once more.

He just sat there for a very long time, deep in thought. The child was obviously the only reason she'd married him. He'd never felt such a strong sense of loss, not even when his parents had died. He felt that he'd lost more than a child; he felt empty, as though he'd lost her, too. And he knew that if he felt bereft, she would feel one hundred times worse. She'd known about the baby for too long not to be devastated. Their child would have taken shape in her mind; it would have learned to walk, to speak and read. She might not love him, but she would have loved their child. And she would think he hadn't wanted it. She would think he was inwardly relieved that she had lost their baby. He was sure she would never forgive him.

It was fully dark when he finally rose and returned to his room, his muscles aching from tension. He knew what he had to do. Eleanor might hate him for it, if she didn't hate him already, but he wanted only what was best for her. He'd made an irreparable disaster of their marriage, but she, at least, had tried. She deserved better.

Mrs. Glynde had stored his valise on top of his linen press, and he pulled it down and opened it on his bed. Packing took only a few minutes. He needed just enough clothes to get back to London, since much of his wardrobe had remained at his town house. He carried his valise down the wide front staircase, passing the closed door of the dining room on the way. Inside, he could hear the sounds of Will and Louisa finishing supper, which understandably they'd started without him. Not the sounds of conversation, since they'd long given up on civility, but the restful clinking noises of silver, porcelain and glass. He wanted to leave before they finished.

Mr. Leonard was sitting rather wearily on an oak hall chair just outside the dining room door, but he rose when he noticed James approaching.

James put his valise down by the butler's feet. "Good evening, Mr. Leonard."

"Good evening, sir." He eyed the case.

"A matter of great urgency requires my presence in London. If you'd have my carriage readied, I'd like to return as soon as possible."

Mr. Leonard nodded. If he found it strange that James should be returning to London so soon after such a tragic event, he made no show of it. It was not his place to comment.

Chapter Twenty

Eleanor edged her heavy chair closer to the fire. The sitting room had grown cold, and most of the fire's heat seemed to be going straight up the chimney. It didn't provide much light, either, and she finally gave up trying to unpick the tangled stitches on the needlework panel she'd been finishing. She laid it on her lap and sighed.

"Oh, do cheer up, Eleanor. Why don't we all travel to London in the morning?"

She smiled faintly at Will, who was reclining lengthwise on the sofa across the room. She hadn't realized he was paying any attention to her, since he'd been silently reading a newspaper for most of an hour. She appreciated his company, even though she was fairly certain he'd rather not spend his evening with her while she stared forlornly at the fire's dying embers. He was obviously just humoring her, along with Louisa, who was upstairs having her presupper nap. Since James had left two days ago, Louisa had acted as if everything was perfectly all right. She'd barely acknowledged his

absence. It was as if everyone thought that even men-
tioning his name would send her into a spiral of despair,
and she wanted to tell them all that she was already as
low as she could get so they needn't bother. The house
had been far too quiet, and she was sick of everyone
treading on eggshells around her.

"I don't think James will want to see me."

Will snorted and put his paper on the floor. "I can assure
you there's nothing he'll want more, although I can understand why you might not believe me. Never seen him like
this before. Started acting strange the minute he met you."

She shrugged. She'd had a dream, when she'd been
sedated, that he'd come to her and told her he loved her.
It had seemed so real she'd thought it had truly
happened when she'd finally woken, feeling nauseated
and groggy from the drug. Will had been the one to tell
her the bad news.

"Perhaps."

"Perhaps nothing, Eleanor. You make him happy."

"Oh, do I?" She didn't want to believe it. Allowing him
to convince her would only break her heart even more.

"Well, you could. He hasn't been happy in years, and
if you don't go after him, he hasn't a chance."

"Then why do you think he left?"

Will sighed heavily. "I don't know. James is…
complicated."

Quietly, she said, "I know what happened."

"What do you mean?" Will asked cautiously, finally
sitting up.

She rose and crossed the room to sit on a chair closer
to the sofa. "I mean I know about Richard. James told me."

"He did?" He sounded truly surprised. "How much did he tell you?"

"Next to nothing. He wouldn't have told me at all if he hadn't discovered me pumping your housekeeper for information. Is Richard the reason James left here when he was sixteen? Did he disown him?"

Will didn't answer right away, obviously balancing her need to know against his loyalty to his brother. "Richard made life here intolerable for James. I suppose he sort of disowned himself, if that makes any sense."

It made no sense at all. "But why? Why did James not go to some relative, if things were so bad here?"

"That wouldn't have even occurred to him, and no one would have taken him in, anyway. Richard told everyone that James was unruly and deceitful, and since his mother hadn't exactly been welcomed into the family, everyone was willing to believe that her son was everything Richard claimed."

"There are no pictures of Richard in this house."

"There used to be. There are still some in the attic, if you'd like to see. Looked a lot like me, but uglier."

Eleanor knew he was trying to make her smile, so she obliged him, even though she felt too sad to put any real feeling into it. "How did he die?"

"Richard was killed—shot, actually. His death wasn't unexpected, considering the way he lived his life. He was a total wastrel—and that's coming from me, so you know he must have been bad."

"James hates him."

"With reason. He was cruel. When we were young, I remember he used to shoot at rabbits on the estate just for fun. By all rights he should have been a pariah, but his title and wealth ensured him a group of friends who were just as privileged and depraved. The sort who belittled servants and mistreated women." He blushed. "I should not be speaking to you of these things."

"No, please," she said, feeling desperate to hear more. "James will not tell me. He doesn't want me to know, but I have to. You understand that, don't you?"

"He was killed in London, in the house where I now live. The night it happened he was…hurting…a woman, and someone seems to have discovered him in the act. Never did discover his killer—she claimed to be too distraught to remember the man's face, but I suspect it might have been a servant, or possibly someone from her family who'd come looking for her. I've tried to mourn his death, but I can't. Whoever killed him saved that girl from a night of humiliation, and he did the world a favor, as far as I'm concerned."

She'd only known Will to be charming and carefree, and it surprised her to hear him speak with such anger. "Perhaps you'll be able to mourn when more time passes."

He shrugged. "Richard was much older than both of us—seven years older than me, and nine years older than James. He inherited everything when I was only eleven, and I suppose the power sort of went to his head."

She was quiet for a moment. "What did he do?"

"Never laid a hand on me, but he used to beat James severely. I…I'm sorry, Eleanor. When you said you knew what had happened, this is what you meant, isn't it?"

She nodded.

"Don't know when it started…might have been happening even before our parents died, and James was just too ashamed to tell anyone. I only witnessed it twice, since I was sent off to school, but I realize now that it happened much more than that. Didn't know it was going on at all, until…well, I must have been fourteen. I saw him striking James for some alleged wrong. I…I'd just returned from school for the summer and Richard didn't know I was in the room. I tried to stop him, but I wasn't strong enough. We tend that way in my family, you know—lanky until we're seventeen or eighteen."

"What happened?"

"Richard stormed out of the room and James, well, I guess he was more embarrassed than anything else. He assured me it hadn't happened before and said he didn't want anyone to know. And if it had happened to me, I probably wouldn't have wanted anyone to know, either, so I told no one at the time."

"But why would anyone act in such a way?"

"Well, I was safe because I was his full brother, and also his heir, at least until he had a son—and thankfully he never reproduced. James's mother was the only mother I ever knew, and I loved her like she was my mother in every sense. But there was talk when she married into my family. I was too young to know of it at the time, but it seems she was more or less scorned. Richard had a weak character, and he was embarrassed by her. I suppose the boys at school teased him relentlessly, and the only person he could take it out on was James."

"That is not an excuse."

"No, it isn't, but he hated James for it, and because

he was older and stronger and naturally inclined to cruelty, he beat him."

"I don't understand how anyone could hurt a child."

"It's despicable. The worst part for James, I think, wasn't the pain, but the embarrassment. Richard hid his abuses from our family, but he didn't keep it a secret from his friends. He'd strike James in front of them and make sport of it. I… You are upset."

"Please, tell me."

"The only other time I witnessed anything, I was seventeen, and James nearly sixteen. It was right around Christmas. We were in the garden, and it was cold, so we borrowed two jackets that we found lying on a table in the hall, not knowing they belonged to Richard and his friend. By the time we returned to the house, they were drunk and looking for us—they wanted to drive back to London, and the jackets were covered in mud. They…they took James into the library and locked me out of the room. I didn't see what happened, and James didn't make a sound, but by the time I was allowed in he was unconscious with pain. I only then realized the extent of what had been happening. His shirt was torn and I could see the scars."

"Could you not have told anyone then?"

"I immediately told both my uncles, but Richard had already been spreading his lies. He'd convinced everyone that James was vicious and disobedient, and to this day the rest of the family regards him with suspicion. I finally convinced my uncle Henry to come to Wentwich with me, just to check on James, but when we arrived he'd already run away. He'd taken some silver and some jewels with him to pawn, since he had to eat somehow, but to my uncle it just looked like theft. James wrote to me six months later, to let me know he wasn't dead, but for years I didn't know where he was. Just a pity he didn't return before Richard was killed, so he could have given him the thrashing he deserved. I've never forgiven myself for not doing more."

"You didn't know—you were a child yourself. But did you never wonder why he wasn't sent to school with you?"

"I asked him a few times, but he said that was what he preferred. I imagine he just didn't want me to know about the humiliations he had to suffer. And I suppose I can understand how he felt."

They were silent for a moment. Eleanor felt a tear slip from her eye.

"It doesn't scare you away, does it?" Will asked.

She shook her head. She still didn't entirely understand why he'd left her, but she could forgive him. As long as he would come back, as long as he'd let her into his life.

"Then I think, Eleanor, you should go find him."

James's solicitor, Martin McAllister, arrived late in the afternoon. He was a slight, nervous man with thinning, blond hair and eyes of such a pale blue that one almost didn't notice them—surprisingly quick and perceptive—behind his round spectacles. James had borrowed Jonathon's office at the theater for this meeting. He did not want Mr. McAllister to come to his house because he didn't want any of his servants to overhear what was about to be said. He didn't want to hear it himself.

"Brandy?" he offered as Mr. McAllister entered the room and took a seat on one side of the partners' desk, looking very uncomfortable.

He shook his head. "No, thank you. I think we should get straight to business. I hope you've received my letter, Mr. Bentley?"

James nodded.

"Then you are aware that an annulment would be out of the question."

James sat on the other side of the desk. "But we've been married for less than a month."

"It is not that simple. You must demonstrate certain irreparable conditions to have a marriage annulled. Insanity is one. Impotence another. Or perhaps you can prove that your wife is also your sister?"

"Bloody hell."

"The only option is divorce, I'm afraid. And you'd still have to prove you've a damned good reason to do it."

James shook his head. He would not, under any circumstances, divorce his wife. Such an action would likely ruin her, and he wanted her to be able to marry again, at least if that was what she wanted. Actually, the thought of her marrying someone else made him ill; he certainly did *not* want to end their marriage. But for once he wouldn't think only about himself. If she wanted to leave him he would not try to talk her out of it. Even if it destroyed him, and he knew it would.

"I know divorce is an ugly word," Mr. McAllister said, "but even an annulment would damage your wife's reputation almost beyond repair. A divorce isn't actually so much worse."

James rose again. His solicitor might not need a drink, but he certainly did. "There must be some other way."

"Perhaps you should simply reconsider. She will face greater censure than you, and it sounds as if she's done nothing to deserve it."

James wasn't ready to give up yet. "But what if I married her under false pretenses? Would an annulment then be possible?"

Mr. McAllister frowned. "I'm not sure I know what you mean."

James knew he wouldn't enjoy explaining this. "Imagine my wife was not fully aware of my identity."

"She wasn't?"

"Not fully."

Mr. McAllister sat forward. "Are you telling me that when you married Mrs. Bentley she thought you were someone else?"

"No, no," James quickly reassured him. "She knew who I was by that stage. But there were circumstances that precipitated our marriage—"

Mr. McAllister blushed again and interrupted James before he could say any more. "I heard the rumors, sir."

"Yes, well, when these events happened, my wife was not aware of my real identity. By the time she found out it was too late. I had…compromised her…and she had no choice but to marry me, even though I wasn't actually who she thought I was to begin with. Is that clear?"

Mr. McAllister was writing this down, shaking his head. "Not really. I…I've never encountered such a situation before. I shall have to check for precedent, but I urge you to change your mind. I must reiterate that even if I can argue for an annulment, the scandal that follows will be unbearable."

But it would be better than staying married to him. Eleanor was strong and beautiful and intelligent, and she'd have little problem marrying again despite any scandal. She could have children without him, be happy without him and forget about him entirely.

"I will show you out, Mr. McAllister."

Both men rose, and Martin McAllister walked to the door. "That won't be necessary. I remember the way."

He left with a nod, and James returned to his seat and put his head in his hands. He didn't know what he was doing, but from where he was sitting it seemed like the most foolhardy idea he'd ever considered. The sort of thing from which he'd never recover. From which she'd never recover, maybe.

It wasn't too late to change his mind.

He hadn't decided on anything yet.

Maybe he really could prove he was insane.

Chapter Twenty-One

Eleanor had arrived on James's doorstep weary and unexpected, only to be informed by his butler that he wasn't in. She'd been riding in the carriage all day and it was growing late, but she didn't accept the butler's offer to take her belongings to a bedroom and prepare her an evening meal. She wasn't going to make herself comfortable until she'd spoken to James. So instead she'd gone to the only other person she could think of who might know where he was.

It was nearly ten o'clock when she reached the theater. Hackney coaches had already started gathering on the street, waiting for the theatergoers inside to emerge. Eleanor still felt nervous, even though she wasn't trying to hide her identity this time, and even though her driver accompanied her to the entrance. She was still a woman, and loitering in the foyer looked a bit strange. She could hear the sounds of a play drifting in from the stage, and of a restless crowd. In just a few minutes the curtains would close, and she wanted to find Jonathon before the foyer was mobbed.

Luckily, he found her first. "Miss Smith?"

She turned around. He'd just entered the room, a pretty young actress attached to his arm. She felt a pang of guilt for interrupting him at such a moment, but it couldn't be helped. "Eleanor will do."

He blushed, realizing he'd addressed her by the wrong name, but he also smiled warmly, and, she thought, genuinely. He whispered something into the young woman's ear, and then left her standing rather sulkily while he crossed the room to speak to her. "This is a surprise. James said you were in the country."

"Is this is a bad moment?" she asked, nodding meaningfully in the woman's direction.

"It would never be a bad moment for you."

She took a deep breath and began. "I'm looking for James and I thought he might be here. Do you know where I could find him?"

"He *was* in my office, but I haven't seen him in a few hours."

"Oh."

He smiled at her gently and gave the pretty actress only the briefest, rueful glance. "I'll show you the way. And if we can't find him there, we'll try somewhere else. Here, come with me."

He led her through the foyer, through a series of doors and down a long corridor. It was all starting to look familiar, and then they arrived at the large room where Eleanor had, so many weeks ago, kissed James for the very first time. Only this time it was empty. They crossed the room to the office. Jonathon knocked, waited, and knocked again. There was no answer, so he tentatively opened the door. Eleanor followed him inside.

She also remembered this room unfortunately well, although it looked rather different now with several lamps burning. A hat and gloves were on a table, and a jacket had been draped across the back of the chair at the desk. Evidence of recent occupation.

"Well, at least it looks as if he hasn't left the building entirely. Why don't you have a seat and I'll go try to find him for you."

She nodded. "Thank you, Jonathon. I—"

"Now, don't get upset. Everything will be fine." He smiled again, and it made her feel much better. "I recommend you stay inside this room until I return. The play will end soon, and those people without anything better to do tend to proceed to the room we just passed through. But I suppose you would probably remember that."

Jonathon walked briskly out before he made any more awkward comments, closing the door behind him.

She wandered slowly around the perimeter of the room, her gaze skimming the spines of the books that lined the walls. She stopped at the table where his hat and gloves lay and picked up the gloves, as if expecting them still to be warm. They were not. She continued to the desk, and she pulled out the chair and sat. The jacket hanging from its back was made of dark blue wool, and it smelled of James. She removed it and pulled it around her shoulders. She inhaled deeply and closed her eyes.

She felt nervous, but also optimistic. She didn't think he would reject her, or at least Will had convinced her that he wouldn't and she wasn't allowing herself to poke holes in his argument. And Jonathon, too, had seemed happy to see her. If James's best friends were on her side, then she must be doing the right thing in coming here. It was never too late to start over, and that was all they needed—a fresh start.

While she waited she picked up one of the many books that were messily arranged on top of the desk. It looked promising, bound in supple, gilt-tooled red morocco, but before she even had a chance to examine its elaborate frontispiece, her attention was distracted by a letter that had been concealed neatly beneath it. She couldn't help it. One word stood out like an elephant walking down Regent Street.

Divorce.

The letter was addressed to James. She picked up the first page with a shaking hand and skimmed through it quickly. It made no sense, so she studied it more slowly, concentrating on every word as if she'd just learned to read. She couldn't actually believe the letter meant what it seemed to mean, even if it stated its purpose in explicit terms. So she read it again, trying to comprehend.

> Dear Sir,
> Further to your enquiry about terminating your marriage, I am afraid I must inform you that divorce would be your only option….

He wanted to leave her. There was no mistaking it. He'd even consulted his solicitor. He must have spent many hours thinking about it. He must be serious.

She hadn't expected this. Not at all.

She scraped the chair back and stood up unsteadily. She left the letter on the desk, but then picked it up and put it down once more. She continued to stare at it. *Could* he divorce her? She didn't think such an action was even possible, although she didn't know the first thing about divorce, since she'd never known anyone who'd even contemplated such a drastic measure. The letter said something about the difficulties involved, but it was too much for her to take in.

She walked to the door, feeling confused and abandoned. The adjoining room had started to fill with laughing, talking people, and for a moment she just stood there, wondering how anyone could be having a good time now. She vaguely registered the same actresses, and again the dissolute gentlemen who'd come to meet them. She lowered her head out of habit and nearly stepped back inside the office. But then she realized it didn't matter who saw her anymore. She simply didn't care.

She straightened her shoulders and crossed the room, ignoring the curious looks that came her way. She walked out the door and into the long corridor, moving quickly, knowing that Jonathon or James might return at any moment—the former might try to talk her out of leaving, and James…if *only* he'd try to talk her out of leaving. But he wouldn't.

She started walking even faster. She passed two women who were walking in the opposite direction, gossiping quietly, and then, at the end of the corridor, a man. She didn't bother glancing up at him, since her peripheral vision alone told her he wasn't James or Jonathon. He was shorter, and his stomach bulged slightly from overindulgence. He moved in a shambling, possibly drunken manner, and she stepped to the side to let him pass, worried that he might weave into her. But he didn't walk past. He stopped right in front of her, blocking her way. He stared at her.

"You're in a hurry," he said.

She kept her gaze on the wall; making eye contact would encourage him. "Yes, I am. Please get out of my way, sir."

He didn't move, though. Just continued to scrutinize her, as if she were horseflesh, or a picture or an expensive new waistcoat, but not a person. "We've met before, haven't we?"

"No," she said flatly. She stepped quickly to the other side of the corridor, trying to get past him, but he grabbed her arm and prevented her.

"I'm devastated you don't remember."

The firm pressure on her arm forced her gaze up to his face. She refused to blink or to cower, even though she was scared. He wasn't as tall as James, but he could still easily overpower her. The skin on his forehead, his cheeks, and around his eyes had lightly wrinkled, and his brown hair was starting to recede and gray. He'd probably once been handsome, but now his drooped shoulders carried the chilling air of decay. His eyes might have been brown, or blue or green, but in the dark corridor his pupils had dilated, making them appear pitch-black, like a beetle's shiny back. And yes, she did remember him. They'd met once before, although she couldn't recall his name, and she'd seen him one other time. That had been here, just before she'd thrown her arms around James and kissed him.

James had said something about this man: friend of his brother, some unresolved problems. He'd seemed truly bothered at the time—angry, in fact, and she wondered why. Perhaps he'd been worried that the man would have greeted him by his real name, which would have caused her to start asking questions. Or perhaps the man knew his secret. She remembered the way James's body had tensed, as if preparing for a fight. And she remembered what Will had told her.

"What do you want?"

"What are you offering?"

She started to struggle to free herself, but the pressure on her arm increased painfully, forcing her to go still.

He continued in a bored tone, as if nothing had happened. "We met at some ball—can't remember which one. Eleanor Sinclair, right?"

"You are mistaken. Now let me pass."

He eased the pressure on her arm, but he leaned his body against the wall, so he was fully blocking her. His protruding stomach brushed against her. "No—no, we've met. I saw you here, kissing that mongrel Stanton— didn't realize it was you at the time, but when I heard he'd been forced to marry you it all started to fit together. Didn't surprise me to see him here, making a spectacle of himself, but you're different. Kissing a man in public—a man like that…must mean you really like it."

"Say what you like about me, but do not talk about my husband."

"Why not? I probably know more about him than you do." He stepped closer and touched her cheek. She jerked her head away, but he gripped her chin hard. She was too scared to fight, and she had no doubt that he would strike her if she tried. "I heard he'd returned to London without you. Tired of you so soon?" His grip eased, and he stroked her face again. His voice was low and insinuating. "And how about you? There's nothing better than a married woman who's bored of her husband."

"I said do not talk about him!" She tried to duck beneath his arm, but he reached out to grab her, preventing her from going anywhere. He didn't grip lightly. His fingers dug into her flesh, and his other hand grabbed hold of her hair. She was pinned in place for the pain.

And then suddenly it was over. James was there to save her.

She hadn't seen him approaching, since she was facing the other way. She knew he was there when the man suddenly let go of her with an agonized howl. She turned around, grabbing the wall for support. James held the man's fist in his, and she could only think that his wrist had snapped as James bent it back. She'd seen him angry several times before, but never like this. His eyes had clouded over with rage, and she could see that he wanted to hurt the man. Whether it was because he'd been threatening her or something else, something deeper, she couldn't tell. The man turned around and tried to swing at him with his uninjured hand, but James easily ducked and shoved him against the wall, cracking the plaster where his head landed. His fist connected with the man's face, once, twice, and again. She didn't know what to do but watch, paralyzed. Jonathon appeared, she didn't know from where, and tried to pull James off before he did any permanent damage. The man tried to slide to the floor, but James grabbed him by his collar and kept hitting him.

She couldn't bear it anymore. "James—James, you'll kill him!"

He'd already cocked his arm back, ready to strike the man again, but her voice made him pause. His breath came quickly, raggedly, and she could tell that he wasn't ready to stop. Without taking his gaze from the man, he slowly lowered his arm and allowed him to drop to the floor. The man slumped unconsciously.

James straightened. Without looking at her, he walked down the corridor toward the large room. He slammed the door behind him.

Eleanor stood there for a minute, too stunned to move. Jonathon, swearing under his breath, had already hoisted the man over his shoulder and was carrying him away.

She looked down the long corridor, staring at the closed door. Then she took a fortifying breath, walked to the door and opened it.

The crowd in the large room continued to chatter, unaware of what had been happening outside. She walked straight through, ignoring the few stares that came her way. She stopped before the office door, taking just a second to summon strength. Then she opened it without knocking.

James was standing in front of the window, looking out. He'd put on his jacket and had collected his gloves and hat, as if preparing to leave. She closed the door behind her.

"James?" Her voice was hesitant and soft.

"I'm sorry you saw that," he said without turning around.

She tried to sound unconcerned. "He'll survive, although I'm not sure his nose will ever be the same. I…thank you. You've come to my rescue again."

He shrugged, but then he finally turned to look at her. His eyes lingered on every plane of her face, checking for any evidence of harm. "He deserved it, Eleanor."

"I know he did," she said quietly.

"No man should ever touch a woman that way."

Or a child, she said to herself, recalling Will's words, and recalling the way James's body had stiffened with rage the first time they'd seen him. "He was the man we saw that night—the night here, when I kissed you."

James nodded.

She crossed the room to stand next to him, and her hand sought out his. "You said he was a friend of your brother. I…Will told me that…" She couldn't say it. She just couldn't, but she didn't need to seek confirmation from James. She knew what had happened without asking, and he knew that she knew. The soured, glassy look in the man's eyes, the mean turn of his lips and his hateful words…it was like being confronted by someone who was truly evil, through to his soul. She'd always been convinced of everyone's inherent goodness, but he'd rattled her convictions.

James just nodded again, though he squeezed her hand. "Robert Petersham was one of Richard's closest friends, which should tell you enough about his character. I hadn't seen him for years until that night, and all my anger... I'd tried to forget about it, but there it was again, right on the surface."

"Why did you not...confront him at that time?"

"Why did I not flatten his face like I did just now, you mean? I wanted to. I—" He paused, realizing that he was speaking to her frankly, for the first time, and without anger. They'd been through a series of traumas, and she knew all his secrets now. It seemed only natural for him to tell her everything. "When I saw him then, I wanted to hurt him like he hurt me, many years ago. I wanted to humiliate him, and make him look weak. I could have, easily. I'm not a gangly boy now."

"But you didn't."

"No."

"Why?"

"Because you were there. I wish to God you hadn't seen it today, Eleanor. I'm not proud of feeling anger like that, having been on the receiving end. I hope you know I would never—"

She touched his arm. "I know you would never hurt me."

"But I have hurt you. In other ways."

"It is nothing we can't recover from, James."

He shook his head. "It is hard simply to forget, Eleanor. For me, anyway. I've spent most of my life trying to forget every bad thing that's happened to me, and tonight only shows I can't. Not permanently. Even though Richard is dead I'll still be reminded every now and then, at least if I'm going to live in London."

"I can help you forget."

"You can't."

She crossed her arms over her chest. "Is that why you want to divorce me?"

His body stiffened and the anger returned to his face. "I *don't* want to divorce you."

She was starting to get angry now herself. "I saw the letter, James. I was in here earlier, waiting for you. I will not let you divorce me."

"*Fine.* I already told you I don't want to." But then, his words softened. "There is nothing I would like less."

"Then why have you discussed it with your solicitor?"

James stepped away from her, putting several feet between them. He appeared to consider his words carefully before speaking. "Because I want you to be free to marry again if that is what you would like. But I'm bloody well not happy about it."

"I do not want to marry anyone else," she said quietly.

"You're not being rational, Eleanor. I've done nothing but make you unhappy. The only reason you married me was the child, but since…since…"

She closed her eyes briefly at the renewed pain. "We could try again, James."

He shook his head.

"Do you not care for me at all?"

He didn't answer right away, and she didn't wait for him to find the words to let her down gently. She couldn't bear to hear him say no. She turned and walked to the door, but he was right behind her, his hand on hers as she tried to turn the knob.

"Where are you going?"

She refused to look at him. Her heart was breaking in a hundred places, and she didn't want him to know it. "Please remove your hand."

"No. I don't want you to leave."

Finally, she turned around slowly, incensed at the way he toyed with her emotions, asking her to leave him one moment and then asking her to stay the next. "Why ever not, James? You are the most inconsiderate man I've ever known. I take back everything I said earlier."

His eyes sparked with irritation. "And you're the most pigheaded girl I've ever known—and I've known a hell of a lot more girls than you have men."

"Well, now you may know many more. I accept your offer of divorce."

She tried to turn again, but he pulled her around to face him, her body pressed hard against his. She started to struggle, but he held her tight.

"Hold still."

"Let go," she said through clenched teeth.

"No, and I revoke my offer."

"Why?"

He leaned in close. "Because I don't want anyone but you." And then his mouth found hers. Impatient, fierce, kissing her with his entire body: hands, thighs, lips, everything contriving to sap her of strength and of the will to protest. He didn't even need to try. She met his kiss with a hunger of her own, with a groan of frustrated want. She couldn't help it. Her mouth opened, her tongue sought out his, and her arms looped round his neck. She wanted more, and she would always want more from him.

It didn't last long enough. Slowly, he pulled away, his

warm gaze searching her face, his eyes so full of tenderness that she thought she must be imagining it. With the soft pad of his thumb, he gently stroked her cheek. "I love you, Eleanor. How can you not know that?"

Sense was gradually returning to her mind, but still she didn't understand. He loved her? "You've a funny way of showing it."

"Probably, but everyone else knows how I feel."

She couldn't believe what she was hearing. His words made her insides rejoice, but only cautiously since they couldn't be true.

"I know that you don't love me."

"You know nothing of the sort, you fool."

She frowned at the mild epithet. "Oh? Then why did you not come to me at night? When we were at Wentwich—before you became angry with me. Even then you were trying to avoid me."

"Yes, because I knew you hadn't wanted to marry me, and every time I touched you I wanted to bare my heart. And I would have if I thought you'd return my feelings."

"You didn't want to marry me, either, you know."

"Yes, I did. I was going to propose before I even knew who you really were. Came to that decision when I was standing on Lady Jersey's terrace, waiting for Will to introduce me to his future wife. I even went to your house the next afternoon, but I arrived too late. What would you have said if I'd asked?"

"I…I thought you hated me."

"I was angry, but I could never hate you."

She walked away from the door and sat on the sofa, utterly bewildered by this revelation. "I was shocked by what I had done. You'd given no indication that you would ask me, and it would have been the last thing I'd have expected. But if I'd thought there was any chance…"

"You'd what?"

She met his gaze. "If I'd thought there was any chance then I never would have left."

"You would have said yes, then?" he asked, sitting next to her.

"I would have burst into song, and probably tears, too. Yes, James. Yes. How can *you* not know that?"

"Because I know you didn't want to marry me even after everyone in town was whispering your name and a child grew inside you." He stopped suddenly. "I should not have said that. I'm sorry."

"It is all right."

He squeezed her hand. "It isn't. I blame myself entirely, and I want nothing more than to spend the rest of my life making it up to you."

"You blame yourself?" She hadn't even considered that possibility.

"If you'd been happier—"

"It was a terrible accident, James. That is all. We could try again."

"I don't know what sort of father I'll be."

"Well, then we will do whatever you propose to lessen the chances of having children. You've said enough times that you don't want children. I do, but you're the only husband I ever plan to have. I love you, James."

"Even if I'm inconsiderate?"

She blushed. "I was exaggerating."

He pulled her onto his lap and wrapped his arms

around her. "And I take back that comment about you being pigheaded."

"And well you should."

He smiled, but his hands were already beginning to wander distractedly over the buttons on the front of her spencer. "So you love me?"

She nodded, feeling shy as the first button popped open. "I am afraid I cannot help it. I would, though, if I could."

"Love at first sight, was it?"

She swatted his hands away. "Absolutely not, you vain man."

"Almost, though?"

She smiled, feeling so happy she didn't know why she was still arguing. "Almost."

"That's jolly good to hear. I plan to make you love me more, you know."

"How?"

"I do want children."

She tilted her head up. "Really?"

"Really."

She kissed him on the cheek. "That's good, since I wasn't actually going to give you any choice."

"No?"

"I was sure you'd come round eventually."

He found her lips, and she sighed in pleasure and contentment.

"Will you tell me you love me again?" she asked. "I think, perhaps, we have to make up for lost time."

"I love you, Miss Smith."

She smiled and snuggled closer. He squeezed her gently to prompt her. "It's your turn."

"I—"

"Ahem."

Jonathon had opened the door without either of them noticing. He was looking pointedly at the wall. Eleanor blushed, embarrassed to be seen sitting on James's lap. She scrambled into a more dignified position and quickly refastened her button.

"I hope this is important," James said darkly.

"Just wanted to let you know that Petersham is gone."

"Gone where?"

"I put him in a hack and paid the driver to take him to Whitechapel and leave him somewhere conspicuous. I'm sure the locals will treat him with consideration when he wakes up."

"Ingenious."

Jonathon grinned. "Rather proud of the idea, I must say. Not my best one ever, but…" He looked back and forth between them smugly. "Are we happy in here?"

Eleanor nodded bashfully.

"All's well that ends well, right?" Jonathon continued. "Even that dreadful scandal served its purpose, didn't it, Eleanor?"

James narrowed his eyes suspiciously, but she didn't notice. "I suppose you're right. I cannot imagine who saw me leave James's house at that hour, though. You didn't tell anyone, did you?"

James shook his head, but continued to look at Jonathon, who was studiously refusing to make eye contact. If this wasn't another ingenious idea of his…one that nearly had her married off to the wrong brother.

He would thank him later. Or shoot him. "Of course not. Shall we go?"

Eleanor nodded, and they both rose. James put his arm around her and they walked from the room. She paused to bid Jonathon good-night, although James just nodded moodily.

Eleanor felt so blissful she could have been treading on frothy egg whites the whole way through the theater. He loved her, and she'd wasted so much time thinking the opposite.

Once onto the street, her driver motioned to draw their attention.

"Whose carriage is that?" James asked.

"My aunt's. It's been waiting for me. I had to get to London somehow."

He waved it on. "We'll take mine."

His carriage was parked just slightly farther down the road, and they walked to it in silence. His driver had already opened the door by the time they reached it, and James helped her inside. As he did so, she couldn't help the thrilling feeling of anticipation that washed over her, the same feeling she'd experienced when he'd helped her into his carriage after their first night at the theater together. Only this time he climbed in after her, and he was her husband. He sat right next to her and pulled her close to his side. She laid her head on his shoulder and burrowed even closer. He felt so right, so solid and warm. His hand rested on her arm, tracing circles.

"We're going home?" she asked as the carriage began to move.

"Yes."

"And we're going to stay there? Together?" She just wanted to make sure.

"Not indefinitely."

That sounded worrying. "No? Why?"

"Don't you think we'll need a larger house?"

"Your house is perfectly large."

"*Our* house, and where will we keep our twenty-three children?"

"Twenty-three?"

"More, if you like. We'll be very busy, so I think we'll have to start tonight. Or right now, maybe."

"You *are* a beast." But she allowed him to kiss her on the nose nonetheless. And then her chin, her neck and a patch of bare skin on her shoulder, exposed by his wandering hands. She closed her eyes and smiled.

Epilogue

*"*Sanctuary. At last." James punctuated their entrance
by closing the bedroom door with a bang of finality.

Eleanor swatted him playfully in the stomach. "Oh,
they're not that bad." She crossed the room and sat on
the chaise longue at the foot of their bed, depositing a
small supply of opened and unopened gifts on the floor
beside her. She kicked off her slippers, pulled up her
stockinged feet and then leaned back against the
armrest. "But they *are* rather trying, even I can admit.
You're doing marvelously."

He rolled his eyes indulgently and sat down next to
her, drawing her feet across his lap. It was Christmas
Day, and they'd been at her father's house for more than
a week, along with her entire immediate family.
Everyone had gathered in the drawing room to exchange
gifts, only to be interrupted when a noisy skirmish had
broken out between Louisa and Helen. James had
jumped at the chance to retreat—literally jumped, as in
up from the sofa, grabbing his wife firmly by the hand

as he did so. Luckily, they wouldn't have to return to the battlefield until supper.

The whole experience was a bit overwhelming for him: the laughter, raised voices, the arguments and the teasing. Large, happy families had that effect on him—he'd sometimes felt the same way around his mother's family, particularly when they gathered en masse. The ease everyone seemed to feel around each other tended to make him feel like an outsider. He didn't feel that way this year, though, even if he wasn't yet exactly comfortable. It was the best Christmas he'd had since he was a child, and certainly better than last Christmas, which he'd celebrated by over-imbibing with Will—which was quite enjoyable in some respects, he supposed, but wasn't quite the point.

Eleanor leaned over to open one of the boxes on the floor beside her. She extracted a confection of a hat and, smiling, placed it on her head. "Well? Beatrice knows my weakness. She's given me hats for the last three years."

He looked at her for several seconds, pretending to examine her hat. Mostly, though, he was once more struck by his good fortune. "I never imagined you'd be so fashionable when I first saw you."

"You don't mind, do you?" she asked somewhat uncertainly.

He didn't. He hadn't known who she was when he'd fallen in love with her, but the more he knew about her, the more his love increased. He'd been learning more every day since she'd told him that she loved him back. For instance, the way she kept losing odd items like gloves and books and cups of tea around the house, and then spending countless minutes wandering around, lost and talking to herself quietly. Or the way she paused over his shoulder every morning to glance at the newspaper, which would have annoyed him if she were anyone else.

But not wanting to sound maudlin or unmanly, he casually replied, "Don't mind at all, but that hat's exactly like the one you were wearing yesterday."

She took it from her head to inspect it. "No…it's subtly different. But I wouldn't expect you to understand."

She dropped it back onto the pile, and then frowned. "Oh—look, we've missed one." She picked up a small, flat object wrapped in brown paper. "It's for you. From Helen."

"For me?"

She handed it to him. "She won't mind if you open it now. Probably just didn't have a chance to give it to you before she stormed off, and if she goes into a sulk we might not see her for days. Louisa simply cannot help provoking her. Or me, for that matter. Or Beatrice."

"She cares about you. She just wants to protect you from wicked men."

Eleanor snorted. "Too late for Bea and me, I suppose. One must pity Helen, though. After the bad example Beatrice and I set, the poor thing won't be allowed any freedom when she has her coming-out." She paused. "They like you, you know."

"They?"

"Beatrice and Helen. They're of a romantic temperament, so they can easily forgive your many misdemeanors—Aunt Louisa, too, although it's rather hard to tell."

"Well, at least the females in your family approve of me. That's a start."

"Yes. I'm afraid Father, Ben and Charles will take a bit longer—"

"I don't expect they'll forgive me anytime soon."

"Oh, they will. I assure you, everyone was more annoyed with me. Charles is still cross at the way I deceived him."

"At least you didn't exchange blows with him."

"Darling, I'm sure he deserved it. Now, open Helen's present."

He did as instructed, feeling rather bemused. Beneath the brown paper was a small, framed watercolor of the gardens at Sudley. Judging by the flowers, Helen had painted it late summer, around the time that he was falling hopelessly in love with one Miss Smith.

Eleanor returned her feet to the floor and edged closer, so she was sitting next to him. "I'd no idea my sister had taken up painting until last week. It seems far too…oh, I suppose *restful* an occupation for her."

"She's very talented."

"I know. She wants to stay with us next year for the Royal Academy summer exhibition. What do you think?"

"That I'll have to assert my husbandly prerogative and refuse her request."

She sniffed, unimpressed. "She asked Beatrice first, but Charles also refused—can't blame him, I suppose, after his experience with me."

He put his arm around her shoulders and pulled her close. "I cannot express how happy I am that he was such an incompetent chaperone."

Eleanor grinned. "I was simply too devious and clever for him." She pulled her feet up again and made herself comfortable against his chest. "Still, though, having my sister to stay might be good practice."

"Practice for Bedlam?"

Still grinning, she looked up at him. "No. For wayward daughters. I feel quite certain we're going to have a girl."

He glanced at her stomach, flat as a sheet of paper. It was hard to believe that already…

She'd told him just two days ago, although she'd insisted that no one else be told. He'd been terrified at first, but the cold hand of fear that had gripped his throat had now subsided to a mere tickle at the back of his neck. In fact, he was delighted, and although he understood why she wanted to wait to tell her family, the more he grew used to the idea the more he wanted to tell everyone he saw. Not doing so was getting rather difficult.

"Are you certain you're not ready to tell them?" he asked.

"Not yet. Wait until we're certain that everything will be—"

He squeezed her hand. "Everything will be."

"And you mustn't tell Will when we go to Wentwich next week."

"I won't, although he's sure to ask. He, for one, is hoping for a son. It would resolve his problem of an heir neatly."

She yawned sleepily. "Perhaps he'll be a father before long."

"Probably already is. Probably has a string of—"

"*James.*"

He immediately abandoned his scurrilous charge. He was feeling too content to insult anyone, even his brother.

"Have you considered a name yet?" she asked after a moment of comfortable, companionable silence.

He had. "If it's a girl, how do you feel about Diana?"

"After your mother? Diana Bentley has a rather nice sound."

"I thought Diana Stanton, actually. That was the name my mother chose, after all. And it's my name."

"Is it?" she asked, sitting up to face him.

He nodded. "And yours."

She smiled and eased back against his chest. "I like Diana very much."

"So you think she'll be wayward, do you?"

"I hope so. Willful and disobedient."

"Well, with a mother like you…"

She pinched his thigh. "You love me in spite of my faults."

"Alas, I do."

"Anyway, I'm sure I'm not *that* bad…but it just seems that disobedience is sometimes the only way to get what you want."

"What do you want?" James asked.

Eleanor didn't answer right away—she didn't know how to. Everything she wanted was in that room. She glanced out the window at the darkening sky. Supper was several hours away and no one would miss them. Still, though, she came from a family of barge-inners rather than polite knockers. Nowhere was entirely safe.

"Perhaps we should begin by locking the door."

* * * * *

"The more I see, the more I feel the need."

—**Aviva Presser,** real-life heroine

*Aviva Presser is a Harlequin More Than Words
award winner and the founder of **Bears Without Borders.***

Discover your inner heroine!

SUPPORTING CAUSES OF CONCERN TO WOMEN
WWW.HARLEQUINMORETHANWORDS.COM

HARLEQUIN

MTW07AP1

HARLEQUIN

More Than Words

"Aviva gives the best bear hugs!"

—**Jennifer Archer,** author

*Jennifer wrote "Hannah's Hugs," inspired by Aviva Presser,
founder of **Bears Without Borders**, a nonprofit organization dedicated
to delivering the comfort and love of a teddy bear to severely ill and
orphaned children worldwide.*

Look for *"Hannah's Hugs"* in
More Than Words, Vol. 4,
available in April 2008 at eHarlequin.com
or wherever books are sold.

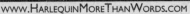

MTW07AP2

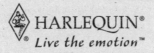

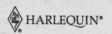

SARAH
ELLIOTT

grew up in Pennsylvania and lived in Massachusetts and Connecticut before eventually ending up in London. She lives there still, and in addition to writing, enjoys walking, baking, art, antiques and watching movies at home in her pajamas. Please visit her Web site at www.sarahelliott.net.

COMING NEXT MONTH FROM

HARLEQUIN®
HISTORICAL

- **TAMING THE TEXAN**
  by **Charlene Sands**
  (Western)
  Clint Hayworth wants revenge—and he'll be damned if he'll allow his
  father's conniving, gold-digging widow to take over the family ranch!
  But something about her is getting under his skin....
  *This is one Texan in real need of taming—and Tess is just the woman
  for the job!*

- **HIGH SEAS TO HIGH SOCIETY**
  by **Sophia James**
  (Regency)
  Ill-fitting, threadbare clothes concealed the body of an angel, but what
  kind of woman truly lay behind the refined mask? Highborn lady or
  artful courtesan, Asher wanted to possess both!
  *Let Sophia James sweep you away to adventure and high-society
  romance.*

- **PICKPOCKET COUNTESS**
  by **Bronwyn Scott**
  (Regency)
  Robbing from the rich to give to the poor, Nora may have taken
  more than she expected when she steals the earl's heart!
  *Sexy and intriguing, Bronwyn Scott's debut book heralds an author
  to watch.*

- **A KNIGHT MOST WICKED**
  by **Joanne Rock**
  (Medieval)
  Tristan Carlisle will do whatever it takes to secure the lands and
  fortune that will establish his respectability in the world and fulfill his
  duty to the king. Even if it means denying his attraction to a Gypsy
  posing as a noblewoman...
  Join this wicked knight on his quest for honor and love.

HHCNM0208